Star Light, Star Bright

Triple Star Ranch series, Book 2

Siobhan Muir

DEDICATION

Dedicated to my bisexual friends. You do count. You deserve love, and you do have a type.

ACKNOWLEDGMENTS

I was in the middle of writing ROPE A FALLING STAR when this long-haired, country-western star sauntered across my imagination. I was all set to ignore him until Paul Henry Serres captured his likeness and it was all downhill from there. I have to thank Paul for giving Henry Bright a face, long before his story was anything more than a couple of character profiles. Thanks to J.M. Madden for allowing me to reference her Lost and Found Investigative Services in my story and connect her series to mine. I was so excited, I couldn't help but squeal every time I thought of it. Thanks also to model Guillaume Charbonneau and photographer Paul Henry Serres for giving Henry Bright not only a face, but the prefect Wyoming rock star countenance. Great thanks to Kris Norris for not only creating this amazing new cover with Guillaume's image and the hot cowboy behind him, but also beta reading the tale to catch my typos, repeated words, and grammatical errors. And thanks to the ARCtic Circle review crew who read the tale, even if m/m romance isn't their usual fare.

THE WESTERN CODE

If I can't help you, I won't hurt you.
I wouldn't ask you for something I wouldn't give you.
I will not cheat, wrong, or defraud anybody in the world
knowingly or willingly.

Al Smith, Mountain Man of Cody, WY

CHAPTER ONE

"You want me to what now?"

Henry Bright stared at his manager, his publicist, and the photographer trying to shoot his album cover with undisguised disgust.

"Oh, honey, don't get so twitchy. I promise to make you look good." The photog gave him a smarmy smile and a wink. "And I'll save the naughty bits for later."

Sweet Jesus, this guy is predatory. Henry scowled. He might be a country star who was out and proud, but that didn't mean he was an easy fuck-toy for every gay predator from New York to New Orleans.

"Come on, Henry. It'll be great." His manager's eyes sparkled. "You know sexy sells. All you have to do is take your clothes off and look over your shoulder with your guitar in front of your ass. Easy peasey, Japaneasy."

"Yeah, but I'll be fuckin' oiled up like a goddamned drill rig." One of Henry's pet peeves took the form of grease on his body. He hated being sticky and he really didn't want to be touched by any of the assistants drooling over in the corner, male or female. "Do you know how hard that shit is to get out of body hair?"

"Oh, don't be so picky, honey. I'll help you clean it out

1

of all your hair anytime." The photog winked again and licked his lips.

"Stop calling me 'honey'." Henry snarled and snapped his guitar case closed. "I ain't doin' it. Shit, they ain't buyin' my music in hopes they'll fuck me. They're buyin' it because it's good."

"That's not why I bought it." The droll comment rolled out of the photog's mouth with his lascivious look and Henry was done. He'd put up with this creep twice before, but this was it.

"Fuck you, all y'all." Henry shook his head and picked up his case. "I'm outta here."

He swung the case around, damn near hitting the make-up woman who'd gotten too close, and strode for the exit of the studio. Like fluttering birds, his publicist and manager squawked and flapped after him, calling his name. Henry ignored them as he headed for the door, but Jordie beat him there by nanoseconds.

"Henry, Henry, calm down. Come on." Jordie stood with his back to the door, blocking Henry's escape. "It's just one photo shoot for your new cover and then it'll be over."

"They want me fuckin' naked, Jordie." He snarled at his manager. "I won't be naked in front of *that*." He lowered his voice and jabbed a finger back in the direction of the photog.

He might be a gay public figure, but he valued his privacy, what little he had, and he only showed his body to select people. He couldn't control much, but he could control that.

"You don't have to be completely naked. I'm sure we can find a thong or bikini briefs that will be hidden behind your guitar." Jordie grasped Henry's arm and turned him back toward the lights and cameras. "Come on. Think of how awesome it'll look and how many albums it'll sell. Everyone will be all over this shoot. And you'll be so sexy, loved by men and women alike."

Henry allowed himself to be hauled back to the set in front of the photog, who licked his lips with a victorious expression. Henry scowled and tightened his grip on his guitar case. *If this asshole gets anywhere near me, I'll beat him over the head with a bale hook.* He still had one left over from the days on his uncle's ranch in Wyoming, though it wasn't close at hand.

"It'll be fine. Come on. Ashley will help." Jordie allowed a young, pimple-faced man to take the guitar case. "We'll just get you undressed and it'll be great. You'll see. Ashley, take his jacket and shirt."

Henry gritted his teeth and disrobed on his own, slapping away Ashley's "helpful" hands. He got down to his Speedo-sized briefs he'd been wearing for his current fuck-buddy and stopped.

"Oh, come on, honey. Just take it all off. It'll be easier."

Ashley approached to do the honors, but Henry swung to face him and dropped his chin. "Touch me and you'll learn why they call me the kick-ass cowboy."

Ashley's eyes widened and he held up both hands in surrender.

Henry switched his gaze to the guitar case and strode over to it as if fully dressed. "Let's get this over with." He pulled the guitar out and looped the strap over his shoulder before he carried it to stand in front of the cheesey sunset-backlighting-prairie backdrop they had for him.

"We'll just oil you up and we'll be ready." The photog looked ready to come in his pants.

"No oil."

"Aw, come on. It'll make you look...slick."

"Try it and see how long I stand here."

The photog huffed. "Fine." He shook his head as if Henry was the most difficult artist he'd ever worked with, but Henry didn't give a shit. He was doing this at the label's request. If it was just him, he'd have called his good friend Lorenzo and took a few snapshots of him standing in the sunshine on a bridge somewhere.

"Stand there and look pretty. Now bring the guitar around to your back and face away from me. That's it."

Henry turned to face the backdrop and slung the guitar to his back.

"Good. Feet apart like you're taking a piss and right foot a little ahead. That's it." The lighting people started moving the lights around while Henry positioned himself. "Good, now turn and look over your left shoulder at me and hold the guitar with your left hand. Yeah, good."

The photog went to work snapping pictures and orders for how Henry should stand, where to put his arms, how to tilt his chin or head. They changed the lighting a few times and fluffed his shoulder-length hair, but he drew the line at make-up. They'd have to go with the real-deal Wyoming cowboy. That's who he was and who he'd always be.

It took over two hours to get the perfect shot, or at least enough of them to be considered, and they even positioned him sitting on a hay bale with one knee up and his guitar artfully positioned between his legs to disguise his assets. By the time they were done, he smelled like sweat and hairspray, and his ass itched from sitting on the hay.

They allowed him to look over some of the raw shots, and he had to admit a few of them were pretty good. They got his hair rakishly over one eye, and he actually looked as if he was hot for someone on the other side of the camera. It was damn sultry if he did say so himself, and it might make a good album cover. *Not that they'll choose the image I like.*

He pulled his clothes on and stuffed his feet into his worn Ariat boots. The clothiers they'd sent him to had tried to make him give up his boots, but he'd refused. He'd be a country star, but not without the country. And his music wasn't the typical Nashville crooning with slide guitar. He had his own western flavor that came from growing up in central Wyoming near Casper, and someone had thought it would sell.

Two albums going platinum might be a good indication that it does.

Jordie clapped him on the shoulder. "See? That wasn't so bad, was it?"

"What's next to do today? Because I'm runnin' out of patience and interest."

Jordie lost his smile and cleared his throat. "Just a few more stills for the inserts and then the music exec pre-release party."

Henry crossed his arms over his chest. "No."

"Come on. It's just a few pictures—"

"Not the photos. I'm not doing the party."

"But it's in your contract. It's part of the promo deal. Come on, it doesn't have to be long. Just show up, schmooze a little, and you're home free."

"No, they aren't for me or the fans, they're only to make the execs feel important. That ain't how this industry should be run, Jordie."

"I agree, but they've got the money and they're spending it on you and your record. And it's only for an hour or so, then you're done." Jordie waved his hand in the air, dismissing Henry's concerns as small. "It'll take a couple of hours, tops. I promise."

Against his better judgment, Henry acquiesced and followed along like a good little performer at the beck and call of the music execs. He endured the few openly gay men trying to get into his pants like the women who'd visit the successful gladiators in Roman times. He used to enjoy these parties and all the glittering excitement combined with the possibility of a good fuck later. But now the glitter had floated away and the chrome had turned to tin foil, leaving behind the sordid efforts of men trying to get ahead by either blackmail or sex.

One night of partying turned into two weeks, punctuated by days of interviews with media outlets like Entertainment Tonight and Rolling Stone and People Magazine. Alcohol and sex flowed like rivers around him, a new nameless lover each night, and finally Henry had had enough.

He woke up draped with a snoring, drooling young man who smelled of sweat, patchouli, and tequila, and wondered how the fuck his life had gone so beyond his control. His mouth had the consistency of gauze and the humidity of the Mojave desert, and someone had vomited nearby. The room sat littered with bodies in various states of undress, empty alcohol bottles and SOLO cups, and cigarette butts. He didn't even know at whose home he'd slept.

Dragging himself to his feet, he was relieved to find he still wore all his clothes, even if they were stained. A headache pounded between his ears as if he'd spent his evening at a club. *Not terribly unlikely.* The smells of unwashed humans, cum, and the various substances people used to forget the world almost overwhelmed him and he hurriedly picked his way through the bodies to the commode.

Holy shit!

He supposed the owners of the golden-veined marble and gleaming chrome bathroom would call it a 'water closet' given its glorious nature. But he simply used it to piss and vomit. He felt better when he was done and took advantage of the toothpaste left on the counter to cleanse his mouth.

Fuckin' A, son. You need to hightail outta this life. Ain't nothin' here anymore.

Despite his fame and fandom, Henry had saved most of the money they'd paid him for this contract. He'd sold a lot of his rights to his music, but couldn't live like this anymore. He didn't enjoy it. Nothing about it felt real. It

6

was all flash and glitter over spun spider webs.

He stared at himself in the mirror, scrubbing his face with his hands. The man looking back at him with bloodshot hazel eyes and lank hair filled with some unknown sticky substance made his gut sink. His beard had been growing in for at least five days to get that length of stubble, and his clothes appeared as if they'd endured far more than just one night's living.

"Fuck. This here shit's gotta stop, son."

He shot a look at the shower and wished he could slough off all the dirt, muck, and grime of the music industry. But he didn't want to be caught with his pants down, literally. He washed his hands and face in the sink with cold water to wake himself up before running his hands through his sticky hair.

Sweet Jesus, son. You're fucked up.

He shook his head and turned away from the mirror. No help for it now but to get back to his temporary apartment, pack his shit, and get the hell out. He straightened his clothes and peeked out the door of the bathroom, listening for anyone moving about. He breathed a sigh of relief when only snores met his ears.

Henry padded his way out to the main room, looking for his phone, his boots, and his jacket. It might be Tennessee, but the fall cold was more bitter than in his native Wyoming. *Damn humidity.* He found his jacket and his phone and keys miraculously remained in the pockets along with his wallet. He expected it to be empty of any cash, but everything appeared to be in the proper places. *Hell, my lucky day.*

He slung his jacket over his shoulders and picked up his boots before heading for the door. He had no idea where this party had taken place, but he could walk toward town and hitchhike a ride closer.

The cool, wet morning met him as he stepped out, and slapped the sleepiness out of him. He took a deep breath and stuffed his feet into his boots. *A lot to do today.* He shuffled past the overly manicured yard and down the tree-lined drive. *God, I hope there's no gate on this estate.* He didn't want to have to climb over wrought iron slimed with moss.

But luck wasn't with him in that aspect. The wealthy owner of the house apparently had precautions against vagrants. It meant increased security, including a wall, a guard shack, and a large, state-of-the-art electronic gate. Henry swallowed his nervousness and hoped he looked respectable enough after the party when a guard stepped out.

"Mornin'. Would you be willin' to let me out?" He hoped his voice sounded sufficiently friendly and innocent. *Yeah, good luck with that.*

"And you are, sir?"

"Ah, Henry Bright. I was here with Lariat Records for the release party." At least that's what he thought it was.

The guard eyed him narrowly before checking the list he held in his hands. "I see your name here. Where's your car?"

"I'm pretty sure it's waitin' on the others in my party to get their asses out of bed." He hammed up his Wyoming accent as if he was a big, dumb, good ole boy just making his way in the world. "I needed some fresh air and a walk. No need to wake 'em up just for me."

The guard snorted. "You said 'fresh air'? You know this is Tennessee, right?"

Henry laughed. "Yes, sir. I have noticed it's a bit more muggy here than Wyoming. But it makes for amazin' sunsets, that's for sure."

"You really are Henry Bright, the Kick-ass Cowboy Western star?" The way the guard said it emphasized his western origins.

"Yes, sir. Born and raised on windy high mountains and deep winding canyons." He gave the guard a lopsided grin.

The guard shot a furtive look around. "Would you, uhm, be willin' to sign your last CD? I listen to it all the time. I'll even call you a cab to take you wherever you wanna go."

Henry raised his eyebrows before he gave a relieved nod. "Sure thing. Bring it here."

"Thanks a lot." The guard shot him a dopey grin and hurried back to the shack. "You can sign it to Arnold, please. I'll just make that call for you."

Henry blinked. Apparently, his luck hadn't completely run out. *You just never can tell who's a fan.* He signed the CD insert for Wyoming Starlight, his previous album, and chatted with the guard as they waited for the cab. Turned out Arnold had a good ear and was an amateur musician himself, but he needed the day job to feed his family.

The cab arrived ten minutes later and Henry bid Arnold goodbye as he told the cabbie to take him to the bank. He'd withdraw the monies he'd been given as an advance on his contract and send them back to the music company. He was done with this life. Hell, they couldn't even pay him to stay.

The bank had just opened and the manager gaped at Henry's withdrawal for the cashier's check, but she complied. He wrote a quick note to the top exec of Lariat Records so they'd know what the hell it was for and sent it certified mail when he stopped at the post office. It wasn't far from his apartment and he hoofed it home to pack up his shit.

The doorman let him in and asked how his music was going. He gave brief pleasantries, but kept moving up to his place. *Just take a quick shower and then I can go.* He didn't know where exactly he was headed, but West and Wyoming each featured in his thinking. He paused to look over the apartment with the designer furniture and decorations. Hell, none of that shit was his. He shook his head and stripped down to shower.

Once he was clean and his hair didn't smell like sex, he dressed and made himself some coffee before typing up an email to the execs of Lariat Records. He thanked them for taking a chance on him and introducing him to the world, and let them know his advance was in the mail as a return. Even if the album had been cut and released, he didn't want to do all the promotion associated with it and felt the money should go back to the company. He left his phone on the counter and headed into the back bedroom to begin packing. He dug in the closet for his two plastic totes and his two guitar cases. One held his favorite old six string acoustic and the other sat empty. His Ferro-Strat sat in the stand in the living room.

Henry stopped and looked around the room. Most of his clothing and costumes would fit into one tote, and his personal knickknacks would fit into the other. He did take the framed platinum records off the wall for his first two albums and the early copy of his newest album with him, but nothing else in this jaded, glittering world appealed to him. *It's all just shit.*

He lugged his shit down to the garage where he'd parked his copper-colored 2014 quarter-ton Dodge Ram pickup. He put the totes in the bed and the guitars in the cab. How pathetic was it that all the stuff he cared about fit into one quarter-ton pickup truck? *And not even overflowing.* He returned to the apartment to check for anything he might have left, but really there was nothing.

Yeah, that's rather pathetic. He poured the coffee into a Lariat Records travel mug and shut off the coffeemaker while his phone chirped. Swiping the face, he found an email from Lariat saying they'd received his email and would respond soon. *Good enough.* He didn't want them to have to guess where he was.

Speaking of that…

He glanced down at the phone in his hand, debating

whether to take it with him or leave it behind. If he left it, he could get away clean and start new, and no one would say he took anything he shouldn't from Lariat. He opened the pictures on the phone, backed them up on his cloud server, and deleted everything off the device. He left it sitting on the counter.

His lease came due at the end of the month, but he wouldn't be renewing. He wasn't coming back. He turned the keys into the manager's office and headed out to the garage. A weight lifted off his shoulders as he sat in the driver's seat and turned on the ignition. He'd need to get a new phone and make some phone calls to friends back home to see if he could crash on their couch until he found a job, but for now he just wanted to get away. It would take him a few days to get to Wyoming from Tennessee anyway.

This is the first day of the rest of your life.

The old line cracked a grin across Henry's face as he pulled out of the garage. Hell yeah, it was. He was going home.

CHAPTER TWO

Henry scrubbed his eyes with his fingers as he waited at the light off the Greeley highway leading into Cheyenne, Wyoming. Holy hell he was tired. The drive across Nebraska on I-80 had been like a bar crawl after he'd had way too much to drink and someone had given him cement shoes to wear. But he'd made it to Wyoming and hoped to find a good breakfast joint to get some food before he headed the last sixteen miles out to his friend's ranch.

He'd called Ransom the first night he'd stopped just outside of Chicago and asked him if he could stay for a bit. He hadn't explained why he was coming home to Wyoming, but Ransom seemed content to wait for him to arrive. *Which just means he must have a lot going on.* Ransom rarely shied away from being in the know. If he didn't ask, it meant he was distracted.

Henry rolled into town and found a parking spot at a restaurant specializing in eggs. He didn't care as long as the coffee was hot and there was plenty of it. Rain sheeted down the windows outside, but folks seemed cheerful for an October morning. He'd found frost gilding his truck when he'd woken in Sidney, Nebraska, and he'd had to dig out a real winter jacket and scarf. *Not used to the Wyoming chill anymore.*

The waitress brought him coffee and took his order without fawning or twittering. He'd forgotten what it was like to be anonymous, just another guy wandering in for a bit of hot food and coffee. He tried to remember the last time he'd gone anywhere and not been recognized. *Not for years.* He swallowed a groan and rubbed his face with his hands. *Twenty-nine and already jaded.*

He sipped his coffee as he thought over his life so far. He'd originally believed the idea that fame and fortune were the answers. They'd cure all his ills and make life easy and fun. But while some things had become easier, others had developed a complexity well beyond his interest, and clouded what was truly important. Turning over the advance and heading west toward home had cleared some of the murk.

I just want a job, some good friends, and a place to play my guitar once in a while.

He was done with the fame part, though he'd have to keep up on social media for a while. *Or not.* Rock stars and musicians faded into the woodwork all the time. He'd stashed away some of his fortune and could live comfortably until he got a job. Henry had spent very little of his income from the music sales beyond living expenses, and he still got paid monthly from the passive income. He'd originally tried living the life of a music star, but he couldn't quite pull it off. After the parties and the social engagements, he'd only wanted to retreat to his small, quiet apartment where he could be left alone.

I'm definitely alone now.

He'd turned his phone off so he could eat in peace. He suspected Jordie and his publicist and even the music execs were blowing up his old phone with texts and voice messages. *I'm glad I have a new number.*

Henry finished his meal and paid for it before taking a deep breath and powering up his phone. As expected the little electronic leash chirped and beeped with a few messages he'd missed, but he scanned the numbers looking for Ransom's. He found one text asking if he was close.

Yeah, 16 miles out. Y'all awake out there in fantasyland?

He climbed into his truck and turned the ignition to warm it back up for the drive out to the ranch. The chill had invaded the warmth from the restaurant and he shivered as the defrost worked on his windshield. *Warm up, dammit.* His phone chirped and he swiped the screen as the rain pattered on the roof of his truck.

You do remember what it's like on a ranch, right? Horses and chickens to feed. Not all of us get to lounge around and sleep in.

Henry chuckled at Ransom's sarcasm. **I thought that's what ranch hands are for. I figured as the owners you get to relax.**

He threw the truck into gear and eased out of the parking lot, letting the rain wash away some of his concerns. Hanging out with Ransom and his family and working with his hands and body might be just what he needed. Music would always be with him and he'd make money off his continued record sales, but he wanted nothing to do with the industry. He wanted a real, normal life.

His phone pinged again just as he turned on to the highway heading north. He left it beside him for a short time as he concentrated on the road. With the rain sheeting down in bucketfuls and his own exhaustion, he thought it best not to be distracted by his electronic leash. Despite his need for concentration, the rain and the road relaxed him. He was home, and ready to make a new life for himself. Music had been a dream until it had gotten tarnished with the bullshit of the entertainment industry.

Been there, done that, got the t-shirt.

He pulled off the highway onto Route 224 and headed west. He passed the drive of the Triple Star Ranch with the tall gate and enjoyed the split rail fencing around it. Something about the ranch gave him a sense of calm and comfort, but he snorted and shook his head. *What a load of horseshit.* He was just glad to be back in Wyoming away from the rigmarole of the music scene.

Five minutes later he pulled up in front of the ranch house of the Fantasy Ranch and shut off the engine. The rain kept up a steady patter on his roof as he scanned the yard. Everything sat quiet in the autumn rain despite Ransom's snarky text. Henry snorted and picked up the phone, swiping the screen.

What a good idea. You said you needed a job, right?

Henry snorted. Yeah, he did need a job and being a ranch hand might suit him, but no use giving Ransom that idea right off the bat. He stuffed his hat on his head and stepped out of the truck. His totes remained sealed tight against the rain, but it would be good to get them inside soon. But friends first.

As if he'd heard Henry's thought, Ransom stepped out onto the porch, his hands on his hips and a smirk creasing his face. "Well, look what the cat dragged in."

"It wasn't a cat, it was a Dodge pickup, but I'm too damn tired of drivin' to argue." Henry stepped up onto the porch and gave his best smile through his fatigue. "You got a place for me to crash for a while?"

"C'mere." Ransom engulfed him in a bear hug. "Of course we do. Tawny is out courtin' investors and Dane's down in Denver lookin' into signature crap like fancy towels and robes and shit." He shook his head as he stepped back. "Runnin' a resort ranch is far more complicated that I thought it'd be."

"I bet."

"Well, come on in and take a load off. Have you eaten yet?" Ransom held the door open.

"Yeah. I stopped in Cheyenne. But I'd like some more coffee." Henry nodded and followed him inside.

"That I can do." Ransom waved at the hat tree. "Hang your coat and hat up. We'll sit in the kitchen with a hot cup. With just me and Clair here, no one's drinkin' it fast enough."

"Oh yeah, can't let coffee go bad or cold. Sacrilege." Henry deposited his coat and hat on the hat tree before he headed for the kitchen. "And good coffee should be savored." He settled himself in the nearest bar stool at the kitchen island and rubbed his hands over his face. Ransom set a large mug in front of him and snagged another stool with his foot.

"You wanna talk about it?"

Henry sighed. "About what?"

"About why you up and left Nashville and your entire country music career behind to come home to Wyoming."

Ransom had a way of getting down to the core of things, but it didn't mean Henry wanted to explain. He sipped his coffee to give himself time to think through what he wanted to say. Most folks wouldn't understand giving up the fame and fortune that came with a successful music career, especially after working so hard to get into the big time.

"It was the right thing to do."

Ransom raised an eyebrow. "That's it? 'It was the right thing to do'? Come on, Henry. I've known you a long time and this was your dream since you were a kid. What the hell happened?"

Why can't anyone take it on faith that I'm right about this?

Because it made no sense in a world that only valued money and fame. *But I want more than that.* Or not more, exactly, but rather a connection to people and music than could be offered in the music industry.

"It wasn't enough."

"What the hell do you mean by that?" Ransom sat back and crossed his arms over his chest. "What wasn't enough?

Hell man, you made money hand-over-fist. You were rollin' in it. You'd hit the big time. Why the hell would you walk away?"

"Because the money wasn't enough." Henry held up his hand before Ransom could bark in disbelief. "It didn't fix the problems. In fact, while it solved some things, it made others worse. I knew people less, and they didn't want to be with me, they wanted to be with Henry Bright, Kick-ass Cowboy Rock Star and overall Music Gigolo. I was nothing more than a notch in a bedpost, a cash cow, a pretty face to make money off of. No one wanted to know me or my music."

Ransom snorted. "It's the music industry."

"Right. Industry. I don't want to be a factory or a machine making someone else look good. That's not what my music's about." Henry shook his head. "The parties, the nameless fucks, the drugs and booze. I woke up one morning and hated everything about my life. None of it was real or had meaning. Even my musical muse flipped me off and went to find better pastures."

He wrapped his hands around the mug in front of him, trying to recapture the heat. "It was too fake to make it. I could donate my funds and try to help others with it, but when I realized money wasn't the most valuable thing in my life, I couldn't stay." He shot Ransom a pleading look. "I know I sound ungrateful, but I didn't want to be fake. I didn't want to waltz around in designer ratty jeans and brand new boots, pretending to be this down-home, good ole boy. That's truly who I am, but not what I was showin' them. It's not the money, Ransom. It's not. And it's not what I wanted."

"So, you walked away? How will that help you? Why didn't you change the system from within?"

"Because it's not set up that way. The execs and the handlers have everything wrapped up in perfect gears to benefit them. Don't get me wrong. The artists and musicians do just fine with the leavings. No one's hurtin'." Or at least not consciously. Most drowned their troubles and fears in drugs and alcohol. "But I'm not that person. I'm not so shallow or heartless as to wander around like I'm God's gift to country. I want to be more than a pretty face with a guitar. I want to get my hands dirty again and really connect with people."

"You know, you could've done that with all the money and influence fame brings you."

Henry nodded. "I know. I thought about it and I could've chosen that route, but it felt like I'd be phonin' it in. Payin' to make the problem go away. That's not me."

"God, Henry." Ransom scrubbed his face. "You worked so hard to get into the big time music industry. You made it, man. You had all that money."

Henry snorted. "I still do. The money ain't goin' anywhere."

"What?" Ransom blinked.

"Yeah, you know my mama was an investment banker. She taught me all sorts of smart investment moves and ways to keep my money safe should I have to make a break of it." Henry grinned. "I'll get passive income from my albums long after my hands are full of arthritis and I can't play. And I set aside most of my money to earn interest and keep me solvent in lean times. I ain't what you'd consider poor, Ransom."

Ransom dropped his hands to the table. "If you ain't poor, why are you crashin' at my place, then?"

Henry shrugged with one shoulder. "I didn't have anywhere else to go. I just up and left, not willin' to stick around for someone to try to talk me out of it. I wanted to come home and see friendly faces who knew me before I was famous, who didn't care about fame or money." He shot Ransom a pointed look and his friend had the grace to grimace.

"Well, all right, then. What are you planning to do

now? Laze around here until you find a place?"

Henry bit his bottom lip. "I was a year and a half from finishing Veterinarian school when Lariat Records signed me. I finished my degree in between my second and this last album."

Ransom's jaw dropped. "You mean to tell me you managed to become a certified vet in between all the parties, concert tours, and public appearances?"

"Yup."

"You're a goddamned overachiever."

Henry grinned. "Yup." He took a sip of coffee. "So, I figured I could get a job as a vet or vet's assistant on a nearby ranch or clinic and make myself a livin' while doing a little strumming on the side." He sat back and met Ransom's gaze. "Unless you need a vet here."

Ransom nodded slowly. "Yeah, I don't. We're pretty good here, but I'll make some calls to the nearby ranches and see if anything crops up. You might want to start with USA Jobs for Wyoming and see if anyone's lookin' for a vet."

"Fair enough. I'll get on that as soon as I've taken a shower. I'm just glad I'm done drivin' for the day." He pushed himself to his feet. "You got a room where I can store my stuff and take a shower? I don't wanna put you out if not."

Ransom snorted. "Yeah, we got a few rooms. We couldn't get the resort open before tourist season ended so we're kinda biding our time until April."

"Aw man, I'm sorry. Anything I can do to help?"

"Nah, Tawny and Dane have it pretty well in hand in terms of promotion and outreach. I'm just working on getting the ranch to be something other than a ranch house and a barn with a few head of horses. It'll all come together." Ransom waved him off. "Come on upstairs. I'll show you one of the rooms that's clean and you can take a load off."

Henry followed Ransom up the stairs to the bedrooms, allowing the tensions of the trip and his monumental decision to leave Nashville to slide away. The homey décor helped relax him as he stepped into a room with a patchwork quilt on the bed and red gingham curtains over the window.

"Will this do?" Ransom switched on the light.

"Yeah, this is fine. Thanks again for lettin' me stay until I find something to do and somewhere to live."

Ransom shrugged. "No problem. You can help around here until then. But go ahead and shower and rest for a bit. I'll see if anyone is lookin' for a vet in the meantime."

"Thanks, Ransom. I appreciate it."

He waved as he stepped out the door and Henry sighed before sitting down on the bed. He'd taken the first step toward his new life. The problem was, he had no idea what that new life would entail.

CHAPTER THREE

"Turn your back to him and wait." Trip Colton nodded firmly to the young man standing in the corral with the skittish buckskin gelding. "This is the point, Mr. Carrick. You're tryin' to gain his trust by keepin' your energy calm. When you're calm, he's calm."

Carrick closed his eyes and took a deep breath, shaking out his hands to relax them. The horse snorted and tossed his head, but Carrick didn't move. The buckskin's ears swiveled and his nostrils flared as he shifted his head from side to side to get a good look at Carrick's back.

"That's it. Make him curious about checkin' up on you." Trip rested his arms on the top rail of the fence, watching the man with the horse through the rain. "Keep yourself steady and relaxed. He'll judge your demeanor clearer than you will."

The rain wasn't letting up for nothing, but Carrick did as he asked. The horse dropped his head and tried to look around the man from behind, but when he couldn't get a good look, he took a step forward. Trip smiled in satisfaction, but held still. *Come on, Sunshine. Find Carrick's calm for me.*

Sunshine took another step, huffing a wet breath out,

21

ears still flicking back and forth. Trip knew this pair was almost there and held his breath in anticipation.

Finally, the horse pushed his body into motion and ambled around the man to bump his shoulder with his nose. Carrick managed not to jump and turned to stroke Sunshine's muzzle.

"Good job, Mr. Carrick. You've done it. Now slowly clip the lead to his halter and lead him around the corral."

The man followed directions and Sunshine chewed contentedly as if he'd found comfort in the man's hands. Trip nodded with satisfaction until a shout from the barn got his attention.

"Mr. Colton! Come quick." One of the ranch hands waved at him from the open barn doors.

"Just keep doin' what you're doin', Mr. Carrick. Angela will keep an eye on you and help you from here. I'll be in the barn if you need me." Trip nodded to the other PTSD ranch staff member as he trotted off to see what had happened.

"What's goin' on?" His gut tightened with the thought of one of the horses being hurt.

"It's Byron. He fell and says his leg won't work." The young man wore his poker face and Trip had to wonder if it was worse than he thought. "He was in workin' on old Mags when she shifted and now he's down."

"Aw hell."

Old Mags was known as Magnificent Feather, but most of the hands called her Malignant Tumor or just Mags with a scowl. The horse was a damn good herdmaster when out in the fields, but she could be a bitch in close quarters. And she hated her vet checkups.

Trip pushed his body a little faster and ignored the creak in his hips. *Damn, this gettin' old shit ain't for wimps.* He nodded to the other hands as he reached the stall with old Mags. Byron sat against the wall with a tight grimace on his face while the mare snorted at him with her ears flat against her skull.

Trip had been around enough rodeo horses to know when they were at the edge of their tolerance, and Mags had reached that point. The problem would be distracting her enough to get Byron safely out of the stall, and he didn't look like he could move too quickly.

"Hey, Byron. If you're thinkin' about takin' a nap, I would've thought you'd pick a better stall to try." Trip kept his voice light as he calculated how he'd get Mags' attention without hurting the man on the floor. "You mind if I come on in there and check on the mare for you?"

Mags' ears let up a bit and she shifted her head so she could keep an eye on Byron while ogling Trip. Trip slid the door to the stall open slowly and let her get his scent along with his presence. The mare snorted and shuffled sideways, closer to the door, planning her escape.

"Easy, Mags. Byron's just gonna set there a bit, and we're gonna move you into a new stall, and someone's gonna brush you down." Trip reached for the lead and halter from a ranch hand and eased his way inside the stall. "Your med check's all done for today. Easy, now."

Mags kept her gaze split between him and Byron, who'd gone a little gray, but she didn't move. Trip hoped she'd stay that way long enough for him to get her out of the stall, but any little noise could set her off. *Time to take your own advice today.* Keeping his own actions slow and calm would allow her to stay calm.

"Easy, Mags." He slipped the halter over her head and buckled the cheek strap. "That's it, darlin'. Let's find you a quieter place, yeah?"

He led the mare out of the stall into the main aisle of the barn and kept going until they left enough space for the hands to go in to rescue Byron. Despite his worry for his friend, Trip kept his attention focused on Mags and stuffed his anxiety down deep. He led her into an empty stall and unclipped the lead, talking to her all the while. The mare calmed down when she found hay in the manger and no one else in her space.

"Dad, is everything okay?" Tom's voice carried to him just as he closed the stall door.

"Well, I guess that depends on your definition of 'okay.'" Trip met his son's gaze and shook his head. "Byron fell while workin' on Mags. I don't know much more than that, but we can find out what Suzie says about it. She's in with him now."

"Aw hell." Tom led the way back to the stall surrounded by ranch hands and Trip paused before he went in. "Y'all get back to work, now. There are folks who need your help and chores need doin'. Get on, now. We'll take care of Byron. Off you go."

The ranch hands disbursed with looks shot toward the stall, but soon it was just Tom, Trip, Suzie, their resident medical doctor, and Byron left. Tom crouched beside the old vet and shook his head.

"Damn, Byron, what were you tryin' to do, dance the jitterbug?"

Byron grimaced as he tried to shift himself into a better sitting position. "Nah, tripped over my damn equipment box and spooked Mags. She slammed into me with her hip and I went down with a twist. Something broke and I howled like a banshee. Scared her more than it did me." He hissed when he moved his leg. "Sonuvaprick, that's bad."

"Yes, it is." Suzie nodded as she cut his jeans back from his leg. The shin and calf sat swollen and darkened with bruising. "I'm pretty sure you broke one or both bones here, but I won't know for sure until we get it x-rayed. You sit tight here for a bit while I go get the wheelchair."

"Aw hell, no wheelchair. I can walk with help." Byron struggled to get up, but Tom held him down as Trip nodded to Suzie to go for the chair.

"Listen to Suzie, now." Trip crossed his arms over his chest. "That isn't a compound break yet, but let's not encourage it. She's good with a chair, and think of it this way. You'll get a pretty woman to wheel you around and compliment you. Right?"

Byron's expression mellowed though he continued to scowl. "I don't need no compliments or wheelchairs."

"Come on, Byron." Tom's voice turned amused. "It'll be like your own private race car. And in a few days, all you'll remember is just the fun parts of bein' cared for by Suzie. When else are you gonna get to spend much alone time with our lovely doc?"

"I don't like doctors." Byron crossed his arms over his chest for a moment before putting them back into the straw to get his weight off his legs.

Good thing because he looked downright petulant.

"Yeah, I hear that." Trip nodded as he looked over his injured friend. "But she's good and she listens to what you say. Which means she'll know when you're feeding her bullshit, so don't. Just let her do her job, and you'll be back to your own self in no time."

"What about the horses, Trip?" Real concern swamped the old vet's face.

"Don't you worry about it. We'll make sure everything's taken care of."

Suzie returned in a rain jacket and hood with a tarp over the seat of the wheelchair and an umbrella tucked under her arm. She nodded to Trip and pushed the chair into the straw.

"Oh, look, your chariot has arrived." Tom grinned. "Let's get you back to the lodge and get that seen to. Dad and I will take care of the horses. Besides, the rain's getting heavier. Good time to head inside for some hot coffee and some of Mrs. Guthrie's pecan sweet rolls."

Tom and Trip helped Byron to his feet and into the chair. He grumbled about being fine enough to hobble to his golf cart, but Trip wasn't taking any chances with him falling off and running himself over. Suzie made sure

Byron's leg sat elevated, handed him the umbrella, and pushed him into the central aisle.

"Well hell." Tom grunted as he watched them go. "We're gonna need another vet while Byron recovers. We can't go without for the weeks he'll be laid up."

Trip nodded. "Maybe you can find one of those interns in vet school. Someone who could trade room and board for workin'."

Tom shot him a concerned look. "Everything okay with the ranch in terms of money?"

"Yeah, yeah, it's fine. Just tryin' to be frugal."

And prepared. After the debacle with Hank Adams' daughter back in August, Trip wouldn't put it past the old bastard to come at them a different way. Their ranch lands were fruitful and they were prospering, both the Triple Star and the Knights' ranch. Hank had hated the Knights since they'd set foot in Cheyenne, and he'd never liked Trip, especially when his daughter came sniffing around Tom like a bitch in heat.

She only came back this summer because daddy wanted to run the Knights off. Or so Tom said, but Trip didn't trust Hank Adams any farther than he could toss a Harley, and his knees wouldn't let him do much weight lifting. So, he'd been saving money, setting it aside in case the rich bastard tried anything squirrelly.

Tom's eyes narrowed, but he nodded. "All right. I'll call around, see if anyone knows someone looking for veterinary work. We might get lucky." He shot a look out at the downpour swamping the yard. "You might want to bring in the folks. It's getting sloppy out there."

"Yeah, you're right. I'll call 'em in." Trip headed for the doors but Tom stopped him.

"You okay? Everything goin' all right?"

Trip dredged up his best smile and nodded. "Yeah, I'm good. Let me get those people out of the rain." He pushed away and hoped his son bought his response.

The truth, however, was much different, and less easy to define. He'd been feeling "unfinished" lately, as if he hadn't completed something important in his life. But he couldn't think of anything incomplete. He'd had the love of his life and a handsome, strong son who'd found a woman to love. He had a ranch that helped people suffering from some of life's afflictions and good friends to help run it. What more could he want?

He helped the staff wrap up the therapy session and brought Sunshine into the barn to warm up and dry off. The gelding rubbed his forehead against Trip in thanks before stuffing his muzzle into the dry fragrant hay and munching with contentment. *Yeah, buddy, I wish it was that simple for me.* To be brutally honest, Trip didn't know why he felt such discontent. Nothing was wrong in his life. In fact, it was damn good, but something was off.

He pulled the collar of his duster up to his ears and headed out into the rain. Maybe a warm cup of Mrs. Guthrie's coffee would do the trick. That, and a good book. Unlike his son, he loved a good adventure story with some romance in it. Yeah, it was uncommon for a man to enjoy those kinds of tales, but who could argue with adventure where the guy gets the girl in the end? He'd bought a Kindle as soon as they came out and had never looked back. Paper or ebook, he read when he had a few moments to himself.

He made it across the yard to the lodge and shook himself off on the porch before he dripped all over the entry floor. Mrs. Guthrie frowned on it even when it technically was his house. He waved to Andrew Martindale at the front desk, the young man they'd hired after the last receptionist had caused trouble with Tom and his girl. *Woman. Amber.* He could hear his deceased wife Olivia's voice and the look of severity she'd give him when he didn't give the ladies their due. *Sorry, Livvy.*

Trip took himself to his apartment before he started

talking out loud to her. She often visited him in his thoughts and dreams, sometimes reminding him through music or phrases he overheard. Other times, he'd smell or taste something and her memory would fill his mind's eye. She'd been his sunshine and moonshine all in one. And her loss had made his shellshock, what they now called PTSD, worse.

Thank God for Tom and the horses. Trip hung up his dripping coat and set his hat on the hat tree. They'd pulled him back from the brink of despair and loss, but he still had his dark moments. And that's when Livvy had been closest to him and loudest. She'd always known when he was in trouble, and even after her death she'd been there, shining a little bit of light down into his darkness.

"You've always pulled my ass out of the fire, even in Vietnam, Livvy."

What else was I going to do, let you flounder around like a calf caught in the mud?

Trip snorted at her dry response. No, she'd never left him to his own devices. She'd been the strongest person he knew, even right up to the end when the cancer ate away at her body. The spirit had been far stronger than the flesh holding it. She'd smiled at him right up to the moment her heart had failed.

Now, stop gettin' all maudlin. That ain't gonna help you or Tom and Amber. He could see Livvy's dry grimace. *Besides, there are plenty of good things comin'. You just wait and see.*

He couldn't stop the tears sliding down his face despite her words of admonishment. Rainy days had been her favorites and he'd loved sharing tea and books with her on them.

"I'm sorry. Can't stop cryin' when I think of you. I know it's been a long time, but some hurts just don't disappear, even after nearly three decades."

I know. But I promise, good things are comin'. Wait

and see.

He nodded and wiped his face. They were her favorite phrases. Good things are coming, wait and see. He yanked his handkerchief out of his back pocket and blew his nose just as someone knocked on his apartment door.

"Aw hell." He wiped his face and shoved the hanky away before he opened the door.

"Hey Dad, I got some good news. Can I come in?"

"Sure. I was just gonna put some coffee on. Want some?" Trip turned away before Tom caught sight of the blotches he suspected decorated his cheeks. He'd always given himself away. Why he'd joined the army. He had to learn to defend himself when the other boys called him a sissy for crying over something.

"Yeah, that'd be great." Tom nodded and closed the door behind him. "I just got off the phone with Ransom Knight. He says he has a friend lookin' for work. Guess what he does for a livin'?"

"What's that?" Trip filled the coffee maker with water and dumped some fresh grounds in the filter.

"He's a veterinarian." Tom clapped his hands and grinned. "Talk about divine providence, right? I told him we needed a vet to help around here until Byron gets back on his feet, and would be happy to take his friend on in the meantime. Whaduya think?"

"Is he certified as a vet?" Trip pressed the coffeemaker's start button and raised his brows. "This place is too specialized to just haul off and hire friends of friends 'cause they need a paycheck."

"No, no, he's certified and everything. Has a real degree from Texas A&M." Tom nodded with satisfaction. "Byron's gettin' on in years. He could use a protégé and assistant so he can eventually retire."

"Now, hold on. Let's not give away Byron's job just yet. He's got a lot more life in him." Byron wasn't that much older than Trip.

"Yeah, I ain't thinkin' of replacin' Byron. I was thinkin' of givin' him backup for when he's busy or hurtin', like now." Tom frowned. "Come on. You know I wasn't thinkin' like that. Byron and you are fixtures here, and I want you around for a long time. But there ain't nothin' wrong with getting backup and help. Right?"

Trip sighed as the coffeemaker burbled happily. "Yeah, I guess so."

"Good. I told Ransom to send him over this afternoon so we can get him up to speed." Tom got two mugs out of the cupboard. "You and I can show him around so he can get an idea of what we do and what we'll need. All he asked for was room and board, and he'd take a lower wage to make up for it."

"You hired him?" Trip raised his eyebrows. "Ain't that jumpin' the gun a bit?"

"Byron might not be done, but his body will take a while to heal. Just the way of things. We can't go that long without a vet." Tom spread his hands in helplessness. "I figured if nothin' else, he'd be able to bridge the gap until Byron's back up to the task."

Trip nodded slowly. "All right then, but you make sure to talk to Byron and tell him why so he doesn't think you're tryin' to replace him. How old is this guy anyway?"

Tom frowned as he searched his memories. "Late twenties, I think Ransom said. Old enough to take on responsibility, but young enough to not be set in his ways."

"Are you makin' a wisecrack at my age again?" Trip shot him a narrow look but couldn't help the smile quirking his lips.

"No, sir, I'd never dream of it." Tom winked and grinned before his smile mellowed. "I'm just stayin' we can train him the way we want him to work with our animals and he'll have the energy to keep up with you and me."

Trip snorted and poured the coffee. "Let's hope so. I don't have time for no-account laze-abouts."

Tom stayed long enough to finish his cup of coffee and share news about his friend Max who'd placed well enough in Cheyenne Frontier Days to make the championship run for next year. While they talked, Mrs. Guthrie called to let them know Byron's prognosis. He'd sustained a badly broken tibia and cracked the fibula just below the knee. He'd have to get surgery at the Cheyenne Medical Center the next day. Trip thanked her, but groaned when he hung up the phone. So much for Byron teaching the new guy the ropes.

Tom left soon after and Trip settled into his favorite reading chair, intending to read for a little to calm his frustrations. But he left the Kindle sitting the side table and let his gaze settle on the rainy landscape out the window.

This is a helluva development. He'd never considered what he'd do if Byron left or got injured. *I guess Tom's solution is the best one.* Trip didn't know anything about this incoming young man, but he hoped he was as good as he sounded. *Ah hell, it's only temporary.*

See? I told you good things were comin'. Livvy's voice echoed in his head.

He snorted. He just hoped she was right this time.

CHAPTER FOUR

Henry pulled his truck into the front yard of the Trip Star Ranch and turned off the engine. He took in the lodge with the wrap-around porch and the clean looking barn with adjoining corrals. The rain had let up, but the clouds had remained, warming enough to melt off the morning's frost.

It doesn't look too bad.

When Ransom had given him the news that the next-door ranch needed a veterinarian, he'd thought his friend was teasing. But Ransom had insisted he meant it and said the ranch would provide room and board, along with a decent income while Henry trained under the current vet. They were in such dire need, they were willing to hire him sight-unseen.

Yeah, but am I willin' to stay?

He sighed and made sure the collar of his coat sat against his neck before he stepped out into the cold. Despite the chill, he heard folks already working in the barn and horses stood sunning themselves in the light. He wished he had the time to do that, but if this was to be his new life, he had to face it sooner or later.

He headed into the lodge and stopped in front of the

reception desk where a cute redhead stood staring at his computer screen intently. After a few moments, the redhead looked up and smiled, his bright blue eyes twinkling.

Damn, that man's cute.

"Welcome to the Triple Star. Are you checkin' in?"

"No, sir. I'm a new-hire today. My name's Henry Bright. I was told to see Tom Colton?" Henry's gut clenched as he waited for the wide-eyed stare and fan recognition.

"Oh, right, the new vet. I'll just let Tom know you're here." The young man nodded and pulled out his cell to type a text without so much as a blink.

I'll be damned. He doesn't know me.

Henry's world slipped sideways for a moment before it righted itself. *I'm still anonymous?* He stood nonplused for a few moments. He didn't have to stand long. A handsome blond man in a black Stetson and worn jeans sauntered into the reception area and Henry tried not to gawp.

Holy shit, that guy's gorgeous. Were all the men on the Triple Star handsome? Henry straightened, glad he'd trimmed his beard that morning.

"Afternoon. I'm Tom Colton. You must be Ransom's friend." Tom held out his hand to shake.

"Yup. Henry Bright, your new vet." He shook Tom's hand, enjoying the calluses on his palm.

"Welcome, Henry. Let me take you out to the barn so you can see the facilities before we get you settled into your new place." Tom gestured for the front doors. "We're awfully glad you're here. When Byron broke his leg, we weren't sure what we were gonna do."

"To be honest, I didn't know what I was gonna do when I got home to Wyoming a few days ago." Their breath fogged in the cold afternoon air as they strode across the yard to the barn.

"Oh, you're from here?" Tom held the barn door open.

"Yeah, born in Casper, grew up in Chugwater." Henry

nodded as he stepped inside. "Just me and my mama. But it turned out all right."

"I'd say so if you got your vet's degree from Texas A&M."

Henry shot Tom a look, waiting for the other shoe to drop. *He's gonna mention the music career, right?* The silence stretched as they passed by stalls and stable hands. The comforting smells of hay, leather, and horse filled his nose, but Tom didn't seem like he had anything to add. *What the hell?*

They stopped at a door near the back of the barn, and Henry realized the veterinary clinic had been attached to give the doc easier access to the animals. Glass double doors opened into a small waiting area to keep the dirt and dust of the barn from the other surgical rooms. Linoleum tiled floors swept from the waiting room to the operating clinic through a solid oak door. It was a simple setup, but had lots of room for the bigger patients. Another set of solid double doors opened to the outside so the larger occupants could be brought in or out easily.

"Wow. Have you always had a live-in vet?"

Tom shook his head. "Yeah, but only because Byron is my dad's old friend and could afford to trade skill for room-and-board. But as income came in for the therapy ranch, we were able to expand and hire him full-time. We still lend him out to the other nearby ranches, but mostly he does his work here."

"Wow." Henry said again. "Will that be part of my duties, too?"

"Maybe, but I think most folks will come here." Tom gestured for Henry to precede him. "Pretty nice, right? We tried to make it as state-of-the-art as we could. We're a bit far to get to the Cheyenne clinics if the timing's critical."

"Yeah, it's real nice."

Tom nodded. "Let me introduce you to my dad, Trip Colton. He runs the therapy side of the ranch. I just clean out the barn." He grinned as Henry laughed.

But his laugh disappeared in a wash of surprised attraction as his gaze rested on the older man who'd been wiping down the metal counters.

Holy hell and damnation.

Steel-blue eyes looked out over a crooked nose and silver stubble filled the man's cheeks. He was currently bare-headed with his gray hair cut damn-near military short and had broad shoulders unbowed by age. Crow's feet marked the edges of his eyes and deep laugh lines framed his sensuous mouth. Henry had the unrelenting urge to kiss them.

Whoa back there, son. He didn't know Trip's sexual orientation and he wasn't about to fuck up his new job on the first day by coming onto one of the co-owners of the ranch.

"Dad, this is Henry Bright, Ransom's friend and certified veterinarian. Henry, Trip Colton."

Trip wiped his hands on a rag and held one out to Henry. "Good to meet you, Mr. Bright." He grasped Henry's hand and froze, surprise lifting his brows. "Damn, I just recognized you. You're Henry Bright, the Kick-ass Cowboy Country star. You have some fantastic music. What the hell are you doin' here workin' as a vet?"

And there it was. Henry knew he couldn't hide forever, and he hadn't really tried, but after no one had seemed to know him, he thought he'd have a bit more time.

He pulled out his best 'aw-shucks' smile. "I got tired of the bullshit in the music industry. There wasn't much that was real anymore. It wasn't really about the music, it was about the music execs and the marketing and the image and the parties. I got so sick of it, I quit and went back to the other thing I loved to do. Workin' with and healin' animals."

"Holy shit, are you serious?" Tom looked like he'd been hit in the back of the head with a two-by-four. "I'm dumber than a bag of hammers. I should've at least recognized the name."

"It's all right. Most folks don't know about my veterinary degree." Henry shrugged.

"And I'd bet dollars to doughnuts most folks wouldn't understand why you walked away from such a lucrative career, either." Trip nodded, a sexy, lazy smile curling his lips.

Damn, that man's sexy. Henry tried to rein in his attraction. This was his boss in some capacity and while Ransom's ranch catered to the LGBTQ community, the Triple Star didn't have that reputation.

"Yeah, the amazement and disbelief are common when I mention it to anyone. So, if y'all would be willin' to not make a big deal out of who I am, I'd appreciate it."

"Not a problem. We'll start callin' you Doc Bright and if you don't spontaneously burst into song, you should be fine." Tom grinned. "Most of the folks who come here are too wrapped up in their own issues to worry about pop culture icons."

"Good to know, but easier when everyone assumes I'm nobody." Henry nodded. "This is a great facility for vet work. I'm impressed."

"Top of the line." Trip beamed as he looked around. "Tom and I have worked pretty hard to get it up and running, and some of those horses need as much therapy as the people out there."

"Looks great."

"Aw hell." Tom grimaced as he pulled his phone out of his pocket. "Sounds like Emery needs help getting the last of the fence repaired before the snow starts for real. Will you be okay showin' Henry around, Dad? I gotta get this done."

Please, oh please, let Trip show me around.

"Yeah, yeah, not a problem, Tom. You got ahead." Trip waved him off and Henry did a mental fist-pump.

"Well hell, what do you want to see next? The patients, the lodge, or where you'll be stayin'?"

"Let's start with the patients and then you can show me the place I'll be livin'." Hell, anything to spend more time with the hot older cowboy. He might not be gay, but that didn't mean Henry couldn't enjoy his company. "I should probably get to know the critters I'll be lookin' at."

"Yeah, you should. And all of them have personalities. Old Mags is probably the most difficult of all of them, but she's too good a horse to just put down, so we put up with her." Trip nodded as he ambled out of the veterinary facilities.

Henry followed behind him. *Because I don't know where I'm going, not because I'm lookin' at his ass.* And what a nice ass it was. Taut and square, hugged by some sexy faded jeans, Henry let himself fantasize about running his hands over those hard muscles. It would probably be the closest he ever got to Trip's body.

"This here's Magnificent Feather, but we just call her Old Mags on account of her orneriness at getting her health checkups." Trip stopped at a stall filled with a large, bay mare with a wide blaze and intelligent eyes. "She's good in the fields and keeps the other horses in line, but she doesn't like vets too much. She's why our last vet got injured."

Henry grunted. "You bring me to the horse who's the worst with vets? Tryin' to get rid of me already?"

Trip blinked then laughed. "Hell no, I just wanted you to know what you were gettin' into. See Mags is one of our therapy horses, but she needs her own therapy. She was abused by someone who used the vet as a punishment so she's got a hang-up about it now."

Henry scowled. "Anyone who abuses horses should be dragged out into the street and shot." He met Trip's gaze. "You say she injured your last vet?"

"Well, I don't think she did it on purpose per se, more like she moved in such a way that his body couldn't take the impact. Byron's not a young man."

Henry nodded. "Mind if I go in and meet her? That way she knows who I am before I have to work with her." And he wanted to show off his horsemanship skills to the hot rancher.

Trip raised his eyebrows. "Are you sure you want to do that before you get settled in?"

"Yeah. Besides, if I get knocked around, I can always take a long soak in the bathtub of my new place." He paused and tilted his head. "It does have a bathtub, right?"

Trip laughed. "I like the way you think, doc. Yup, it has a bathtub."

"Then we're all set. Give me a moment to get to know Old Mags here."

Henry opened the stall door and pushed it just wide enough to let him inside. But instead of stepping in, he waited to see what the horse would do. Mags raised her head and pricked her ears at him, blowing out through her nose as she got his scent.

"Hey, Mags. My name's Henry. I'm gonna be helpin' old Byron out by lookin' after you." Henry moved into the stall and backed against the wall closest to the door. "Tell me how you're feelin', darlin'. Everything okay, or are you hurtin' at all?"

One of the tasks he'd excelled at in vet school was his interaction with the live animals. Ever since he was a "sensitive artist kid" as one of his mother's boyfriends had called him, he'd been able to sense where the energy pooled in an animal's body, causing a conflict. It made him look like a genius when he could pinpoint where the problem was happening. While he couldn't tell exactly what was wrong, he could sense its location.

Looking at Mags, he recognized the signs of something wrong. It wasn't a sickness, but her stance and the way she moved showed her distress. Despite that, her curiosity overrode her discomfort and she stretched out her nose to sniff his hand.

"Hey there, honey. Whatcha got goin' on?" He ran his hand up to her jaw to rub the juncture between neck and head then slid it down her sleek neck to her shoulder. He closed his eyes and tried to see where the energy "bunched" in conflict.

His hand followed his "eyes" as he scanned her body. Her heart, lungs, and digestive track seemed in order and he breathed a sigh of relief. Digestion issues in horses were the worst ailments. But the closer he got to her back end, the more tense she grew and the energy showed a jumbled, tangled mess around her left inner thigh.

"Easy now, Mags. I just want to see where we stand. I ain't gonna touch anything just yet. Easy." Henry opened his eyes and met the mare's gaze. She'd raised her head and turned it just enough to watch him, her ears turned back to listen. "I know you're worried, darlin', but I'm just goin' to look. I know you're not feelin' well, but I need to see it to make it better, all right?"

Henry patted her rump as he walked around behind her close enough to keep those powerful legs from knocking him on his ass. She didn't move, but she'd stiffened.

"Easy now. I'm just gonna squat down here and take a look at your left thigh. That's what's botherin' you, isn't it?" He slowly crouched beside her, keeping one hand on her right leg while he pulled out a penlight from his pocket. "See? Nothin' goin' on here but lookin', Mags. I promise. Let me take a look and we'll see what can be done."

He knew most folks thought him a crazy person for talking to the animals, but he'd learned most animals were more aware then people gave them credit for. Horses, dogs, and cats in particular, but all animals responded to voice and energy signatures from human handlers.

Mags patiently waited to see what he did. *Probably plotting my imminent demise if I hurt her.* He shined the flashlight up between her legs. Her udder and nipples looked fine, but as he slid the light down the inside of her left, he found a small sore the size of a dime leaking fluids. That was the source of the energy tangle.

"All right, I see what's goin' on, Mags. I'm gonna stand up and talk to Mr. Colton about what we can do. Easy now." Henry took his time rising and patted Mags' hip. "Thanks, honey. Just give me a moment." He walked up to her head and brushed her muzzle with his fingers before he stepped around her to the front of the stall.

"What's goin' on, doc?"

"She's got a festering sore on her inner thigh. Looks like she got bitten by somethin' and it got infected. Not a big deal, and we'll put some antibiotic ointment on her, but enough of a problem to make her more ornery than usual, I'd bet."

"Aw hell. How long do you think she's had that sore?" Trip looked stricken.

"Hard to say, but I'd guess no more than a week or the rest of the leg would be swollen." Henry nodded back to the mare. "Since I'm new, can you bring the ointment you have back here? I'll stay with Mags and let her know we're gonna fix her right up."

Trip nodded and strode away toward the veterinary area. Henry watched him go a few moments before turning back to the bay mare.

"He's awful handsome, Mags. Don't tell, okay?" He stroked the mare's blaze. "I don't wanna get in trouble, but Mr. Trip Colton's gonna be in my mind for a long time. It'll be our little secret."

The mare whuffed a breath that sounded all too amused, but if she planned on telling Trip, she didn't let on. *Thank goodness horses don't talk like we do.* He just hoped he could hide his attraction for the older man long enough to keep his new job.

CHAPTER FIVE

Trip stood corrected. He hadn't expected the country rock star-cum-vet to be any good. How good at working with animals could a guy be who spent all his time strumming a guitar? But Henry, with his melodic tenor voice, wooed the most ornery mare in the barn and Trip along with her. He had a damn near magical way with the horses and all of them fell under his spell. The young man laughed easily and spoke to the animals as if they were old friends, and the critters responded better than Trip had ever seen.

"I think I've met everyone, right?" Henry shot Trip another one of his killer smiles.

"Yeah, yeah, I think so. Want to see your place now?" Trip had to clear his throat at the fluttering in his stomach with that smile.

"Yeah, that would be good. I'd like a shower since I smell like horse. I'd forgotten how pungent they are and how much it sticks to body and clothes."

Henry closed the stall door and brushed himself off. Trip followed his motions, enjoying the play of his muscles in his arms and shoulders. *What the hell is wrong with me?* Why was he even looking at another man with those kind thoughts? The last time he'd felt anything remotely similar was with his wife Livvy. Since her death, he'd never noticed anyone else, let alone a young man.

"Can we stop by my truck to get my things before we head to my new place?" Henry's gave Trip a hopeful smile and Trip's traitorous heart fluttered.

"Uh, yeah, we can do that." Trip cleared his throat again to get his head back in the game. "In fact, why don't we take your truck to your staff cabin? It's not far, but you wouldn't want to haul your shit that distance by hand."

Henry grinned. "Especially with how cold it is outside. Hell, I wouldn't want to haul it by hand when it's warm."

Trip had a flash of what Henry might look like without his shirt on while carrying an armload of stuff, and his cock started to fill out his jeans. He forced a laugh and turned to walk out of the barn in hopes Henry wouldn't notice his reaction.

Fortunately, Henry didn't say anything and they headed for a metallic-rust colored Dodge pickup. *Livvy would call it Burnt Copper or something.* Despite its newness, the truck looked as if it had some miles on it from all the dust and dead bugs.

"Nice truck." Trip climbed in the cab on the passenger side.

"Thanks. It's been pretty damn useful, 'specially recently. I can fit all my shit in the back." Henry snorted as he started the ignition. "I'm not sure if that's good or pathetic."

"I'd say it's pretty good. It's my understanding most folks from your line of work have too much stuff to fit in the back of a pickup truck."

"My line of work?" Henry raised an eyebrow as he backed the truck up.

"Yeah, country rock stars. With that much wealth comes that much stuff, doesn't it?"

Henry threw the vehicle in gear and nodded slowly.

"Yeah, for most of them, that's true. For me, I didn't want all the stuff. I lived in a two-bedroom apartment that was filled with rented furniture. Hell, it wasn't really my apartment, just an opulent storage unit really."

"Opulent? That's a helluva word."

"Creates a specific image, don't it?" Henry chuckled. "But it's true. The place was fancy and professionally decorated, but it really was just a locked space for me to store my shit when I wasn't usin' it. I basically slept there. I did my livin' elsewhere."

Trip didn't say anything as they pulled up in front of the staff bungalow. This had once been Amber's place before she moved in with Tom, and they'd had to refurbish it after the building had been damaged. As a result, Henry got the most updated bungalow on the property.

"This place looks nice. Does it have a little fenced in yard back there?" Henry parked the truck.

"Nope, but it does have some shrubs as a privacy screen." Trip got out and headed for the front door. The cold made his hips ache a little, but he'd turned the heat on the day before and looked forward to stepping inside.

They'd managed to clean this bungalow up after the pipes had been sabotaged to leak all over. Amber, Tom's woman, helped select the carpeting and furnishings to replace the ruined ones. Trip wasn't into interior design at all, but he had to admit Amber had done a good job selecting items to make the space calm and restful.

"Hey, this is pretty nice." Henry came in with a plastic tote in his hands. "Does every staff member get a place like this?"

"Yeah, anyone who wants one. Byron lives a couple bungalows over, but he'll be stayin' in town because of his injuries." Trip flipped on some of the lights. "This one is newly renovated so it's pretty state-of-the-art. Should fit a man like you."

Henry stopped and shot him a solemn look. "A man

like me?"

"Yeah, used to some of the finer things in life after a career in music." Trip backpedalled. He didn't want to insult Henry.

"Oh, right. Nah, them finer things were nice, but not really my thing." Henry shook his head with a rueful smile. "The only things of mine there were my awards, my guitars, my clothes, and my toiletries. That's it. I'm pretty low-maintenance for a country star."

For some reason that made Trip terribly happy. Men who required primping took too much energy to entertain. *Not that I need to entertain him or even worry about it.*

"Well then you should fit in pretty well here. Most of the staff eat on their own though Mrs. Guthrie does have lunch foods at the lodge for the staff who can't get away to run home." Trip waved at the full kitchen. "But you can cook here if you like. Every now and again the staff has group dinners for holidays and such, especially if they live far from family. And of course, there's Sunday supper at the lodge."

Now why had he mentioned that? Only family and very close friends were invited to Sunday supper. It had always been the case because it was Trip's rule.

"Thanks. I'll think about it." Henry nodded with a smile. "I'm just gonna get settled in here, set my computer up, and try to figure out my new life. Thanks for givin' me a chance." He held out his hand to shake.

Trip took it and the moment his hand closed around Henry's, the world seemed to stop. Trip's heart thundered and all external sounds ceased. He fell into the hazel gaze and experienced the oddest sensation of coming home. He wanted that, wanted more of it, and wanted it now. Trip damn near dragged Henry into his chest for a hug, but stopped the urge before he did more than tighten his grip.

"Uh, yeah, sure. It's not a problem at all and I think we were pretty lucky to get a man of your skills on such short notice." He released Henry like he'd been burned, hoping his intent hadn't been obvious. "So, I'll leave you to it. Let you get settled in and all. I'll, uh, leave my cell number if you need me or Tom for anythin' regardin' the horses." He retreated to the kitchen where he found a pad of paper and scrawled his cell number on it.

Not that I want him to call me or anything.

"Thanks...Mr. Colton." Henry didn't move.

"Yup, sure. And call me Trip. Ain't no reason to use a title." He gave a perfunctory smile. "All right then. I'll catch you later, Doc Bright."

"Yeah, okay." He sounded as lost as Trip felt.

Trip damn near bolted out of the bungalow and headed straight for the river. The cold air slapped him enough to wake him up so he didn't fall, but he moved as fast as he could away from Henry Bright. *What the hell is wrong with me?* Trip hadn't experienced this kind of uncertainty and anxiety since he'd first met Livvy and she'd come to the Hay Bale Dance with her best friend.

The cold air made Trip cough and he slowed his steps as he neared the river. Frost decorated the autumn grasses and gilded the edges of the fence posts and barbed wire. If it had been sunny, the whole place would've glittered. Trip usually loved this time of year with the cool weather, hot coffee, and a good book to read when not working with the animals. But now in the grayness of the overcast day, he found himself panicking.

He stopped at the bank of the river and looked across the slowly moving water. Ice crystals had already formed at the edges and periodically broke off to flow with the current. That's what his life felt like at the moment. Pieces slowly breaking off and shifting downstream. Maybe they'd find a place to rest on the shore or maybe they'd just keep going. All the things he thought he knew about himself were snapping off and floating away.

He took a deep breath and tried to figure out what the

hell was going on. Excitement, need, and anxiety swirled in a tornado of emotion inside, and he shoved his hands in his jacket pockets in frustration. Where were all these emotions coming from? He wished he could remain oblivious, but all of them centered around Henry's arrival.

If he didn't know better, he'd say he was attracted to Henry Bright. *But that's plum insane.* Not only was the man a man, the gender Trip had never been attracted to before, but he was way too young. Hell, Trip was pretty sure Henry was younger than Tom.

That ain't right.

But he'd definitely felt the connection the moment he'd seen Henry. And shaking his hand? Sweet glory, it felt as if he'd touched a live wire. Everything zinged and tingled. Nothing in his life had done that since Livvy had died. So, what did it mean? Was he really attracted to Henry?

"Aw shit, Livvy. What the hell is goin' on? I took one look at Mr. Henry Bright and I got the same feelin's I got when I looked at you. What the hell does that mean?"

His words puffed out in white steam and fell into a pool of silence. The world had grown still and quiet. Not even the usual ever-constant Wyoming wind skated over his part of the world. Despite the stillness, things had shifted and changed right out from under his feet. The world had grown strange and alien, and yet still felt comfortable like a warm coat.

Trip dropped his gaze to his boots in the frosted grass. "I don't know what to do about it. Hell, I can't even begin to sort out what being attracted to a man means. It just don't make any sense."

Stop trying to make sense of it, Trip, and tell me how you feel.

"Shit, I don't know." He kicked the frosty turf. "Twitterpated. Is that still a word they use? Like I did when I first saw you. Unsettled, excited, terrified, and foolish all wrapped up in stupid. I wanna strut around and show off for him, but I'm too damn old to strut, and who the hell am I tryin' to impress, anyway? And what will Tom think, me moonin' over some young buck? Shit."

You like him, don't you?

"Hell yeah, I like him. I liked him from the moment he came out on the music scene. He wrote some damn good songs." Trip tucked his chin against his chest. "But now that I've met him in person..." He shook his head and kicked the turf again. "He's gay. But I don't know if I am."

You might try using the word "bisexual." Although I think that might be too broad for you.

"Broad?" Trip snorted. "How is 'bisexual' too broad to describe me?"

In his mind's eye, he could see Livvy tip her head and narrow her eyes. *Because it's not the body or gender that attracts you, but rather the person. The first person you fell in love with happened to wear a female body. Now you're interested in a person who's wearing a male body.* She shrugged. *That means you love beyond the outer appearance. You always have. Hell, honey, you've loved horses as much as people.*

He shook his head. "Ain't never wanted to sleep with horses, though."

No, thank goodness for that. Otherwise I'd've had competition. She winked and grinned. *Don't worry too much about labels. Focus your energies on love and people, and you'll win every time.*

"It don't unnerve you at all? It unnerves the hell outta me."

Give yourself time to think it through. Henry didn't come on to you, did he?

"No, ma'am. I did this all on my own." Trip shot a look back toward the bungalow where the country star resided. "Thank God I didn't tell him or say anythin' about it. That would've been a helluva intro to the Triple Star."

Take is slow and natural, then. She smiled and patted him on the shoulder. *It'll work out. I promise.*

Her words faded as motion across the river caught Trip's eye. A robust ten-point Mule deer buck paused and met Trip's gaze. The big buck had scars on his hide and a notch in one big ear, but he carried those ten-point antlers with quiet strength and determination. The buck dipped his chin a moment before turning his head to continue on his way. Behind him, six does came out of the grass, all healthy and sleek, and evidently this year's harem. The buck sauntered on, completely confident with his place and his mates.

Trip raised his chin. The buck still had it, even at his age and experience.

"I don't know if I still have it, Livvy, but I'm thinkin' I might give it a try."

Take it slow. It'll work out. Let Henry come to you, but don't shy away when he makes his own efforts. Livvy looked over her shoulder with a sly smile. *You know men like to take their time and come on their own terms.* And she winked before she faded.

He snorted. Yeah, he knew that. She'd been referring to him taking his time courting her in their younger days. This time he'd try to be a little less stoic. He wasn't the best at communicating his feelings, but Livvy had taught him a few things in their short marriage. It still spooked him to think he might be attracted to a man, but she was right. It wasn't the gender he liked, it was the person, and he liked Henry's person.

The only question he had as he retreated from the river was how would he tell Tom?

CHAPTER SIX

Henry ended the call and sat back in his new armchair, rubbing his forehead. He'd just spent the last several hours on the phone with his accountant and the little bank back in Nashville to find out what the hell was going on.

When he'd taken off about a week ago, he'd pulled all his funding from the little bank and took it with him. He'd notified his accountant that he'd be changing banks and how much he'd withdrawn. He'd set up some new accounts in a local Wyoming bank and given the accountant the information about his new employment. Everything was fine until the accountant received a call from the Nashville bank saying the closed account was severely overdrawn to the tune of nearly three grand.

"What the fuck?" Henry said it out loud even though he sat alone in the bungalow.

According to Nashville, he'd made a withdrawal the same day he'd closed the account, with his card and pin number. But because the money was already gone, some glitch in the system recorded it as overdrawn, and now Henry had to scramble to figure out what was going on.

Fuck.

He'd been enjoying the autumn in Wyoming after the

heat in Nashville and he thought he'd left his life there for good. But something about this didn't ring right. Once he'd made it to Cheyenne, he'd contacted everyone in the music industry to say he was done. The execs weren't happy, but they hadn't argued when he'd returned their advance monies.

He'd have to report it as fraud and hope the banks would honor it. It would be tricky because it was his card and pin, but he'd reminded them to check their security vids of him emptying his account before the withdrawal came through. Still, who could have done that?

He scowled at the blissfully calm day outside until his phone rang again. He almost snarled at the caller until he recognized the number.

"Hey, Ransom, what's up?"

"Hey, Henry. How are ya fittin' in over there at the Triple Star?"

How was he fitting in? Great, and yet not great enough. Oh, he and the animals got along great, but he'd gotten very little time with Trip Colton. The man featured in damn near every dream and fantasy Henry had endured for the last few days and he didn't foresee them quitting anytime soon. But the man in real life remained polite and distant. Dammit.

"Real good. I'm learnin' the ways of the ranch and which critters are the most obstinate." He chuckled. "You ever met Old Mags here?"

"Can't say as I have."

"She doesn't like anyone, apparently, but she seems easy with me." He didn't tell Ransom about his energy-sensing gift. "All the hands were in awe of me givin' her shots and checkin' her over. None of them would come in the stall with me."

"That's real good. I'm glad it's workin' out for you so well." Ransom cleared his throat, his voice growing cautious. "Hey, I'm callin' because I keep gettin' these

50

phone calls from some guy back in Nashville who seems to have a hard-on for you. He's been tryin' to get a hold of you for the last week he says and kept askin' what your number is. I told him you haven't been around my place, but said I'd pass on the message if I heard from you." He sighed. "I didn't know if he was a rabid fan or somethin' so I didn't want to give him your number."

Unease slithered through Henry's gut. Stalkers were a real problem when fame put him in the spotlight. He'd had one bad one in the years he'd been onstage, but the cops had reported they'd caught him.

"Did he happen to leave his name?"

"Yeah. He said it was Jordie Heathrow. Sound familiar?"

Relief surged and Henry sat back in his chair. "Oh, yeah, that was my manager when I was singin'. Did you get his number?"

"Yeah, I wrote it down. Let me get it for you." Rustling of papers sounded on the other end of the phone. "Just a heads-up, though. He sounded a bit unhinged, like border-line hysterical. That's why I didn't give him your number."

Henry frowned as Ransom rattled off the number. Jordie should have had his cell number. He'd called or texted all his important contacts when he bought a new phone on the way to Wyoming.

Guess I forgot to tell Jordie.

"Thanks, Ransom. I'll give him a call here soon. You said he sounded unhinged?"

"Yeah. You know, panicky, as if he had somethin' important to talk to you about." Henry heard the shrug on the other end of the line even if he couldn't see it. "It wasn't enough for me to give out your number, especially not knowin' him, but he was freaked out not bein' able to get in touch."

"Huh, that's weird. Well, I'll give him a call here in a

bit and see what's up. Thanks again, Ransom."

"You bet."

Henry ended the call and stared at the paper with Jordie's number on it. He didn't really want to call his erstwhile manager. He'd left that world behind and all its craziness. He liked the quiet of the Wyoming open spaces and the way the land turned golden as the year advanced. He'd missed this in the midst of all the parties and promoting. He could hear the music again. It wasn't drowned out by the constant need for attention and money.

"Aw shit." He set his phone and the number down on the kitchen counter and threw his coat over his shoulders.

He needed to do his rounds on the animals who'd taken ill or were on the mend. He stuffed his hat on his head and headed out the door. He could drive to the barn and stay warm, but he let the temperature shock the stresses and worries out of his system as he strode through the frigid, clear afternoon.

The cold did the trick and by the time he'd reached the barn, he was ready for the heat again. *Damn, I'd forgotten how fuckin' bitter it can be in Wyoming.* He stepped through the doors and sighed in relief as the heat flooded over him along with the scents of hay, horse, and leather.

"Hey, Doc Bright." Several of the ranch hands waved to him as they went about their duties.

He liked the new nickname and the anonymity. No one rushed after him for autographs or hounded him for selfies or photos. They accepted him for his skills and left it at that. Only two people on the ranch knew about his flashy past and that was enough. He'd even closed his Facebook and Twitter accounts. The official fan pages were still there, but he didn't manage them.

Henry pushed open the veterinary center and stopped dead, his heart hammering in his chest. A hot man lay on the floor of the clinic, his upper torso and shoulders hidden under the sink. But the powerful thighs encased in taut denim flowing down to feet in scuffed boots made his cock stand up and salute. *Sweet Jesus, please let him work on the sink all day.*

"Everything okay down there?" He called out to the man under the counter to let him know he'd come in.

"Yeah, should be right in a minute. Just had to replace the U-bend down here to stop it leakin'." Trip's voice echoed hollowly as his triceps bunched with his work under the sink. "There, that should do it." He wriggled his way out from under the counter and sat up.

Henry damn near swallowed his tongue. Despite Trip's age, he still had hard pecs and ripped arms. The man carried his years very well and Henry had the unreasoning urge to tear his t-shirt off to count the abs. Instead, he shoved his hands in his jeans pockets to keep from grabbing Trip, and to hide the burgeoning bulge in his crotch.

"Now it should work." Trip pulled himself to his feet using the counter and turned the water on.

A groan rent the air before a huge clunk sounded and water sprayed out from under the sink like a power-washer wand. Trip yelped and reached for the taps while Henry jumped in the same direction. Trip managed to get the water turned off, but his feet slipped and he headed for the floor. Henry leapt for him to keep Trip's head from hitting the counter and they collided, which made Trip lose his grip on the tap. They landed hard in a heap on the wet floor with Henry wrapped around the older man.

Damn he smells good.

"Are you all right?" Henry didn't want to release Trip from his embrace, but he didn't think the older man would appreciate a hug while they sat in cold water.

"Yeah, thanks for the save. I don't wanna lose my teeth quite yet." Trip reached for the counter and hauled himself up. Henry let him go with regret. "Damn, that woulda been worse than riding a Brahma bull. Here, lemme give you a hand."

Trip reached for him and Henry took his hand. The moment he closed his fingers around Trip's wrist, a curious tingling, milder than electricity, zipped up his arm and hardened his cock against his fly. The clinic faded away and he no longer felt the water or his cold jeans sticking to his ass. His world focused down on pale blue eyes and a crooked nose over full sensuous lips. *Sweet glory, I wanna kiss him.*

"Dammit, your jeans are soaked clean through." Trip tilted to get a good look at Henry's ass and Henry resisted the urge to wiggle it. "We should get changed."

"Not if that pipe is still leaking. We'll only get more clothes soaked." Henry took off his coat and hat, and rolled up his sleeves. "Come on. Let's get the pipe fixed and we'll worry about being dry later."

Trip raised an eyebrow. "You know how to fix pipes as well as fix horses?"

Henry laughed as he picked up the flashlight. "No, sir, I figure you can fix the pipes, I'll just hold the light and hand you the tools."

Trip chuckled and accompanied him on the wet floor again. "All right, then. Let me turn off the water valve first. No need to get wetter than we already are."

It was a smart thing to do because even though they'd closed the valve, water still showered them from the loose pipe when they took it off. The next forty-five minutes would be etched in Henry's memory as an unofficial wet-t-shirt contest. By the time they'd gotten the pipes reattached, they both wore sopping clothes and wet towels.

"She-it." Trip shook his head as he leaned against the cupboard doors beside the sink. "I hope to God it's fixed now, but I dunno if I want to test it."

"Tell you what, let me test it and we'll go from there." Henry pushed himself up and reached for the tap. "Ready?"

"Hell no. Give me a moment to at least turn on the

valve. God help us both."

He hid a grin as Trip reached under the sink and turned the valve wheel. "Okay. That should do it. I hope. Let 'er rip."

He took a deep breath and twisted the taps. The water ran through the faucet without the tell-tale thumps or whines. "Did we do it?"

Trip whooped like a bronc rider. "She's done." He scooted out from under the sink and stood up. "Thank God."

They grinned at each other, and Henry couldn't help letting his gaze drift down the older man's wet body. His shirt stuck to his chest and his nipples pressed against the soaked cloth. Swirls of hair matted down showed beneath the fabric and Henry's cock flexed in salutation. *God, I wish he was interested in men.*

An errant breeze fluttered through the clinic and Henry shivered.

"Aw hell, we're both soaked to the bone." Trip shook his head with a grimace. "And it ain't warm out there. I'm sorry, Henry."

"Don't be. It's all good. I'll just head home and get changed." He waved Trip off with a smile.

"Walk home? To your bungalow soaked like that?" Trip raised his eyebrows. "It's snowing."

"Sure, but it's not that far."

"Son, you've been away from Wyoming too long. You'll be frozen stiff by the time you make it half-way." He shook his head and grabbed a large plastic bag from under the counter for the wet towels. "Come to the lodge with me and we'll get you fixed up. Hot coffee, maybe a hot meal and a shower in there, you'll be good as new. Then I'll give you a ride to your bungalow after you're dry."

"Yeah, you may be right, Mr. Colton."

"Didn't I tell you to call me Trip? Come on. Let's get

back to the lodge. I'll have Mrs. Guthrie add these to the laundry." He held up the towels then shot a considering glance at Henry. "And maybe those, too." He gestured to Henry's dripping jeans. "I'm sure I can find something for you to wear while we wait on your clothes. Come on."

Trip threw his coat over his shoulders and zipped it up as he headed for the doors. Henry blinked at him, following along because he couldn't stay in the barn. *He'll give me something to wear?* Did that mean Trip expected Henry to get naked? *That can't be right.* But the lovely fantasy kept his mind off the cold that clobbered him as soon as they stepped outside. His ass froze damn near instantly and his balls shrank to the size of raisins with the cold. *Holy fuck!*

They made it to the lodge in record time and Henry's teeth chattered hard enough to rattle his skull. Trip nodded to Andrew, the young man at the front desk, and asked him to send Mrs. Guthrie to his place as soon as he saw her.

"Sure, Mr. Colton. Will do."

"Thanks, Andrew." Trip nodded to Henry. "Come on. Let's get out of these wet clothes and have some hot coffee."

Henry gaped. *Did he just offer to get naked with me?* He mentally shook his head. He had too much sex on the brain. He expected Trip to ask for a key so Henry could clean up in one of the lodge's rooms, but Trip waved to Andrew and headed toward a door down a hallway to the left of the desk. Henry nodded to Andrew and followed, wondering where the hell they were going.

The door looked a lot like a typical front door complete with little bevel-paned window in it. Trip unlocked it and pushed it open, striding across the threshold. He left it open for Henry to follow.

A modestly appointed apartment with wood floors and homey comfortable furniture came into view. It took Henry a few moments to realize this was Trip's personal apartment and he'd invited Henry in. Giddy excitement flooded Henry's chest as he took in the framed family photos on the wall behind a comfortable chair and end table with reading glasses. *I'm in his home.* The air smelled of leather, vanilla, and pumpkin spice, and Henry smiled at the odd combination.

"Did you make a pumpkin pie in here?" Henry paused at the edge of the dining room encased in a large wall of windows like a sun room. No sun today with the heavy clouds and wind. A few small flakes of snow skidded past the glass.

"Aw hell. No, not me. But Mrs. Guthrie probably lit the pumpkin spice candle she got for me. She said it'd make it smell homey." Trip snorted as he set his hat and coat on the hat tree and sauntered for the kitchen. "Yup, there it is. If you put it on the table, the whole place smells like it."

"She's right, you know. It does smell homey or at least festive." Henry grinned. He wanted to stay in this festive place. *Rein it in, son.* Instead, he removed his hat and coat and placed them beside Trip's.

"It's somthin'." Trip shrugged, tightening his wet shirt against his chest. The cold made his nipples stand out and Henry swallowed against the urge to lick them. "The bathroom's right through there." He pointed down a hallway that sported two more doors. "Towels are in the closet right outside the door. Why don't you warm yourself up and leave your clothes out. I'll take 'em to Mrs. Guthrie to have 'em dried."

"Are you sure? I can wait." Henry hesitated, not wanting to take advantage of the older man.

"Nah, I'm good. I'll be fine. I have dry clothes here whereas you're soaked. Get in the shower and warm up. I'll make some coffee while I'm waitin'."

Henry nodded and dragged his frozen ass to the bathroom. Someone had decorated it like a backcountry cabin with taupe colored hand towels and beveled crystal covers on the lights. Wrought iron towel racks and a matching mirror increased the rustic feel. A paned window looked out on an LED lit mountain scene, but when he touched the rocking clasp, it opened to reveal the medicine cabinet.

That's cool.

He closed the cabinet and pulled off his clothes. The flannel shirt and his dry-wicking long-sleeved shirt were stiff with cold water. He didn't look forward to wrestling with the jeans. At least his cock had returned to normal. Damn, Trip Colten made his blood flow hot and arousal flare in his chest. He'd never noticed older men before, but something about Trip set him on fire.

He finally stripped all his clothes and gathered them to set outside when he realized he hadn't grabbed a towel from the linen closet. He groaned and closed his eyes. How the hell would he get one now? He couldn't put his wet clothes back on. *Shit.*

Taking a deep breath, he reached for the door just as Trip knocked on the other side.

"Everything okay in there?"

Aw hell.

"Yeah, but I realized I'd come in here without a towel. Would you be willin' to hand me one?" He grimaced and shook his head. How could he face Trip? His cock would give him away and Trip knew he was gay. *Dear God, just shoot me now.*

Trip laughed. "Yeah, not a problem. Just drop your wet things outside and I'll hand you a couple towels."

Henry took a deep breath and cracked open the door. He dropped his clothes with a wet splat on the floor and raised his gaze to Trip. The man had changed into a plush fleece robe tied loosely at the waist. His silver chest hair showed throw the gap at the top and Henry's gaze stuck there, his mouth drying out. Jeez, the man was sexy no matter what he wore.

"Here's your towels. I'll make sure Mrs. Guthrie gets your wet clothes." Trip paused when Henry stared at him. "Everythin' okay?"

"Yeah, uh, yeah. No, it's all good." He grasped the towels. "Thanks. I'll be out real quick." He closed the door quickly before his cock waved.

"Take your time. Coffee should be ready by then." Trip's voice carried through the door.

Henry snorted. Oh, he'd take his time all right. He had to get rid of the hard-on and figure out a way to be normal around him, because the man was sexy-experience walking.

Maybe I'll take a cold shower. Yeah, not his first choice, but Trip heated him up too much to be necessary.

CHAPTER SEVEN

Trip bundled the clothes up in the bag and set it beside the front door just as someone knocked on it. He opened it and Estelle Guthrie bustled in, a dry look on her face.

"What in the world did you need, Trip? I was in the middle of making cinnamon rolls for breakfast tomorrow." She tilted her head and put a hand on her hip, irritation seeping out of every pore.

He cleared his throat. "I'm sorry, Estelle. I didn't mean to interrupt. I thought Andrew would have you stop by when you had a moment. I was wonderin' if you could drop these by the laundry and have them cleaned and dried? Henry and I were fixin' the sink in the clinic and we got all soaked and dirty. I wasn't gonna send him all the way to his bungalow in this cold to get changed."

"Henry? You mean, Henry Bright, the new vet?" Some of Estelle's irritation morphed into curiosity. "He's here?"

"Yes, ma'am. He's takin' a shower to get warmed up."

Trip gritted his teeth, hoping he didn't show off his interest in the younger man. *Shit, I can't even imagine what Estelle would think of me bein' sweet on Henry.* She'd known him since high school.

"Do y'all need some soup? I have a big ole stew

simmerin' on the stove. I can bring you two bowls and some bread to go with." Estelle eyed him. "What about you, Trip? Are you headed for the shower to warm up? We can't have you catchin' cold."

"Yes, ma'am, as soon as Henry's done. I made some coffee, but the stew would be awful nice."

Estelle nodded slowly, eyeing him with concern. "Trip, level with me. Why is Henry really here?"

He shrugged uncomfortably. "I told you. He was soaked to the bone and with the snow, it was too far to walk to his bungalow. My place was closer."

"Yeah, but you could've given him a ride to his place. You've never brought anyone you barely know into your home. Why him and why now?"

Trip clenched his jaw, but refused to look away. "This is not the time to share." He shot a look at the bathroom door as the water cut off. "I'm still workin' it through in my own head, but don't you worry about me. I'm sure it'll all work out."

She nodded again. "All right, then. You just take care of yourself, though. I'll get these laundered and bring y'all some stew when it's ready."

"Thanks."

Trip let her out of the apartment just as Henry stepped out of the shower and Trip couldn't help locking the door. He didn't want anyone walking in on him. *Why the hell do I feel so nervous and guilty?* Maybe because the idea of loving someone of the same gender had too much societal rejection. *And who says I'm in love with him?* He wasn't, at least he didn't think he was, but he certainly liked Henry in ways he'd only associated with women.

Screwing up his courage, he turned to meet Henry's gaze, only to gawk at him like a country bumpkin. The younger man rubbed his long hair with one towel while another sat wrapped around his waist, showing off hairless pecs and abs, but a sexy happy trail from his navel disappeared into the towel. He wanted to peel it off him just to see what lay under it.

Henry glanced down at himself then back at Trip with a raised eyebrow. "Somethin' wrong? Did I miss a spot?"

"What? Oh, no, you look fine." *More than fine. Sexy, handsome, relaxed, attractive. Get a grip.* He cleared his throat. "Did you leave me some hot water or will I be takin' a cold shower?"

Now why the hell had he said it like that? He resisted the urge to smack his forehead.

Henry chuckled and the sound wrapped around Trip, making his stomach flutter and his cock harden. *Aw hell.* He didn't want to give the man any ideas, especially when he didn't understand them himself.

"There should be plenty of hot water left."

Henry's rueful smile made excitement rise in Trip's chest. *Holy shit, did he have to take a cold shower?* He tried to rein in his wayward thoughts before they showed under his robe.

"Oh, all right. Good. Uh, Mrs. Guthrie took our clothes to be washed and dried, and she should be bringin' some stew for us to eat when it's ready." Trip nodded sharply. "I'm gonna shower. Coffee should be ready and I'll see you when I get out."

"Sounds good. I'll have a cup waitin' on you." Henry rubbed the towel over his head again and Trip took the opportunity to escape into the bathroom.

Unfortunately, it smelled like heat and Henry. Trip closed the door and leaned against it, closing his eyes as his cock throbbed. *Quiet, you.* But it wouldn't stay down and eventually he shoved off the door and started the shower. He adjusted the heat and shed the robe before stepping under the spray.

Trip let out a long breath as he ran his hands over his head, trying to push away the arousal pounding through his chest. He gritted his teeth as his cock insisted on flexing at the image of hot water running down Henry's mostly smooth chest and abs. *Glory be, he's fuckin' handsome.*

Trip grabbed the shampoo and soaped up his short hair, the arousal ignoring his efforts at distraction. The image in his head only became clearer and he dropped one hand down to massage his throbbing shaft. The moment he touched it, the image changed from Henry bathing to Henry kneeling between Trip's legs, fisting his cock.

Trip moaned. The adoration and sultry smirk on Henry's face as he slid his hand up and down on Trip's shaft made Trip's balls tighten with impending pleasure. Henry's smirk widened as he leaned forward to take the tip into his mouth. Hot, slick ecstasy flared from Trip's groin, burning a fiery path all the way up his back.

"Oh, glory, Henry."

Trip's whispered words made the dream-Henry tighten his lips over Trip's cock and stroke harder. Trip threw his head back against the tiled wall and held out as Henry worked him over, scraping his tongue along the edges of the head and squeezing the shaft. At the last moment, he dug his tongue gently into Trip's slit and Trip was lost.

His orgasm tore through him, painting thick ropes of cum on the wall of the shower as his pleasure exploded.

"Henry…" He couldn't hold back the name or the feeling of desire that came with it. Trip had never had trouble getting sexual gratification from masturbation, but this was the best he'd experienced in a long time.

Aw hell. Livvy's right. He was interested in Henry. Now he just had to figure out how to tell Tom and Estelle. *And Henry.* Would the young man even be interested in a broken-down cowboy with PTSD, twice his age? *When you put it like that, I'm not sure I'd be interested. Either.*

Trip leaned his head against the wall as the hot water poured over him and wished life could be simpler.

****

Henry scrubbed his face with his hands. Holy shit, he'd heard Trip moaning his name in the shower and it had made his cock flex. *Easy now, son. Don't jump the horse quite yet.* Trip might want Henry, but that didn't mean he was ready to admit it to the rest of the ranch. *And he might have been moaning with frustration.*

Yeah, not likely with the tone of voice he'd used, but still something to pursue carefully. Being gay in Wyoming wasn't a particularly safe life. Matthew Shepard had been brutally beaten only eighteen years and forty-five miles west of them, and while awareness was up, homophobia ran deep. Henry had known his sexuality from when he was a tween, but he'd been careful to cultivate friends of all genders to keep it hidden until he was old enough to defend himself.

Trip came from an older generation, where hypermasculinity forbade men from showing emotions, showing "weakness", or vulnerability. And loving another man was the ultimate weakness. Henry didn't know if Trip could acknowledge his interest to himself, much less to his friends and family.

Henry groaned and wished he had a brush to work through his hair. If nothing else, it allowed him to turn his brain off and focus on something easy when his mind ran around in little gibbering circles. Masturbation worked, too, but he didn't think Trip would appreciate Henry getting cum on his towels.

Coffee. I need coffee. He could distract himself with a hot cuppa joe and hopefully get his erection under control. He forced himself to move away from the enticing sounds coming from behind the bathroom door and went through the cupboards to find some mugs.

He'd just found two matching mugs with a southwestern design when someone knocked on the door of the apartment.

"Trip? Why is the door locked?"

Henry bit his lip, but strode to the door and opened it. The woman had stylish silver-gray hair cut short and brown eyes. She gasped and frowned.

"Sweet mercy, who are you?" She clutched a container of what looked like hot stew covered in a plate wrapped in cling wrap.

"Henry Bright, veterinarian." He stood back out of the way. "Come on in."

"Thanks. Nice to meet you." She bustled past him and set the container down on the counter before meeting his gaze again. "I'm Mrs. Guthrie."

"Pleased to meet you, ma'am." Henry bobbed his head with a smile. "Trip has mentioned you a time or two. I'm sorry about the towels, but you have my clothes in the laundry and this is all I've got. Thanks for takin' care of them."

"Uh, yes, not a problem." Mrs. Guthrie narrowed her eyes. "You look familiar, but I can't place where I've seen you. Have we met before, Mr. Bright?"

"No, ma'am." That was true enough, though she'd probably seen him on TV or in a video on YouTube. "I did grow up around here and just recently moved back." He didn't really want to mention his music career if she couldn't peg him with it on her own.

"Hmm." She nodded slowly, though her gaze remained narrowed. "Well, I brought some stew and a plate of freshly cooled brownies for y'all. Make sure he eats. Trip's been known to forget."

"Yes, ma'am. I will." He nodded earnestly and hoped the towel didn't ride too low on his hips. There'd been many a woman, regardless of age, who'd taken a low-riding towel as an invitation for more than just ogling.

"Good." She turned to leave, but paused at the edge of the kitchen. "Mr. Bright, may I ask you a personal question?"

"Yes, ma'am."

"Are you gay?"

No point in denying it. "Yes, ma'am."

"Are you interested in Trip?"

"Uh..." How did he answer that one? "If you're askin' if I find him attractive, yes, ma'am. But I haven't made any moves on him or talked to him about it. And before I tell you anything about my plans, I'd rather discuss it with him first."

"But you're plannin' to discuss it with him?" She raised an eyebrow.

Henry raised his chin. "Well, ma'am, I figure that's my business."

She scowled. "You do know he was married and had a son, right?"

"I figured that's where Tom Colton came from. I might be gay, but I did take biology in school."

"Don't you get cocky with me, young man. I've known the Coltons a lot longer than you. Trip was married to my best friend, who was the love of his life, so don't you be thinkin' you can just mosey on in here and warm Trip's bed because you're cute."

Trip was married to the love of his life? The knowledge of Trip's wife cooled some of Henry's arousal, but the older woman's meddling ways pissed him right the hell off. Trip was old enough to make his own decisions if they discussed it. *If I ever get the courage to ask him about it.*

"Respectfully, ma'am. It ain't anyone's business but Trip's and mine, and I haven't talked to him about it. I don't know if I ever will." He worked at keeping the edge out of his voice. "But right now, all I expected was a place to warm up for a time. I have no designs on Trip Colton."

"You best keep it that way, Mr. Henry Bright."

"Best keep what what way, Estelle?"

Trip appeared around the corner dressed in his robe

with a towel draped around his shoulders. Henry wanted to hand him a cup of coffee, but his anger made his hands shake and he didn't want to spill it. Instead he shifted them to the side and turned around to lean against the counter, waiting to see what Mrs. Guthrie would say. It pissed him off that she felt she needed to defend Trip, as if he was a wayward child or fresh out of a divorce or death. Henry idly wondered if she'd do the same to a younger woman interested in the elder Colton.

She raised her chin. "I told Mr. Bright that he needs set aside any designs he has on you in an attempt to make a name for himself in Wyoming."

Henry tightened his lips over a disbelieving smirk. *Make a name for myself?* Shit-oh-dear, he already had half of the country drooling over him from his music alone. He didn't need Trip to make a name for himself.

Trip dropped his chin to his chest as he gathered his thoughts for a few moments. "I appreciate you tryin' to protect me and all, Estelle, and I realize that Doc Bright might seem threatening to you as far as I'm concerned. But you don't have to worry. I can take care of myself. Have been for years."

"You ain't never had a hot young thing marchin' around here to defend against." Estelle leveled a gimlet look at Henry. "You better watch yourself, mister. Trip Colton isn't your stepping stone and he's not a quick screw."

"Ease up, Estelle. Doc Bright hasn't done anything and we haven't talked about it. Plus I'm pretty sure he doesn't need me to make a name for himself." Trip used a voice full of understanding and compassion, but firmness. "Thank you for your concern, but I'm all right." He gestured toward the door. "Thank you for the stew and goodies, too. And let me know when the laundry's done. I'll be happy to come get the clothes."

He ushered her out the door while Henry waited in the

kitchen, trying to figure out if he was more insulted or amused. True, he wanted a chance with Trip if it was available, but not because he owned a thriving ranch or had plenty of money. *Damn, money isn't what I wanted.* He'd left behind his music career because he wanted something else.

Love. Respect for himself. Control over his art. But not money. At least not the kind he hadn't earned himself.

He'd count himself lucky if he found a man to love who loved him for the person he was rather than the fame he had. He crossed his arms over his chest and stared at his feet. Ah hell, he would've liked the chance to explore with Trip, but he was pretty sure his opportunity had evaporated.

"I'm sorry about that." Trip reappeared with a grimace. He stood with his feet braced apart, but still managed to look uncertain. "She doesn't recognize you and she seems to think you're here to get into my pants for a share of the ranch."

"Yeah, I got that." Henry ran a hand through his hair. "Look, Trip, it's no secret I'm gay and, if it isn't obvious, I do find you handsome. But unlike a lot of homophobic rhetoric, I don't hit on guys who aren't clear on their sexuality. And I'm not here to get into your pants and take your ranch. I do have my own money."

"I know that, Henry. She's just bein' protective against gold diggers."

He shrugged. "Could be. Or it could be a problem with the widower of her late best friend havin' a young gay man in his home after marryin' a woman."

Trip's brows lowered and he nodded as he rubbed his chin. "Yeah, could be. That gave me pause, too." He shoved his hands in the pocket of the robe. "The thing is, I uh, well, I'm out of practice with…"

He struggled to find the words he wanted, but Henry kept his mouth shut. Trip had to get this out on his own without help.

He sighed. "Other than my late wife, I haven't dated anyone else. After her death, it wasn't worth it and I didn't find anyone else I was interested in. At least, not until you."

Henry raised his gaze to meet Trip's, resisting the urge to drop his jaw. "You're interested in me?"

"Yeah, uh, yeah." Trip cleared his throat. "I'm not too good with words and I don't always know how to say things right. But, uh, I sure do like spendin' time with you and I, uh, would like to get to know you...you know. Better."

The happy tattoo of excitement and pleasure thundered in Henry's chest. *Trip likes me and wants to be with me.* He couldn't have asked for a more promising thought. But he didn't want to screw it up and forced himself to take it slow enough not to scare him off.

"Are you sure, Trip?" He had to give him an out. "You haven't known me that long and I don't want to overstep anything. Technically, I'm an employee."

Trip snorted and waved his hand. "You don't work for me. You were hired by my son Tom, and technically you work under Byron. Or you will when he gets healed up."

"But you haven't known me longer than a few days. You're sure?"

He sobered and nodded, confidence shining in his expression. "I'm old fashioned, Henry. I might not have known you for very long, but I know my own self pretty damn well, and my gut's rarely wrong. If you're willin' to take a chance on an old man gettin' back into the datin' game, then I'd like to try it with you."

Henry couldn't believe his luck. Trip wanted to try with him? But reality wouldn't let him celebrate.

"What about Mrs. Guthrie? She's pretty sure I'm a gold digger, and I know she's known you a long time." He grimaced. "I don't want to cause a rift here at the ranch. To be honest, I'm kinda worried what your son will think about this, too."

SIOBHAN MUIR

Trip sighed and rubbed his face with his hands. "Yeah, Tom's a question. I honestly don't know how he'll react. He's okay with Ransom and his family, but I don't know what he'll think about his dad being interested in men." He shrugged. "No point borrowin' trouble over it. But don't worry about Mrs. Guthrie. It ain't her business about our relationship."

"No, but she could make it her business."

"Yup, she could. People are always gonna think what they want. I can't change them. But I can be honest with you and me and Tom." He rubbed his chin again. "I'm not real good with words, as I said, but I don't wanna hide anything with you." He frowned as if searching for the right things to say. "That said I'm not overly affectionate in public, even with Tom and Amber, so it might seem like I'm hidin' stuff. I haven't had anything like this in damn near thirty years. Fortunately, we got rid of the gossip monger on the ranch a couple of months ago."

"That's a relief. I didn't spend much time in the tabloids, but keepin' a low profile is kinda where I was hopin' to be." Henry screwed up his courage and stepped closer to him. "I'm willin' to take this slow and easy."

Trip's brows lowered and he bit his bottom lip, cranking up Henry's arousal.

"You're sure you want an old man like me?"

"Age is just a number, Trip. Yeah, you've had thirty more years of life in this world than me, but I'm old enough to know what I want and who."

"It don't matter to you that my son's older than you are?"

"Nope. Does it matter to you?" He stopped in front of Trip and met his steel-gray gaze. "Attraction has never been worried about age differences, and neither have I."

He waited for Trip to move away or punch him. He'd experienced both, especially with men uncertain about their sexual leanings. But he waited and Henry took a chance.

70

He brushed his lips over Trip's and prayed to anyone listening that he wouldn't get decked.

Trip tasted like coffee and masculine beauty, and Henry's cock flexed against the towel. He loved the sensation of the stubble on his cheeks and chin, and wanted to deepen the kiss. But he held back from slanting his head and taking control. Yeah, he would've liked to feel Trip's tongue in his mouth, but he didn't want to unnerve the older man.

Pulling back, Henry met his gaze once more and hoped he wouldn't see revulsion. *Or panic.*

"That was...different."

Somehow, the tone of voice Trip used sounded disgusted. Henry sighed and stepped back. *I just kissed a straight guy curious about gay men. Fuck.* He'd truly hoped Trip wasn't one of those gay-for-you men who just wanted to see what the gay scene was about, but he was pretty sure that was Trip all the way. He ran his hand through his hair and over the back of his neck.

"Different. Yeah. Right." Henry nodded. "I'm gonna..." What? He had no clothes so he couldn't get dressed and leave. And he couldn't cause a scandal for Trip if he walked out into the lodge in just a pair of towels. *Shit.* Now what could he do?

"Henry, I didn't mean... Aw shit." Trip reached for him only to pull his hand back. "I'm sorry. I've never kissed a man before and I spoke out loud before I thought. It was different than kissing a woman, but it wasn't bad."

"Are you saying it's "not bad"?" Henry couldn't help the dry tone.

"Yes, no. Fuck!" Trip shook his head. "I liked it. That's what I meant. I liked it. I don't think I was any good at kissin' before, but I liked it. If you're okay with my inexperience, I'd like to do it again." He suddenly smirked. "You know, so I can get better at it."

Henry laughed. "Are you sayin' you wanna practice

kissin'?"

"Yes, sir. If you're interested and all." He grinned and looked terribly boyish for all his silver hair and laugh lines.

Henry looked pointedly down at the tenting towel then back up at Trip. "Oh, I'm definitely interested." He returned to stand damn near nose-to-nose with him. "Do you trust me?"

"In terms of kissin'? Yes, sir."

"Good." Henry cupped Trip's head with his hands and tilted his face. "Because I'm gonna kiss the hell outta you."

And he sealed his lips to Trip's.

The first kiss had been gentle, a test and a taste. This kiss was everything Henry had hopped and then some. Trip didn't hesitate and opened his mouth as soon as Henry pressed his tongue to the seam between his lips. Again, Trip tasted of coffee and masculinity, and his tongue tangled with Henry's. They both moaned, and Henry took it as encouragement to wrap his arms around the older man and pull him against his chest.

To his delighted surprise, Trip buried a hand in Henry's hair and fisted it as he tangled his tongue with Henry's. Henry's cock flexed and brushed against a similar ridge under Trip's robe. The unexpected contact sent arousal flaring through Henry's chest and he rubbed his hips against Trip.

Trip broke the kiss and threw his head back. "Aw fuck."

Is that an invitation? Henry took advantage of the neck exposure and peppered kisses along Trip's jaw and throat, heading for the silver-gray chest hair between the lapels of the robe. When he reached Trip's collar bones, he buried his nose in the hair and inhaled. *Holy fuck, he smells good.*

Henry slid his hand under one side of the robe and over Trip's hardening nipple as he kissed Trip's chest. He could easily imagine himself snuggling up to the older man every night and falling asleep in the delicious scent of Trip's hairy chest. *God, if you grant wishes, let this one be mine.*

"Just to be clear, you're okay with kissin'. Is that any kind of kissin' or just on the lips?"

Trip opened his eyes and met Henry's gaze. "What kind of kissin' did you have in mind?"

Henry slid his hand down to the front of Trip's robe and grasped his scrotum without breaking eye contact. "I'm of the mind to kiss you here."

Trip blinked, the thoughts chasing each other across his face too fast for Henry to interpret.

"You wanna give me a blow job?"

"You said you were okay with kissin'. Blow job is a form of kissin'." Henry gave him his best sultry smile. "How 'bout you sit in your comfy chair over there and I'll help you relax."

Trip nodded reluctantly and headed for the chair, his shoulders tense. He sat down, the robe closed over his chest and Henry mourned the loss of the view. But he followed and knelt in front of Trip's legs, gazing up into the gray-blue eyes.

"Are you okay with this, Trip?"

"Yeah, sure. Why wouldn't I be?"

Henry shrugged. "Because you look like I'm gonna attack you with a bale hook."

Trip grimaced. "I just don't know if I, uh, well…"

He raised an eyebrow at the stiff flesh tenting the robe's folds.

"Oh, I can get hard, Henry. I just don't know if I can come." To Henry's surprise the older man blushed. "I sort of came in the shower just now…"

He smirked. "Were you thinkin' of me when you came?"

Trip looked away as the rosy hue suffused his cheeks. "Yes…"

Pleasure and excitement heated Henry's chest as he took in his chagrin. "I think I should repay the favor. Or at least make good on the fantasy." He spread the robe open over Trip's lap and took in the lovely masculine sight.

Though not more than average length, Trip's cock rose in a thick, curving line from a thatch of silver and black hair. Heavy testicles rested against his muscular thighs and He inhaled the earthy, heady scent.

"Damn, Trip, you smell fuckin' wonderful." He nuzzled the heavy sac and the thick shaft flexed with arousal. "I'm gonna pleasure the hell out of your cock and if you come, then it's gravy for me."

"I'm not sure I can come again so soon, but I ain't gonna say no if you wanna try." His blush still stained his cheeks, but his steel-gray eyes glittered with arousal. Henry didn't wait to see if he'd change his mind.

He grasped Trip's thick cock and dragged his tongue over the plum-sized head. The salty, rich taste of his skin and pre-cum hit his tongue like ambrosia and he damn near swooned. *Glory be, he tastes so good.*

Trip gasped as Henry explored the edge of the head and traced the robust veins in the shaft. Emboldened by the response, he fit his lips around the glans and pushed down on Trip's cock. Pleasure and arousal ripped through him as the hard, hot flesh filled his mouth with his taste.

There was so much to explore, Henry didn't know what to do first. But he wanted to do it all. He started with dragging his tongue over the edges of the head as he tightened his lips around the shaft. Pre-cum dripped onto his tongue as he squeezed the shaft below his mouth with his fist.

Trip moaned. *Glory, that's a sexy sound.*

He slowly pulled his mouth off the broad head and dropped his face to nuzzle Trip's balls, licking them at the last moment.

"Sweet Jesus, Henry." Trip's hands fisted in the soft fabric of his robe as he dropped his head against the back of the chair.

Henry took the exclamation as approval and kept licking and suckling the soft skin. Trip's cock flexed with each swipe of his tongue and Henry gripped it, stroking him with firm but gentle motions. He moaned and his hips jerked, the knuckles on his hands growing white from the pressure.

Henry moved back to the straining, plum-sized head of Trip's cock and sank down over it, squeezing with his lips. He whimpered as Henry took him as deeply as he could and swallowed. The hot, solid flesh in his mouth stiffened more and he savored the texture of it against his lips. He swirled his tongue around the smooth shaft, enjoying the tangy pre-cum coating his mouth.

When Henry accidentally scraped the edge of the head with his teeth, Trip hissed and grabbed his hair with his hands, holding him there.

"God, yes, Henry. Right there. Like that."

The guttural command set Henry's blood on fire and he increased the pressure on the hot cock in his mouth. He happily took it deeper, swallowing and drooling around the shaft until his hand grew slick with it. Trip whimpered and moaned, his hips rocking as Henry increased the pace of his suckling.

When he tickled the skin of Trip's balls, the man gave a deep groan and his cock stiffened to silky steel in Henry's mouth. His hands tightened in Henry's hair and cum filled his throat in hot spurts. Henry greedily swallowed all of it, licking and slurping with abandon, his own cock stone-like between his thighs.

At last, Trip went limp in the chair, his chest rising and falling with his settling breaths. His hands remained locked in Henry's hair as he slowly relaxed. Henry lovingly cleaned his cock with his tongue before easing back to look up Trip's body. Pleasure and satisfaction greater than he'd ever known filled his chest. He'd made Trip happy and relaxed, and it was almost better than getting his own blow job.

"That had to be the best blow job I've ever gotten, bar none." Trip didn't open his eyes, but his voice held the same satisfaction as shown on his body.

"You know I'm going to hold onto that honor and compliment." Henry rose and sat on the couch beside the chair, just wanting to look at his satisfied lover.

'Cause that's what he is. My lover.

The understanding thrilled him.

CHAPTER EIGHT

Trip floated. That was the best he could describe the euphoria after Henry had sucked him off. He'd received blow jobs before, from Livvy and a few whores while he'd been in Vietnam, but none of them had been this erotic or satisfying. *Sorry, Livvy.* To be honest, he'd never cared about them much. But Henry made him feel like a king and Trip wasn't going to ignore his gift.

"I hate to suck and run, Trip, but I gotta get back to work. If my clothes aren't done, can I borrow something so I can get to my place and change?" Henry relaxed on the couch, his body as luxurious as satin sheets. Trip resisted the urge to reach over and touch him.

"Do you want any stew? If you stay for lunch, it might give your clothes a little more time to dry." Did he sound as hopeful as he thought? He wanted more time with Henry, but they both needed to work, too.

Henry tipped his head and chewed his bottom lip. "Yeah, I guess. But if we get done eatin' and the clothes ain't done, I'd still like a ride to my place. I gotta check on the animals and fill out the order forms for supplies."

"Are we low on anythin'?"

"Yeah, we need some wormin' meds and our antibiotic

stash is low. Plus, even though I'm all right, I gotta make some money. I can't live on my savings forever."

"And you deserve to be paid for the work you do. Yeah, I get it. Let's eat and we'll see where your clothes are." Trip nodded as he rose.

"Sounds good." Henry followed him and Trip wished they had more time.

Yeah, put wishes in one hand and spit in the other, and see which one fills up first.

They shared the stew and it was as good as usual, but something about sharing it with Henry made it taste even better. Their conversation drifted to ordinary ranch issues and when they thought Byron would be back on his feet. Part of Trip hoped the man would take as long as possible to heal. Then Henry would stay much longer. But another part of him wanted his good friend to get better. *Maybe I can convince Byron to keep Henry on.* It would be better to have a backup vet should Byron have another accident.

By the time they were done with the stew, Trip wished Henry could just while away the afternoon with him. To keep himself from mooning over the younger man, he excused himself to get dressed on the pretense of checking on the laundry. Irritation over Estelle's misplaced defense stuck in his craw and he wondered what her problem was. He pulled his jeans over his hips and stuffed his cock and balls into the fly, remembering the vision of Henry's lips stretched over his girth.

Shit-oh-dear, that's sexy.

His fingers shook a little as he buttoned up his flannel shirt, but he ruthlessly stilled them. What the hell was Estelle's problem? She seemed fine enough with the Knight family and they weren't heterosexual at all. Why would it matter if Trip was interested in men?

"I'll go get our clothes and you can be back to work in a few." Trip ambled out into the main room of his apartment and stopped dumb.

Henry sat in his favorite chair, reading a book. The light fell over his glorious dark locks of hair and painted sexy shadows on his stubbed cheek and jaw. Instead of lust, tender attraction filled Trip's chest, and he wanted to settle beside the younger man just to cuddle and read. *What the hell is wrong with me?*

Henry looked up. "Sounds good. I don't mind if they're a little damp. It'll get me to the barn a helluva lot faster if my balls are cold."

Trip laughed at the image that conjured. "Right. Let's hope they're completely dry."

He left the apartment and headed for the laundry at the back of the lodge, the smile fading from his lips. He liked having Henry in his place, but he needed to think about how he'd present this situation to his family. He didn't know how Tom or Amber would take it. It was already apparent Estelle wasn't pleased. They were all used to him being the single widower, ambling along, contented with his lot. But that was no life. In his soul, Trip understood change came when least expected. Henry represented a huge change and he didn't know how his loved ones would handle it.

How am I going to handle it?

Estelle stood at the dryer pulling out clothes when he arrived in the laundry room. Heat and the scent of fabric softener perfumed the air, chasing away the cold from the winter world outside. She paused in her work and looked at the clothes in her hands before she pulled them to her face and inhaled. Her shoulders shook with silent sobs and some of Trip's confidence slipped. Why was she crying?

He'd known Estelle Guthrie since they were kids out of high school. She'd been the best friend of the prettiest girl he'd ever seen and he'd courted that girl, Olivia Murray, until she'd agreed to be his wife. He'd married her and promptly got drafted for Vietnam. They had fourteen tumultuous years together, and he'd never stopped loving

Livvy. Even now.

Estelle had seen them through it all as Livvy's best friend and confidante, and when her own husband had died a few years before Trip was gored by an ornery bull, Trip had stood with her and held her hand. They'd been friends a long time, but he'd never seen her this upset.

"Estelle? Everything all right?" It was an inane question, but he wanted to give her time to find her equilibrium.

"Oh, Trip. Uh, yes, I was just collecting the clothes to bring to you." She straightened her shoulders and sniffled a little, boxing up her emotions like they always had. "How did you like the stew?"

"It was real good, thanks." He waited for her to finish gathering up the clothes. "Do you want me to take those? I don't want to add anything to your chores."

"Sure, that'd be fine." She handed him the warm pile of clothes, but wouldn't meet his eyes. "You best be getting those back to Doc Bright so he can get back to work."

"Yup, that's where I'm headed." He wanted to say more, to ask what was really going on with her, but he didn't know how and except for with his wife and son, wasn't good at confronting emotions. "Thanks for doin' this for me."

Coward.

Yeah, at the moment, he was, but until he understood what he wanted for himself, he'd have to be that way. Trip turned and strode back to his apartment, dodging guests and keeping his head down. He had a lot of things to think on, and he couldn't do it with people around him.

He pushed into his apartment and found Henry where he'd left him, still reading.

"The clothes are dry. Your balls should be safe."

Henry looked up and laughed. "Good to know." He rose with youthful grace and Trip's cock flexed a little. *Down, boy.* "I'll get changed and out of your way." He took the clothes with him to the bathroom.

Trip busied himself with the kitchen, tidying up from their lunch as he waited for Henry to appear. He turned over the events in his mind, trying to make sense of how he felt and what it meant in the long run. He hadn't reached any answers by the time Henry reappeared, dressed and ready to go.

"Thanks for the warm meal and lettin' me give you a little pleasure." Henry smiled. "I enjoyed it."

Heat warmed Trip's cheeks, but he smiled. "You're welcome, and thank you, too. It felt amazin'." He cleared his throat and rubbed the back of his neck. "I really enjoyed your company. Would you be interested in sharin' supper tonight? It ain't gonna be fancy, but it'd be nice to have some company this evenin'."

Henry paused and unease slithered through Trip's gut. "Yeah, uh, I have some stuff I gotta take care of tonight, but how 'bout we do it tomorrow night? It's Friday, after all."

Trip's gut released. "Yeah, okay. That sounds good. I usually eat around six-thirty. That work for you?"

"Sure, that's good." Henry nodded with a smile that didn't quite reach his eyes, but he held out his hand and pulled Trip into a back-slapping hug when they closed palms. "I'll let you know about the supply situation so we can make an order as soon as I have it."

"Sounds good." Trip didn't want to release Henry's hand and held it just a minute longer. "I really enjoyed today, Henry. Never doubt that no matter what else happens, okay?"

Some of the warmth returned to Henry's smile. "I enjoyed it too, Trip. And I do want to spend more time with you, I just gotta take care of some things. So, tomorrow at six-thirty, right?"

"Yeah."

"See you then."

Trip released him and let him head out of the apartment. The space seemed smaller with his absence, but Trip shook his head. *Don't be stupid.* He didn't need to moon over the younger man. But he recalled feeling the exact same way whenever he'd said goodbye to Livvy when they first started going out. She'd filled up the space, no matter where they were, and he missed her when she wasn't there.

He sighed. *Good god, Livvy. Is this okay? Henry fills my lonely heart like you did.*

He didn't get an answer, but he didn't expect one. Instead, he picked up his phone and his reading glasses to text his son Tom. He really needed to talk to him and get some perspective, because one thing he knew for sure. He wanted more time with Henry.

****

Henry settled into the clinic and wrote down all the supplies he needed to order so they'd be set for the next couple of months. He didn't know how the older vet Byron did it or kept the order forms, but he wrote everything down and planned on talking to Tom about the suppliers so he could make the orders directly, either online or by the phone.

He managed to distract himself until suppertime when he had to face the dark and cold to march across the ranch to his bungalow. *You jackass, you could've had dinner with Trip in the lodge.* Instead, he wrapped his scarf around his neck, stuffed his head into his hat, and hoped his fingers wouldn't freeze considering he hadn't brought his gloves that morning. He locked up the clinic, turned off the lights, and shoved his hands into his pockets.

Fortunately, the Coltons had wisely chosen to light the driveways and paths around the ranch with solar lamps. In the snow, they sparkled like holiday lights and he enjoyed the beautiful sight despite the wind cutting through his coat. It was damn near magical.

Yeah, kinda like this afternoon.

The heat of arousal and pleasure from sucking off Trip's cock carried him all the way to his bungalow. Snow decorated his truck, the roof, and front walk, but he didn't mind. Something had changed and happiness edged out his usual frustration with winter weather. *It was a damn good blow job.*

He hadn't given one in weeks. Hell, he hadn't had one in longer than that, but giving pleasure to Trip had been far more satisfying than any cock-sucking he'd received in years. Henry liked the way Trip's body tightened up and all the muscles in his belly and chest stood out. It had given him great satisfaction to watch Trip's pleasure.

Best fuckin' blow job ever.

He let himself into the warm interior of the bungalow and sighed. Trip had enjoyed it and shared lunch with him, but they'd talked about ranch issues during the meal. Trip hadn't seemed to regret their sexual interaction, but he also hadn't lingered over their stew. Henry wished he could have more time with Trip, just getting to know him, but this wasn't a gay men's resort and they both had jobs.

Henry hung up his coat and pulled off his boots before snooping through his refrigerator for anything edible. Nothing looked good beyond the can of soup in his pantry so he dumped it in a pot on the stove and pulled out his phone to call Ransom.

"Hey Henry, what's up?"

"You got some time to talk, Ransom?"

"Sure. What's goin' on? You call that guy back yet?" Ransom sounded like he was moving from one room to another.

"No, but I'll do it this weekend. Gotta figure some shit out first." Henry stirred his soup. "What do you know about Trip Colton?"

"Tom's dad?" Ransom's surprise came through loud and clear. "I know he's a widower and a Vietnam vet. I know he used to be a rodeo bullfighter until he got gored. Tom damn near lost him to it and that's kinda what made them set up their ranch. Why?"

"Do you know if he's closet gay?"

Silence stretched on the other end of the line. "I don't, but he's a widower and I've never heard of him dating or seeing anyone. Why? What happened, Henry?"

He squirmed as he watched the soup. "I, uh, I sort of...kissed him." *Very loose translation.*

"You what? Where?"

"In his apartment in the lodge." Henry rubbed his forehead with one hand. "He was okay with it. I didn't force myself on him."

"Trip Colton was okay with kissin' you?"

"Yup." *And then some.* Henry pulled the soup off the stove before it boiled. "He told me he wanted to practice kissin' so he could get better at it on account of how long it's been."

More silence came through the phone. "Well I'll be damned. I didn't think Trip was gay. He didn't give off that vibe. Of course, it might be more ageism on my part."

"Ageism?" Henry ladled some soup into a bowl and took it to the table to eat. "What do you mean?"

"You know. He's older, from the previous generation. We all know intellectually gay folks have been around since the dawn of time, but the myth that no one in the previous generation was gay persists." Henry could hear Ransom's shrug. "He was married and had a son. He never dated anyone so I just assumed he was straight."

Henry nodded. He'd made the same assumption at first. "Yeah, I think everyone does. Mrs. Guthrie accused me of bein' a gold-digger goin' after Trip's ranch to make a name for myself."

"Mrs. Guthrie the housekeeper there?" Ransom

whistled. "She saw you with Trip?"

"Well, not really saw us together, just found out I was in his apartment in just towels."

Ransom laughed. "Son, you're gonna have to explain a bit more. Did she catch you after you had sex with him? I thought you said you only kissed him."

"No sex." *Not while she was there.* "We'd been fixin' the sink in the clinic in the barn and got soaked. Trip brought me to his place to warm up and dry out. I was fresh out of the shower when she came in with stew and brownies."

"Where was Trip?"

"In the shower."

"You weren't there together, were you?"

"No, separate showers." But the idea had merit. *Focus!* "But she didn't recognize me as Henry Bright the Kick-ass Cowboy, and accused me of taking advantage of Trip. As if the man isn't old enough or lucid enough to make his own decisions."

Ransom chuckled, but it sounded sad. "Here's the thing. Mrs. Guthrie as far as I can tell has been around Trip since forever started. She's known him as only one thing— widower and father. You just represented two very big changes to her. Not only are you younger than Trip and he seems interested in you, but you're male, which means he's at least bisexual if not closet gay. Neither of those things are easy for people to accept."

"Yeah, I know." He pulled the soup off the stove and poured it into a bowl as he held the phone to his ear with his shoulder. "But I like him, Ransom."

"This ain't one of your flings, is it?" Ransom's voice held unease. "I might not be into the man myself, but Trip Colton isn't one of those guys you can love and then leave. If you're thinkin' about gettin' involved with him, don't do this for the quick and dirty."

Henry scowled at the phone. "It's not like that at all. I

really like him. I don't care if he's older than me, I just like him, and I want to see if it can go somewhere. I don't want to hurt him."

"I'm glad to hear that." Ransom still sounded cautious.

"I'm just worried about Mrs. Guthrie."

"What about her?"

"She could really make things rough and I don't know what to do. I have to work here."

"Well, you're gonna have to take things slow. Your relationship with Trip is what matters, right? So, he's the one you have to make your feelings clear to, got it? She's gonna be uncomfortable until he sets her straight, but he's gotta know you're serious." Ransom sighed and Henry wondered if he spoke from experience. "If he knows and you know, and you're both clear on that, it'll work. Otherwise, he'll start listenin' to those who don't want y'all together."

"But this just started today."

"Damn, son, you work fast." Ransom laughed. "Look, no matter what, try not to think with your dick. You're pretty smart when it comes to people from what I remember. Feel the situation out and you'll be fine."

"I hope you're right, Ransom. Shit, I've never been in this kind of situation before. All my previous partners have been…well, my age and tryin' things out." Henry rubbed his head. "They've never been established as somethin' other than they are."

"Yup. This is a new opportunity for you not to screw up."

"Thanks." Henry snorted.

"Anytime." Ransom laughed again. "Just be you and be honest. Nothin' more you can do."

"Right. Thanks anyway. I'll talk to you later."

"Yup."

Henry ended the call and shook his head. *Just be you.* Ransom's words echoed in his head, and he grimaced as he grabbed a piece of bread to eat with his soup. He had been himself, and he was happier as himself with Trip. *After only one afternoon?* It didn't make sense. Love at first sight didn't exist except in movies. Attraction and lust were easy, but love? That took work. Work he'd never had to do before.

How do I work on love with a man who's lived twice as long as I have?

He didn't know, but his gut told him he'd never give up trying.

CHAPTER NINE

Trip tried to busy himself after Tom's response to his text, but his mind kept running around in circles. Tom wasn't available until after work, but he said he'd bring Amber with him when they came for dinner. They had something important to talk about. Trip's gut sank and he had to swallow against fear a few times. Had Estelle talked to Tom first?

Aw hell, worryin' will get me nowhere.

The only thing that worked at turning off his squirrely thoughts was exercise. As he'd gotten older, ranch work became increasingly difficult and hard on his joints. Remembering the times in the Army had him researching exercise equipment and he'd bought an elliptical to keep his body at least limber. It had worked to keep him moving and functional without causing extra strain on his joints. And it shut off his mind.

He changed into a t-shirt and jogging shorts, and set out to do a rigorous workout. Despite his pushing as hard as possible, he couldn't outrun his anxiety and unease. What would Tom say when Trip admitted his interest in Henry? What would Amber say? In the state known for the Matthew Shepard killing, violent responses to homophobia weren't out of the question. Trip might be an adult, but that wouldn't stop other men from taking their fear out on him.

He ran himself damn near ragged and only the ache in his knees forced him to stop. His breath sawed in his chest, and he staggered to the bathroom to shower away his sweat. For the moment, his mind remained blissfully quiet and he stepped under the hot spray with a weary sigh.

He let the hot water pour over him and his mind slowly refocused. He thought about Henry and his gut tensed with excitement and desire. He growled and shoved the thought aside, only to be hit with Tom and Amber, and the concerns over what they'd think.

Shit.

Now, don't go worryin' over nothin', Trip. You know better than that.

Livvy sat on the bathroom counter across from the shower and shook her head at him.

But Tom's our son and the only family I got left. He ruthlessly scrubbed his body with soap, trying to outrun his concern.

Yes, he is, but Tom also loves you, and so does Amber. If you make it clear how you feel about Henry, they won't begrudge you a second chance at love.

He groaned. *Even if that second chance is with a man? You know how folks around here feel about that.* He rinsed his body and shut off the shower, pushing the door open. Livvy shot him a look that said he was being an idiot.

"What?"

And how do folks 'around here' feel about that? Are you referin' to the Knights next door? What about Henry?

"What about Matthew Shepard?"

You're not a young freshman at college. You're a man with a life and a business.

"And if someone like Hank Adams finds out, that life and business will be done." He dried his body with his towel, trying to settle down, but the fear kept rising up.

I need you to understand somethin'. Are you listenin'?
He raised his gaze from his toes to the serious expression on the ghost of his wife. When she used that tone of voice, he'd learned to pay attention.

"Yes, ma'am."

Good. You can either be who you are without apologies or flash, or you can run, hide, and lose a second chance at happiness because of fear. She narrowed her eyes at him and raised her chin. *I don't recall thinkin' of you as a coward, Trip Colton.*

"No, ma'am." He scowled, but couldn't meet her gaze.

Then you better make it clear this is what you need for your own happiness. And have a little faith in your son. Livvy hopped off the counter and shook her head. *He's more understanding than you give him credit for. Especially now that he has Amber.*

"I don't know about that."

Trust me.

He looked up to protest, but she'd gone, and his shoulders slumped. Nothing like being reprimanded like a wayward child by the ghost of one's wife. Still, she was right. He couldn't run or hide. He didn't have to broadcast his romantic liaisons far and wide, but he wouldn't walk around on eggshells either. Who he slept with had no bearing on his capabilities as a man, but if he didn't accept that, no one else would, either.

All right, Livvy. I'll man-up and tell Tom.

He didn't receive an out-loud response, but he immediately felt better and hoped it meant Tom wouldn't be too upset. He headed for his kitchen and started dinner of salad, soup, and toasted cheese sandwiches. Comfort food to ease the uncertainty. The words of Tom's text still gave him some hitch in his giddyup–*Something important to talk about.* Trip gritted his teeth as he cut bread.

"Hey Dad, are you in here?" Tom's voice echoed through the small apartment.

"Yeah, in the kitchen." He hoped his voice held steady.

Tom appeared around the corner with Amber and her dog Nimbus in tow. "Good to see you. Thanks for havin' us over for dinner."

"Yeah, no problem. Everythin' okay with all y'all?" He kept his voice light though his heart pounded in his chest.

"Yeah, everything's good, Trip." Amber snuck into the kitchen and kissed his cheek. "How are you doing? How's the new vet working out for you?"

"Uh, good. Good, real good." He tried to smile, but the memory of Henry's mouth around his cock derailed the attempt. "Are cheese sandwiches and soup okay for you tonight? I was thinkin' it would be nice to have some comfort food in this cold."

"Sounds perfect, Dad." Tom set a bottle of sparkling apple cider on the counter as he helped Amber out of her coat. "We brought Nimbus's food dish tonight. That okay?"

"Sure." Trip shot a look at the dog to assess Amber's mood. The blue-heeler mix seemed relaxed despite her service-dog vest and he breathed a sigh of relief. *At least Amber's not upset about it.*

"Can I help with anything?" She returned to the kitchen.

"If you don't mind workin' on the salad, that'd help." He nodded to the vegetables on the counter.

"Sure, I'd be happy to." She gave him a speculative look. "Are you all right, Trip? You seem nervous."

He'd forgotten how intuitive Amber was, but he wasn't ready to say anything. *Better to deliver this kind of news over food.*

"Yeah, I'm good. Got a lot on my mind about the new vet and all." That was the understatement of the week. He tried to smile. "Part of the reason I wanted to talk to y'all tonight."

"Oh, right. I'd heard Tom hired someone new. Do you

think he'll be a good fit at the Triple Star?" She shredded lettuce into a bowl.

Definitely. "Yeah, I think so. But I wanted to talk to you about Byron and how Doc Bright will work with us."

"Doc Bright, huh?" Tom laughed as he helped set the table. "That makes him sound old, and he's about my age."

Trip swallowed hard against his unease. Tom had three years on Henry. What would he say when he expressed interest in the younger man? *This is all sorts of messed up.*

"It's good to get some young blood around here. Balances out the experience." Amber winked as she put the salad together.

They finished up the dinner prep and Trip tried to keep the conversation light though his gut sat in knots tied from knots. Tom and Amber shot loving glances at each other and he couldn't help but feel both proud and envious. He wanted them to be happy and settled, and he was hoping to hear about a marriage proposal. But he also wanted a similar kind of happiness for himself.

Tom brought the bottle of apple cider to the table and opened it while Amber handed him the good crystal glasses. They all sat down to dinner and said a short grace before Trip offered the plate of cheese sandwiches.

"So, what all did y'all want to talk to me about?" He served himself salad and hoped his hands didn't shake from nervousness. *Please say it's not Estelle's news about Henry.*

Tom shot a look at Amber, nodding for her to tell the tale.

"I had a doctor's appointment today." She smiled as she drizzled salad dressing over her vegetables.

"And?" His gut froze. Was she all right?

"And I'm pregnant." She bit her bottom lip to curb a wide grin. "Tom and I are going to have a baby."

He stared, the words not quite making sense. "What?"

Tom laughed. "You're gonna be a grampa."

"Grampa?" He'd be so wrapped up in his concern about his relationship with Henry, Tom's real news took a while to sink in. "Wait, pregnant? You're sure?"

"Yes. Just confirmed it today." Amber beamed.

Trip whooped and launched from his chair as much as his bad hip would allow. "Well hell! That's the best news I've heard in weeks." He dragged Tom from his seat and hugged him. "I'm so pleased for both of you. When's the little rugrat due?"

"May of next year. The doctor said I'm about eight weeks along." She squeezed him when it was her turn for a hug. "We'll have to be extra careful because of my advanced age, but all my blood work looks good for a healthy pregnancy."

He snorted as he sat back down. "Advanced age. Honey, you're still young."

She grimaced. "Not in terms of having my first child. The body doesn't know what it's getting into, so I'll have to baby it, no pun intended, to make sure everything works right."

Trip couldn't stop grinning. "Aw hell, we'll all help if we can. I'm so pleased for all y'all." He shook his head as he sipped his apple cider. "Another little Colton wanderin' around. That's a damn fine development." He raised his glass. "To Tom, Amber, and the little May cowpoke."

They all raised their glasses and toasted the good news, and some of his unease fled. *Did you hear that, Livvy? I'm gonna be a grampa.* He missed his wife in that moment, but the sorrow was bittersweet. She'd have loved to see Tom's child.

"So, Dad, now that we got that out of the way, what all did you want to talk to us about?"

His sandwich turned to dust in his mouth and he swallowed hard, wiping his mouth to give him time to organize his thoughts. He didn't want to ruin the mood and their possible reaction to his news scared the hell out of him.

"Trip?" Amber laid a hand on his arm and her face creased with concern as the silence stretched. "What's wrong?"

"I need to talk to y'all about somethin', but it's a sensitive issue and it's gonna be a shock." He pushed his salad around his plate with the fork, but he couldn't think of a way to come out with his interest in Henry.

"We're here for you, Dad. Whatever it is." Tom's brows lowered in concern. "What's goin' on?"

He rubbed his hands on his thighs, still unable to get the words out.

Just say it. You might be surprised at their reactions. Livvy leaned against the couch with her arms crossed over her chest. Trip met her gaze and swallowed again, bucking up his courage.

"Come on, Dad. You're scarin' the hell outta me. What's going on?"

"I really like the new vet, Henry Bright." He said the words, but it didn't seem to be enough.

"I'm glad to hear that. The animals seem to be doin' well. What's the big deal about that?" Tom's frown hadn't lifted yet.

"I, uh, didn't say it quite right, Tom." He met his son's gaze. "I think pretty highly of him, and…I, uh, I'd like to spend time with him socially."

"Socially? You mean like goin' out for a beer?"

"No. Well, yeah, but that's not what I mean." He rubbed the back of his neck and couldn't stop the flush from staining his cheeks. "I like Henry, Tom, the way you like Amber."

A silence as thick as a January snowfall settled over the room. He shot a look at Livvy and she waved at him to keep going, but he couldn't seem to find any more words. Instead he turned his gaze to Amber, afraid if what he'd see.

Instead of flat implacability or denial, she wore a look of consideration, and he took courage in her lack of anger.

"Trip, I'm just trying to clarify here. Are you saying you find Henry attractive and would like to go out with him?"

He swallowed the panicked saliva built up in his mouth. "Yes, ma'am."

"I see." She nodded and looked at Tom. Trip couldn't help but follow her gaze, terrified of what he'd see.

"Are you gonna say anything?" Where he got the courage to ask that question, he'd never know. But he needed to hear what Tom had to say. *Glory, please don't let me lose him forever.*

"I'm tryin' to understand." Tom clenched his jaw and straightened his shoulders before he met Trip's gaze. "Are you tellin' me you're gay, Dad?"

His immediate reaction was to deny it, to go back to where everyone thought he was a good ole heterosexual widower and leave it at that. But he couldn't do that to himself or Henry. They both deserved better. *Even if I'm scared shitless.*

"No, I don't think I'm gay. I think the proper description is bisexual, being that I loved your mom and all." He took a drink of his apple cider to whet his throat. "Y'all know I've been alone for a long time and I ain't never met another person who sparked my interest like your mother. She was one of a kind and no other woman has tempted me since." He clenched his hands into fists under the table. "I thought that was the way it would always be until I met Henry." He met Tom's gaze again, trying not to interpret the scowl on his face. "There's somethin' about him that makes my heart pump faster. I haven't felt this way about anyone since your mom."

Another silence ensued and he couldn't sit still. He gathered his plate and took it into the kitchen while he waited for the condemnation to come from his little family.

God, please make this all right. He couldn't help how he felt about Henry, and he had Livvy's blessing for it, but while his dead wife approved, his living son might not be so willing to accept it.

As the silence stretched, he sighed heavily and dropped his shoulders. "I like him, Tom. I know relationships between men are uneasy for most folks, and you didn't expect it of me, but I'm hopin' you'll give it a chance and won't be mad at me for too long. I didn't do this to hurt you or make your life harder."

"Oh, Dad, that's not what I'm thinkin'." Tom's voice sounded strained and sad, but Trip couldn't look. "It's just a surprise, is all."

He nodded. "I know. Was for me, too. I hope you can understand it's not all men I'm interested in, just Henry. Hell, I wasn't interested in all women, either. Just your mom."

"Speaking of Henry, how does he feel about this? Does he know about your interest?" Amber's voice remained light and curious.

"Yes, ma'am. He, uh, he feels the same. We discussed it this afternoon." He forced himself to turn around and face them.

Tom wore his stoic cowboy's mask while Amber appeared to be considering all angles.

"You know he's younger than me, right, Dad?" He rubbed his chin.

"Yup. That was one of my concerns, too. I didn't want him to saddle himself with an old man, but he said attraction never worried about age differences and neither did he." Trip ran his hand over his graying hair. "I know I'm stompin' on thin ice, what with Henry bein' so much younger than me and being male, but I like him." He met Tom's gaze. "He lights my campfire."

Tom took a deep breath. "Are you serious, Dad?"

"Yup."

"What does that mean?" Amber switched her gaze between them, her eyebrows up. "Is that some special guy code for something?"

Tom laughed a little. "Nah, it's Colton code for 'love of your life'."

"Did you say that about me?" She tilted her head.

"Yes, ma'am, I did." He grinned before he returned his gaze to Trip's. "Henry lights your campfire." He shook his head with a rueful smile. "Aw hell. You know I've always wanted you to find someone again. I just figured it would be some older woman lookin' for a companion. I never thought it would be a younger man."

"Yeah, me either." He bit his bottom lip. "Are you okay with this? I wanted to tell you in person, but I know it's a big adjustment. Wyoming isn't exactly homosexual-friendly."

"No, it ain't." Tom shot a look at Amber before he smiled. "But the Knights next door are mighty fine people and Ransom's gay. I never had a problem with him."

"I know, but family can be different."

Tom nodded. "Yeah, that's true. The thing is, if you and Henry are good with it, I'll be good with it. Though it might be a little unnerving for me at first if you kiss in front of me." He held up his hand as Trip opened his mouth to protest. "I can't say I won't get over it, it just might take me a little while."

Trip nodded slowly. "I can understand that. I'm not big on public displays of affection anyway. My generation always preferred to do that behind closed doors. But you're really okay with this?"

"Yeah. Or I will be." Tom stood and approached him in the kitchen. "I love you and want the best for you. I didn't know the best would be a young man, but if it is, I'm good with it." He opened his arms for a hug and Trip slapped his back with relief.

He stepped back and narrowed his eyes. "But if he

hurts you, I'll beat the living shit outta him."

"Tom!" Amber rose to her feet.

"Hey, that's guy code for 'you fucked up and better make it right.' Ain't no other way around it." Tom raised his chin while Trip nodded and she scowled.

"I'll be sure to let him know." Trip sighed and managed a real smile. "Thanks. I was real worried about tellin' you."

"I can understand that." Tom nodded. "Have you told Mrs. Guthrie yet?"

He lost his smile. "Not exactly, but she knows."

"Oh?" Amber raised her eyebrows.

"Yeah, she found Henry here this afternoon. He needed to get warm and have his clothes dried after he helped me repair the pipes under the sink in the clinic." He shrugged, but his unease returned. "She accused him of bein' a gold-digger and tryin' to make a name for himself by shackin' up with me."

Amber's jaw dropped and she barked a laugh. "She did not."

"Yes, ma'am, she did."

Tom shook his head. "Henry Bright, the country rock star, a gold-digger tryin' to make a name for himself with you?"

"Wait, wait. Henry is *the* Henry Bright, the one who won best new artist at the CMA's a two years ago?"

"Yup." Trip smiled. "That's him."

"And he's now our vet?"

"Yup. Apparently while he was writin' all that music, he took some time to finish his veterinary schoolin'. He's certified and everythin'."

"Wow. I should head over to the barn to get his autograph." She shook her head with a smile. "Then he definitely doesn't need you to make a name for himself." She met Trip's gaze with a concerned look. "How did she take the news you were interested in Henry?"

"We didn't really get to that. She was more concerned with Henry bein' interested in me."

Amber frowned. "So, she doesn't know you're bisexual?"

Trip rubbed the back of his neck as she started the water in the sink for dishes. "I dunno, to be honest. I think she thought Henry, bein' gay, was hittin' on the old man. I don't know if she thought I'd be welcome to it or not."

"Is that why you didn't invite her tonight?" Tom carried the dishes in from the table and loaded the dishwasher.

"Partly. I didn't want her to tell you before I had a chance to do it." He grimaced. "But also, this was somethin' I needed to share with family only. I needed to know what I would have to face before I dealt with her issues too."

"You're gonna have to talk to her about it at some point, Dad."

"Yeah, I know. But I'd rather share the news about y'all and your new little one." Excitement bubbled up inside him. "I'm really happy for both of you. I wanna ask all sorts of questions, but I figure if you just found out today, you haven't given much thought to things yet."

Amber laughed. "It's too early to tell you much of anything except I'll have to be careful so the little Colton will come out okay."

"Anything I can do to help, y'all let me know." He grinned.

"Oh, we will." Tom sipped his apple cider.

"Good. Now how's the plans for the weddin' going? Y'all workin' on that, too, right?"

He groaned and rubbed his face. "Yeah, we're tryin', but with the ranch, and winter comin' and now the baby, it's been kinda pushed back."

"And I'd like a warmer wedding." She shrugged. "That's not until May, which is after this little person makes an appearance. Not sure which would be better. Round as a ball with no baby, or slender again with a newborn."

"I'm not gonna tell you what to do, but having had some experience with newborns…" Trip shot an amused look at his son. "I'd suggest you do the weddin' earlier than that. They rarely give you enough time to do what you want to do and weddin's are a bit long for them to hold out."

"Was I a newborn at your wedding?" Tom frowned.

"Nope. But you were a newborn at someone else's weddin', and it was a trick to keep you quiet durin' the ceremony." He shook his head with a smile. "If you can pull it off before the baby shows up, I think you'll be happier."

"That sounds…good." She held her hand over her face as she yawned. "Oh dear, I get so tired these days. Being pregnant isn't for wimps."

Trip laughed as Tom helped her up. "No, ma'am, that's why men don't do it. Only the strong can bring a baby into the world."

"Hey, now. Are you callin' men wimps?" Tom held up her coat so she could shrug into it.

"Yes, sir. Until you see what she's gonna go through, you have no idea the amount of strength it takes. You're only along for the ride." Trip clapped him on the shoulder. "Just back her up and you'll be fine."

"Oh, stop scaring him, Trip." Amber laughed. "I need him to be there when the baby comes. But I'll consider what you said about the wedding. You have some good points."

"Thanks for tellin' me about the little Colton comin', and for hearin' me out." Trip hugged her before he turned to Tom. "I was real nervous about tellin' y'all. But you needed to know."

"Thanks for letting us know." Tom moved forward and opened his arms for a hug. Relief cascaded through Trip as they embraced. "You're still my dad and you're not interested in every man around here, are you?"

"Nope. Just Henry."

"Well then, that's just fine if Henry's okay with it." Tom smiled a little sadly. "I'd considered that you might be interested in someone else, but even if it had been a woman, it would've taken a little gettin' used to."

"Whereas since it's a man, it's gonna take a lot to get used to?" Trip grimaced.

Tom opened his mouth to deny, but shut it and nodded. "Yeah, there's no way to get around that. It's different when it's family."

"I know."

"Yeah, I'm gonna work on viewin' it like I do Ransom Knight." Tom tugged Amber to his side. "Have you talked to Dr. Emily about it yet?"

He shook his head. "Nope, but I have my regular appointment tomorrow mornin' and I thought I'd stop in to visit Byron, too. See how he's doin'." He eyed his son. "You ain't gonna have it out with Henry, now, are you? We're both adults and we both made this choice. He didn't coerce me into anythin'."

Tom hunched his shoulders in chagrin. "How'd you know I was thinkin' that?"

"'Cause I know how family works when they feel their loved ones are gettin' railroaded." He shrugged. "You ain't the first to get twitchy about changes like this and you won't be the last. Just don't take it out on Henry. I know what I'm gettin' into and even if you run him off, it won't go back to the way it was."

"Oh, he's so got you figured out." Amber snorted as she poked her fiance's chest. "Have you been watching Lifetime movies or something? That's the most typical trope when someone comes out as gay."

"I think it becomes a trope because it often happens that way in real life." Trip nodded, trying to smile. "But makin' Henry leave won't change how I feel about him, and besides, he's a damn good vet."

"Yeah, he seems to be." Tom allowed Amber to tug him toward the door. "Just make sure you square it away with Byron. That old man might feel like you're replacin' him and that ain't right."

"I'll make it clear we're not replacin' him, but bringin' in someone who can back him up." Trip sighed as he followed them to the front door of his apartment. "To be honest, we should've done that a while ago now, but there never seemed to be time."

"Yeah, no time like the present, I guess." Tom smiled as he opened the door. "Thanks for lettin' us know about you and sharin' dinner with us."

"Thanks for tellin' me about the new Colton headed our way." Trip smiled, love and excitement rising his chest. "I'm so pleased for all y'all."

"Thanks, Trip." Amber waved. "We'll see you tomorrow."

"Yeah, y'all have a good night." He closed the door behind them and leaned against it for a moment. "Well, Livvy, I'm gonna be a grampa."

He couldn't hear anything specific, but he could picture his wife laughing and slapping her thigh with one hand in delight. It made him grin as he ambled back to the kitchen to finish cleaning up. At least he'd have something good to tell the shrink at his next appointment.

His smile faded. *Along with a lot of unnerving revelations.* Thank God Tom and Amber were good with his interest in Henry. Trip didn't know how Byron would take it, especially when Henry currently had his job. Trip didn't want to replace him, but the man was no spring chicken and it was good to have backup. The Army, hell even the rodeo, had taught him that.

Livvy appeared as he returned to his bedroom. *Don't be too hard on Byron. Change is difficult while you're doing it. Again and again, it comes down to what you really want and who you are at your core.*

"I know, but some folks can't take too much at once and I have a lot to tell Byron."

Have faith in him. He's wiser than you know.

Trip hoped so. He didn't want to lose more than he'd won.

CHAPTER TEN

Henry started his Friday like any other day, but something felt different, as if he was missing an important detail. He frowned as he trimmed his beard. Nothing had changed, but he felt different. He studied his face in the mirror, noting the deeper creases around his eyes and mouth, though the latter were disguised by his scruff.

What the hell's wrong with me?

The answer came in the form of a text from Ransom, saying the idiot trying to get in touch with Henry had called again. *Jeez, what the hell kind of bug crawled up Jordie's ass?* He shook his head as he poured a cup of coffee and dialed the number Ransom had given him.

"Hello?"

"Hi Jordie. It's Henry Bright. I heard you called?"

"Jesus, Henry. What the fuck took you so long to call me back? Why the hell didn't you answer my messages?"

Nothing like having a friend appreciate my efforts or anything. It took him a few moments to figure out how to respond without telling his erstwhile manager to fuck off.

"Yeah, having a job and workin' each day as a vet will do that. What's so damn urgent?"

Jordie must have heard something in his voice,

because his tone changed immediately to a lighter, relieved sound. "I'm sorry. I was just really worried. You lit outta here so fast without telling anyone, and I thought for sure something had happened to you."

Something about his response didn't ring true, but Henry ignored his gut. "Yeah, well, I was done with that life. It was time to go home. Sorry I wasn't more clear, but I couldn't do it anymore."

"Couldn't do what anymore?"

"The rock star life. It wasn't me. I was tired and the music wasn't flowing." Henry shrugged.

"What are you talking about? Your career was just taking off. The sky was the limit, and your songs were hittin' the charts left and right." Jordie sounded incredulous.

"Those songs were, true." Henry sipped his coffee. "But there was nothing to follow them up. And you know as well as anyone that a musician is only as good as his next release. I didn't have anything comin'." He shrugged again. "So, I got out while the gettin' was good. Best decision I've made in a long time." His mind filled with a hot, older Wyoming cowboy and his cock started to swell in his jeans.

"But you'll be back, right? After a sabbatical to get your head on straight?" A wheedling tone filtered into Jordie's voice.

"No, that's what I'm tellin' you. I'm out, done, finished with the music industry. It's not my life anymore." And he wanted a new life, a quieter life with Trip and the Triple Star Ranch.

"You can't be serious." Jordie's voice had risen in pitch and volume. "You had a lucrative and growing music career. Why the hell would you just throw it all away to be some Podunk veterinarian in BFE nowhere?"

"It's not even close to Egypt." Henry sighed as he rubbed his forehead and looked out at the autumn sunshine gilding the turning trees. "I'm in Wyoming, I have a job, and I like it. If they can't understand that back in Nashville, it's just too bad."

"There is no money—"

"For you, maybe, but I'm happy here and I'm doin' what I want."

"Please, come back and just talk to the music execs. We'll renegotiate your contracts so you have more control." The wheedling tone returned.

"No. I'm done with that now. As I said, I'm happy here doin' what I want to do." Henry clenched his hand around the phone before he threw it across the room. "Thanks for checkin' with me, but I gotta get to work here in a few. Good to talk to you." Not really, but he had to say something to end the call.

"How about I come to you, then? You're in Cheyenne, right?" Clicking sounds came from the other end of the phone as Jordie pecked on the keyboard. "Where the hell is that...Oh, up I-25 from Denver. I see. Jeezus, you're way the fuck out in nowhere. Do they have indoor plumbing there?"

"Try not to show your ugly east coast ignorance. It makes you look bloated." Henry rubbed his forehead and scowled. "Seriously, Jordie. Don't come out here, just let it go. I'm not going back into music. The muse is silent and I need to step away."

"No, no. This is good. I can come out there, no problem." More clicking sounded in the background. "I can get a direct flight from Nashville and be there tomorrow. We can meet in Denver—"

"I'm not drivin' to Denver. I have a job." He didn't want to see Jordie. He hadn't missed his wheedling voice, the business deals, the partying.

"Oh, come on. It's Friday. You can't come see an old friend in town on the weekend?"

"No." Glory, it felt good to say that.

"How about if I get a place in Fort Collins? That's closer, right?"

"I'm sure there are other young musicians in Nashville who could benefit from your help. You don't need me."

"That's not true. I do need you. You're my friend. Let me come out to Fort Collins and we'll just visit and talk." The wheedling tone returned once more. "Please, just meet with me. We'll talk and if it doesn't work out, I'll come back to Nashville and leave you be. What do you say?" The keyboard clicking sounds continued, unabated.

"I gotta get goin' and make my rounds to check on the animals."

"Please, Henry. You get to work and I'll call you when I'm in Fort Collins, okay? Now I have your number."

Henry immediately wondered if he could get a new number.

"Yeah, fine, Jordie. I gotta go." He didn't want to say 'nice talking to you' or 'talk to you later', but he couldn't leave the conversation where it was at. "Have a good day." It sounded lame, but he wanted out of the conversation fast.

He didn't allow Jordie to respond before he'd terminated the call and hoped to God the man wouldn't immediately call back. Just to be safe, he set his phone to vibrate. *I should make him a specific ring tone so I know his calls before I see them.*

Something turned his stomach about keeping in contact with Jordie. Henry couldn't put his finger on it, but he didn't want to reconnect. He'd left the party-life and wanted peace, quiet, and real friends around him. *And a hot, silver-haired fox cowboy to love.* That wasn't too much to ask, was it?

He sighed and finished his coffee before he threw on his hat, coat, and gloves. He hoped the day would improve. *I know tonight's gonna be great. I have a date.* That happy thought carried him all the way to the barn.

****

Trip stepped out of the cute brick house in downtown Cheyenne and breathed a sigh of relief. Dr. Emily, his psychotherapist, had been pleased and proud of him for coming out to his family. She cautioned him on taking it slow with everyone, and reminded him he didn't have to tell anyone if he didn't want to. She insisted it was no one's business who he slept with but his own, and if Tom and Amber were fine with it, they were the only ones who needed the information.

When he mentioned Byron and Estelle, she reminded him he didn't need approval from anyone on his sexuality or his relationships. Despite that, he understood he needed to talk to Byron and clear the air with Estelle. Both of them would see him with Henry often, and he didn't want to hide his relationship.

He squinted in the cold October sunshine and strode for his truck. He needed to stop by Byron's daughter's place to see him before heading back to the ranch. Trip didn't know how he'd get through the coming conversation, but it was something he had to do.

Byron's daughter, Seychelles Abernathy, owned an antique store in town and did a brisk business with both the tourists and the local junk collectors. Trip never said anything to her face, but he didn't understand collecting crap either too broken to use or anything already improved upon. But she made money and had a nice house in the Avenues so he couldn't complain.

And she's takin' care of Byron when he needs it.

He pulled up in front of a blond brick one-story house and parked his truck. He stared at the door for a few moments, trying to plan his approach.

It ain't gonna get any easier, Trip. Livvy's voice wrapped around him as she appeared sitting on the front steps of the house.

"Yeah, I know. But I have to word it just right and you know how I am with words."

You're better than you think, especially when you speak from the heart.

He sighed and got out of the truck, but still dragged his feet on his approach. He hadn't come up with a good enough plan by the time he reached the door. He didn't want to knock yet, but there was no more time to stall. He raised his hand and thumped it against the door, hoping maybe they weren't home.

"Hey, Trip, how are you?" Seychelles stood at the open door with a welcoming smile.

"Oh, hey, Seychelles, I'm good. And you?"

"Real good. Come on in. I guess you're here for my dad, yeah?" She stood back to let him through before she pushed her glasses back up her freckled nose.

"Yes, ma'am." Trip nodded and removed his hat as he stepped across the threshold. "How's he doin'?"

"Good. Stubborn and cranky as ever, but good." Seychelles shook her head with a rueful smile. "I think he's been expecting you. Just go easy on him, okay? He knows you're gonna make him retire, but can you shore up his ego a bit before you let him go?"

"Let him go?" Trip frowned. "What load of horseshit is this?" He grimaced. "Sorry, ma'am. That wasn't proper to say in front of a lady."

She snorted. "I've heard worse from him. So, you're not here to lay him off?" Relief loosened her shoulders as she led him toward the sunroom on the side of the house.

"No. Is that what the fool is tellin' you?" Trip gaped at her.

"Something to that effect. He said he knew he was getting old and you'd be looking for a new vet soon." She paused at the door to the sunroom. "The doc says he'll be laid up for another seven weeks at least so keep that in mind, too."

"I will. But I'm tellin' you now I ain't firin' him."

"Good to know. I'll bring you some coffee." She nodded and headed back toward the kitchen.

Trip shook his head and scowled. *Layin' Byron off. Shit. That ain't even in the program.* He pushed into the room and found his old friend reading a veterinary journal with his reading glasses perched on the end of his nose like an olden-day school marm.

"Hey, Byron, how're you holdin' up?"

"Hey yourself, Trip. What brings you out here to Cheyenne?" Byron set the journal aside and pushed his glasses to the top of his head. "Have a seat. It's good to see you."

The words were friendly, but wariness lined Byron's expression and shoulders. He pushed himself higher in his chair and grimaced at the ungainliness of his casted leg.

Trip sat. "I was in town to talk to Dr. Emily and I wanted to see how you're were comin' along. What did the doc say about your leg?"

"Oh, you know, somethin' about old bones takin' forever to heal and me needin' to not overdo it anymore at the ranch." Byron shook his head. "He said it'd be at least another seven weeks before I can use it again. That's why you're here, isn't it? To let me know I'm done at the Triple Star?"

Trip scowled. "Hell no. I really came by to see how you're doin'. There ain't no talk about layin' you off or askin' you to quit. That's a load of horseshit you been tellin' yourself."

Byron's gray, bushy eyebrows went up. "You tellin' me I still got a job if I want it?" He frowned. "Who's takin' care of the horses while I'm here?"

"Yeah, you still got a job, and yeah, we hired a new vet while you're laid up." Trip allowed some of his joy at Henry's presence warm his chest. "His name is Henry Bright, and he's a certified vet. Nice young guy, and knows his way around both Wyomin' and horses. But while he's not a temporary hire, I don't want you to think we're replacin' you."

Byron rubbed his chin, the frown still etched on his features. "He's not temporary, but I ain't bein' replaced?"

"Nope." Trip squared his shoulders. "I figure when your leg's better and you come back to work, you and he could share the work load. See, you have the experience and knowledge, and he has the strength and ingenuity. He can benefit from your experience at the Triple Star, and you can benefit from having a knowledgeable partner who has the youth to do all that damn hard work." He grinned. "Make him do the heavy liftin'."

Byron chuckled, but his expression remained wary. "What's he think about this?"

"I haven't told him yet. I'm pretty sure he's gonna have the same reaction as you did, thinkin' I'm gonna lay him off after you get back." Trip shrugged as Seychelles came in with two coffee mugs and the carafe. "I don't want to get rid of either one of you. And think of it this way, it'll be nice to split the duties so you're not on call all the time. Hey, thanks, Seychelles." He took the mug of coffee from her.

"He set you straight, Dad?" She raised her eyebrows as she dipped her chin to meet her father's gaze.

"Yeah, yeah, we're gettin' there." Byron took his own cup.

"Good. I don't want to hear any more bellyaching about how Trip is gonna throw out years of friendship over one broken leg and kick you to the curb." She shot Byron a dry look.

Trip added his own wide-eyed stare. "Is that what you thought?"

"Aw hell, yeah, of course it is. You know I ain't as young as I used to be and your expenses wouldn't be as high if I didn't wander around on a golf cart all the time."

"To hell with that. It ain't nothin'." Trip waved the concern away with his free hand. "That's small potatoes in the grand scheme of stuff. You're not young, but neither am I, and experience counts a helluva lot more than people give it credit. So, here's what I wanna do. I want to have you and Henry workin' as vets at the Triple Star. That way he can face Old Mags instead of you, and he'll have the agility to get outta the way."

"Shit, how's she doin'?" Byron frowned again as he set his coffee aside. "Did you ever figure out what was botherin' her so bad?"

"Yeah. Henry found a sore high up on the inside of her left hind leg. That's what was makin' her so ornery."

"Shit." Byron shook his head. "I never would've found it."

"Maybe, maybe not, but that's why I'm thinkin' two vets are better than one."

"He's right, Dad. A younger guy could benefit from your experience and knowledge that you can't learn in books." Seychelles tapped her chin with one finger. "You have a lot to teach a newer vet, especially one who's not stealing your job as you thought." She snorted while Byron ducked his head. "Take Trip up on this. It's good for all y'all. I'm gonna head to the grocery while you folks visit. I'll have my cell on me if you need anything. Good to see you, Trip."

"Nice to see you, too." Trip waved as she left the room. "Your daughter's turned out to be a great person. How's she doin' in her antiques shop?"

"She's doing good, and I'm glad of her help, but you ain't gonna distract me with her." Byron pointed a finger at Trip. "You serious about me and Henry workin' together? No one's gettin' replaced?"

"Yeah, I'm serious."

Byron let out a long breath and his shoulders sagged in relief. "Well, all right, then. I won't worry anymore."

"Good." Trip was glad to hear it, but now that the work situation had been hashed out, the relationship between him and Henry had to be addressed. And it scared the hell out of him. "Speakin' of worries, I got one gnawin' at me and since you're my oldest friend, I thought I'd mention it to you."

Byron took a moment to sip his coffee before he met Trip's gaze. "What's it about?"

"It's about Henry Bright, actually." He swallowed against the fear crawling up his throat. "I, uh, well, I like him."

"That's good. I'm glad he's workin' out for you at the ranch."

"Yeah, yeah, he is, but that's not what I'm talkin' about." *Shit, how the hell am I gonna say this?* Trip turned his head to scan the big cottonwood trees framing the edges of Seychelles' yard. "I really like him and am thinkin' of spendin' a lot of time with him."

Byron froze, his expression turning stoic. "I don't think I'm understandin' what you're tellin' me, here. You better spit it out clean."

Trip sighed and took a gulp of coffee, burning his tongue. The pain gave him a little more time to gather his thoughts, but they kept running away from him. *Fuck, I'm scared.*

"Henry and I are an item. We're havin' a relationship." It sounded stupid when he said it aloud, but that didn't diminish the truth of the words. He took another gulp of coffee, burning his tongue more before he met Byron's gaze.

"A relationship." Byron tasted the words. "As it, you're goin' out with him, like on dates and stuff?"

"Yeah, somethin' like that." Trip nodded.

"Are you gay?"

Unease made him set his cup down before he burned his tongue a third time. "No. Near as I can tell, I'm bisexual because I wasn't fakin' it with Livvy. But here's the thing. I'm not attracted to any other men. Just Henry. So, don't think I'm gonna ask you out for dinner or nothin'."

Byron snorted, but he didn't smile. "Yeah, I probably wouldn't have taken you up on that." He tightened his lips a moment and scratched his jaw with one hand. "Is this why you told me you're keepin' both of us on as vets?"

"No, I really do want two vets to make the job easier. But I figured you'd see me and Henry together, and I wasn't about to hide my relationship with him from you." Trip rubbed his hands on his denim thighs. "I really like him, even if he's young. He makes my heart flutter like when I first met Livvy. He lights my campfire."

"Aw hell." Byron sighed and rubbed his eyes with both hands. "You're serious?"

"Yes, sir, as a heart attack."

"Shit."

Byron didn't say anything else for a while as he stared out the windows of the sunroom. Trip wished he could read his friend's thoughts, but the man resembled the sphinx. He hoped he hadn't lost Byron as a friend, but sometimes that was the price of honesty. *And I ain't gonna hide this from friends and family.* He'd just have to deal with the outcome if Byron couldn't handle it.

"Did I ever tell you about Bo?" Byron still hadn't looked at him, but at least he was still talking.

"No, I don't think you have. Who was he?"

"Back when I was young, just startin' my rodeo days, I hung out with a lot of young cowboys and Bo was one of them. He wasn't too different from anyone else, but I noticed he spent most of his time with the other boys and not so much with the ladies. He was friendly and all, but while the other men were hookin' up with buckle bunnies, Bo didn't seem to ever find one he liked well enough."

Trip didn't like the sad expression on Byron's face, and he had an inkling of where the story would go.

"Bo was damn good at ridin' broncs, like Tom, a real natural, and most of the boys liked his steadiness. But one day, about a year into my rodeoin', a group of drunk cowboys cornered him outside the Albany and beat the livin' shit outta him." Byron swallowed hard. "I was there, watchin', and I didn't do nothin' to stop them. I just froze like a scared 'possum. I was so ashamed. Bo had a broken jaw and his face swelled up like it'd been stung by a whole hive of bees. He had two black eyes and a broken arm. I took him to the hospital, but he never spoke to me or rodeoed again."

Byron met his gaze, his expression bleak. "He retreated from everyone, and we didn't see him much. Then I found out a few months later he'd died. Official report said gunshot death, but we all knew he'd suicided." He dropped his gaze and shook his head. "I don't know, but I suspect one of the boys who'd beat him up was his lover, too afraid of bein' outed to the others."

He picked up his coffee mug and his hands shook. Trip didn't know what to say, but suspected the story wasn't over.

"I gave up rodeoin' right then and there, much preferrin' the company of animals to people. I couldn't deal with the guilt for having done nothin' for my friend. It was easier for me to figure out silent pain of those who couldn't speak, than deal with those who could." Byron swallowed hard. "I didn't do anythin' for Bo, and I should've. It's a regret that follows me all the time. I was a fuckin' coward because I didn't know how to deal with the idea that a man could love men."

Trip cleared his throat. "Well, it's not an easy concept."

"That's bullshit!" Byron snapped, his eyes hard. "Lovin' anyone is natural and easy as pie. The body people wear is just outward shit. Hell, you love Tom, don't you?"

"Well, yeah, but he's my son."

"Don't make him less of a man. And you love your horses and Amber's dog, Nimbus, right?"

"Yeah."

"See? They wear bodies that aren't even human, but you love them just the same." Byron waved his hand. "I couldn't do right by Bo. I didn't have the courage or experience, and he killed himself. He didn't know there were people who had his back even if he was attracted to other men. See, he never hit on anyone where others could see it. He was careful, but it still killed him just the same." He shook his head, the edges of his mouth pulling down. "I guess what I'm sayin' is you ain't alone, and if you want to be with Henry and Henry's okay with it, you ain't gonna get any grief from me. I got your back."

Trip couldn't speak for a few moments, his voice locked in his throat from all the emotion welling up. He hadn't known Byron before the man became a vet, but he'd liked him the moment he'd met him. He cleared his throat and shook his head.

"And it don't bother you that I was with Livvy first and now with Henry?"

Byron shook his own head. "How long's Livvy been gone now?"

"It'll be thirty years in February." Not that he'd been counting or anything.

Byron nodded. "It's been long enough to find someone new to love. You're not meant to be alone forever. How old is Henry?"

"I don't rightly know. I think he's a little younger than Tom. Why?"

Byron raised his chin and a thoughtful look fell over his features. "Has it ever occurred to you that Henry might be the reincarnation of Livvy?"

"Oh, come on, Byron. You know I don't believe in that New Age mumbo-jumbo." Trip waved him off, but his friend only shrugged with a half-smile.

"Just food for thought. You always struck me as a one-love kinda guy. It would make sense that Livvy knew that too, and made sure to come back to be with you in whichever way she could."

"Henry's nothin' like Livvy." Trip shook his head.

"You sure about that?" Byron wouldn't be deterred.

"Yeah, I'm sure. That's crazy talk right there."

Byron shrugged. "Just think on it. It don't change how you feel about Henry or how you treat him, it's just somethin' that came to mind. I've known you a long time, and you've never been interested in anyone like this except for Livvy."

"Yeah, but reincarnation? This ain't the 1960s."

"Don't make it less true." Byron held up his hand as Trip opened his mouth the protest. "I know you're done talkin' about it. That's just fine. The upshot is I'm okay with you and Henry bein' more than friends, if you take my meanin'. And I'll do my best to support you in it."

"Thanks. You and Tom and Amber are the only ones so far."

"Aw hell. Mrs. Guthrie?"

"Yeah, she ain't too thrilled about it. She's convinced Henry's a gold-digger tryin' to make a name for himself and hittin' on an old widower who's straight." Trip rubbed the back of his neck. "She don't know that he's Henry Bright, the Kick-ass Cowboy, and he comes with his own fortune."

"Shit, the Henry you hired as a vet is *the* Henry Bright? The one whose records Seychelles listens to almost every night?"

"Yup, the very same."

"Well, damn, son. You found yourself a Rockstar. We should all be so lucky." Byron winked.

Trip chuckled. "Yeah, if he doesn't get bored with my old ass."

"You'll just have to show him all the interesting things

about Trip Colton that the rest of us know and love." Byron shook his head with a smile before he sobered. "Seriously, be yourself. Livvy liked you just the way you were. Henry will, too, I'm sure."

"Livvy was my own age. Henry's quite a bit younger." It was a fear that lurked in the background, rearing its ugly head from time to time.

"Age is just a number."

He blinked at his old friend. "Henry said that."

"See? The man knows what he's talkin' about." Byron chuckled as he sipped his coffee again. "Damn, Seychelles really makes good coffee. I need her to come out to the ranch and school Mrs. Guthrie."

"Oh, now, don't let Mrs. Guthrie hear that. She'll skin you alive." Trip grinned.

Byron frowned. "She ain't thrilled about your connection to Henry, huh?"

"Yeah." Trip sighed, losing his smile. "I thought it was the age difference, but I caught her cryin' in the laundry room afterwards, and I'm wonderin' if there's more to it than just a young thing comin' in to steal my affections."

Byron rubbed his chin. "Yeah, well, she's known you longer than I have, hasn't she?"

"Yup." Trip nodded as he picked up his mug again. "She and Livvy were best friends."

"Think it's possible she might've been thinkin' you'd eventually turn to her for comfort now that she's a widow?"

Trip blinked, the coffee turning to flavorless water on his tongue. "Shit. It never occurred to me to turn to her." He swallowed hard and hunched his shoulders, his gut sinking. "I didn't think about it. After Livvy, there hasn't been anyone else until Henry showed up. No matter how nice Mrs. Guthrie has been to me, I was never interested in her." He shook his head again. "Aw hell."

"Now, I ain't sayin' that's what's wrong, it's just an idea." Byron gave him a sympathetic look. "But maybe she's takin' this so hard because she never thought you'd be bisexual."

"Hell, I didn't know I was until I saw Henry. I wasn't interested in anyone." He kept Livvy's visits and suggestions to himself. *No point in makin' Byron think I'm more crazy.* "But it's too late now. Henry's captured my attention and lights my campfire. It ain't logical or easy, but it is what it is."

"Yeah. What do Tom and Amber think about it?" Byron frowned. "You said you told them, right?"

"Yeah, yeah, I told them first." Trip scowled. "But they're good with it, though Tom said it'd take some gettin' used to. But they aren't mad or nothin'. And Amber's pregnant. I'm gonna be a grampa."

Byron whooped and slapped his thigh, then hissed with pain as his hand connected with his bad leg. "Damn, son, congratulations! When's the baby due?"

"Sometime in May, Amber said. She's tryin' to decide when to do the weddin'. I suggested before the baby's here."

"Oh, hell yeah." Byron nodded vigorously. "You don't want a little one suckin' at the teat when you're supposed to be sharin' intimate time with your new spouse."

Trip laughed. "Yeah, I hadn't thought about that one. Maybe I'll text her about it."

"You do that. And thanks for stoppin' by. You gonna see Henry tonight?"

"Yeah, I think so." Trip hesitated as he rose. "Are you okay with this? Me bein' involved with a man more than half my age?"

"Trip, I may be old and set in my ways, but I've always been honest with you. As long as you're not sackin' me, and Henry knows we'll be workin' together, it'll all work out fine." Byron met his gaze with warmth in his eyes. "I don't want him nervous about losin' his job, neither. And like you said, backup is good. So, you keep bein' yourself and let the details work out on their own."

Trip let his unease out on a long sigh. "Thanks, Byron. Seven more weeks, right?"

The other man nodded. "That's what the doc says. I'm hopin' to be back at the ranch sooner, even if I'm sittin' in my chair there."

"Sounds good to me. Take care now and I'll see you again soon."

Trip waved to his friend and took his coffee mug to the kitchen on the way out, more relieved than he'd been after seeing Dr. Emily. So far Tom, Amber, and Byron seemed to be okay with him having a relationship with Henry. *What am I gonna do about Estelle, Livvy?*

She didn't answer him this time so he set the concern aside until he made it home to the Triple Star. He had sixteen miles to think on it. *And tonight I get start spendin' time with Henry.* He allowed the thought to go through his mind, the smile curling his lips the whole way home.

CHAPTER ELEVEN

The workday started out well for Henry, especially with the thought of the date he had with Trip that night. But it quickly soured as Jordie sent several texts, an email with his itinerary, and tried to call three times. Henry seriously considered getting a new phone number when the last call finally stopped ringing. *What the fuck, Jordie?* Apparently, he hadn't made it clear he was done.

Trip didn't seem to be at the ranch, which ruined more of Henry's mood, but he tried to keep his frustration from affecting the animals. *Where the hell could he be?* He shook his head as he cleaned his hands after checking on Old Mags. *Damn, I sound like a possessive nag.* The mare was healing well and seemed less ornery than before, her ears pricked forward each time Henry came to see her.

Henry tried to let the concern go, but his mind kept circling around to Jordie, and he finally gave in to checking his email. He'd gotten a few offers from online dating sites for gay singles and a couple of emails from old friends in the music biz, but otherwise only Jordie's itinerary for his trip to Denver appeared. One way. *Shit.* That meant he was staying for an unforeseen duration.

If he asks to meet, I'll make sure to do it in Fort

Collins. He didn't want Jordie to track him down to the Triple Star Ranch.

He didn't respond to the email and went back to work, but the afternoon dragged on until quitting time. Most of the animals were in good shape, although one of the PTSD geldings had developed a bout of thrush that would take some tending. Despite the medical issues and the worming that needed to be done, his mind wouldn't leave the issue of Jordie. Something didn't feel right about the man's desperate need to find him, and he definitely didn't want to see his former manager.

According to the itinerary, Jordie would arrive on Tuesday. *Gives me a little time to figure out what I'm going to do about him.* But what could Henry do? It was a free country, and Jordie could go where he wanted. Henry wished it was anywhere but near him.

At last the end of the day rolled around and Henry was out the door at the first chime of five. He checked his phone for messages from Trip as he climbed into his truck. The cold of the seat seeped into the ass of his jeans, but he ignored it in hopes a text had come through without him noticing. Disappointment hit his gut with no message notifications and he cranked the engine over, willing the unhappiness to fade.

He made no promises and his family might not be thrilled with him. Mrs. Guthrie definitely wasn't happy with Trip's interest.

The truck rumbled gently as Henry allowed it to warm up. He scrubbed his hands over his face and grimaced. They stank like horse and meds. *I definitely need a shower.* Too bad he couldn't shower with Trip. Despite his sad thoughts, he chuckled. *Yeah, we'd never get clean.*

He threw the truck into gear and headed for his bungalow. The trip didn't take long enough for him to sort out his thoughts, but at least the sunset painted some pretty colors on the ranch as he drove. He parked in front of the house and hurried inside. With sunset came increased cold, and he didn't want to freeze his balls off.

No one to warm them up if Trip doesn't call.

He shoved the unhappy thoughts aside and stomped into the shower to clean up. He let his frustration flow out in his intensity for cleaning his body. Nothing killed the mood in bed more than the scent of horse, and after seeing *The Godfather*, he made doubly sure horse didn't come to bed with him.

Not that I won't be alone tonight. The thought made his mood plummet and he finished his shower with a scowl. He dried off and wrapped the towel around his waist before he wrapped a second one around his head to keep his hair from dripping on his shoulders. A plume of steam followed him from the bathroom as he stomped into the kitchen to start some coffee and think about dinner.

His phone lay on the counter beside the coffee container and he ignored it as he filled his coffeemaker with water. *No point in lookin' when there's nothin' there.* He set up the coffee and trudged back to the bathroom, his footsteps mirroring his rising disappointment.

He thought Trip was interested in seeing him again. *Maybe I didn't read him right.* Why one missed opportunity for intimacy bothered him so much, Henry didn't know, but he ripped a brush savagely through his hair in rising anger. *Dammit, Trip, what the fuck?*

His anger had reached incandescent levels when someone knocked on his door.

"Sonuvaprick!" He snarled as he ripped the towel off his head and stalked over to the door, tearing it open. "What?"

Trip stood on the front step, a grocery bag full of savory food in one hand and a bottle of something that looked like whiskey in the other.

"Trip? What are you doin' here?"

"I thought I'd come by for supper. Didn't you get my

text?" He ran his gaze over Henry's bare chest before returning it to his eyes. "Everything okay? Did somethin' happen?"

"Uh, yeah, everything's fine. Come on in." He stood back to let Trip in out of the cold and gather his thoughts. "Let me check my phone. I was just in the shower."

The older man stepped in and kicked the door shut before he set the bag and bottle down on the kitchen counter. He removed his hat and held it in his hands as Henry retreated to grab his phone, feeling like a dumbass. Sure enough, a little red one showed on his messenger icon. The text had come in while he'd showered. *And I didn't bother to check.*

"Oh yeah, here it is." Relief and something like excitement pushed all the earlier frustration away as he waved the phone. "I'm sorry I'm not dressed, but I'm glad you're here. I wasn't sure you were comin'."

"Hell yeah. I said I wanted to share supper with you, and I meant it. It's been a helluva day and I wanted to unwind, so I brought along the mead. You ever had mead before?" Trip grasped the bottle and held it up.

Henry shook his head as he set his phone aside. "Nope. What is it?"

Trip set his hat down and rotated the bottle until the label was visible. "It's honey whiskey. Well, more like honey wine. They have a couple of different flavors at this brewery, but this one is my favorite."

Henry took the bottle and tried not to inhale Trip's scent. *Damn, the man smells good.* His cologne had hints of sandalwood that tickled Henry's nose and he forced himself to step away from his handsome guest. The label had an elegant rendering of a honeybee in gold on a black background with the name of the meadery and the flavor.

"You like this better than whiskey?" Henry raised his eyebrows.

"Yeah, it's sweeter and smoother without the fire."

Trip nodded as he rummaged through the drawers of the kitchen. "Want to try some?"

"Yeah, I do. Thanks for bringing it." He set the bottle down and smiled, resisting the urge to close the distance between them for a welcoming kiss. *He's too new to being with a man.* But it didn't stop Henry from wanting to show his affection.

"Yeah, well, I needed something to take the edge off." Trip shrugged as he found a corkscrew to work on the bottle. "But tell me how your day went. Everythin' okay with the critters? Any problems we gotta face?"

Henry suspected Trip wanted to take his time relating his news so Henry focused on the events of the day. "Nothin' too serious. Old Mags is doin' better and the sore is healin'. Her movement is more relaxed. And Kipling has thrush, so we're keepin' an eye on him. Everything else is pretty good. I caught a couple of scratches and slivers on three of the newer horses where they've been rubbin' against some old fence posts, but nothin' real bad."

Trip poured the mead into two small shot glasses he found in the cupboards.

"That's it?" Henry picked up the shot glass.

"Believe me, that's all you need. It's sweet so you don't want to drink too much in one sittin'." Trip raised his own glass.

"You're not gonna warn me against drinkin' too much of it because it's got punch?"

"Nah, you're old enough to know how to drink and I figure it'd be pretty patronizin' to tell you how." Trip shrugged. "I will say I don't tend to drink more than a little of it myself before I've eaten anythin'."

Henry chuckled. "Become a lightweight, have you?"

Trip shook his head. "Just smart enough to know when I've had enough. It wasn't always the case, and I damn near died from it. I'm older and wiser now."

Henry bit his lip as chagrin cascaded through him.

"Aw hell, I'm sorry, Trip. I didn't mean to be a jackass. It hasn't been a great day for me either, and I'm kinda takin' it out on you."

Trip frowned. "I thought you said it wasn't bad."

"Yeah, well, the past came knockin' and I didn't want to answer the door." He sipped the mead and let its sweetness dismantle some of his frustration. "Damn, that stuff is good, and I can see how it'd be potent if you took too much."

"Uh huh. What about your past came knockin'?"

Henry shook his head. "Let's set up supper before we talk about it. It ain't worth rehashin' on an empty stomach. And I'll get dressed."

"Don't get dressed on my account." Trip shot him a half-smile as he dug into the grocery bag. "I don't mind sharin' the space with a half-naked man like you. Sure is a nice view."

Henry blinked. He hadn't expected Trip to be so forthright. *And that's my ageism showing right there.*

"You know, I could be all naked if I take off the towel."

Trip's smile bloomed into a grin. "As much as I'd like to enjoy that spectacle, I think you might want to keep those sensitive parts covered while we eat hot food. Just speakin' from experience."

Henry laughed, some of the day's tension fleeing. "Yeah, true, and it's a little cold in here, which doesn't create much of an impression. I think I'll get a shirt and some sweats. Be back in a bit."

"I'll serve up supper while you're changin'."

Warmth filled Henry's chest as he hurried to his room. He liked having Trip in his space, serving up supper like a domestic couple. *Whoa, now, son. Don't get ahead of yourself.* He didn't know how long their relationship would last, but something about doing ordinary things together made Henry happier than he'd been in weeks. He shrugged into a long-sleeved t-shirt and a pair of light fleece pants before he padded back out to the main room.

Trip had set out plates, silverware, and the food, along with two lit candles that gave the space an intimate feel even with the lights on. The man himself sat in one of the chairs at the table, setting out paper towel napkins beside two plates with burgers and fries.

"Wow, looks good. Where's the food from?" Henry settled into the other chair and nodded at the plates.

"Two Doors Down. Local place in Cheyenne. You okay with chicken?"

Henry blinked. "Chicken? We're in Wyoming. What's wrong with beef?"

Trip grimaced as he dumped ketchup on his real potato steak fries. "Stops my system up. I hit fifty and the body had had enough." He shrugged. "Gotta listen to the body. It's the only one I got."

And it's fuckin' sexy. "Yeah, that's the truth for sure." He'd never considered the restrictions that came with age, but he figured he'd be learning a lot in the next few weeks. *If this relationship lasts that long.* He hoped it would. He wanted it to last.

"So, tell me about what happened today that twisted your tail." Trip took a bite of his burger and Henry had to look down to keep from reaching out to wipe away some mayo on his chin.

He cleared his throat. "You know I was a musician for a while."

Trip snorted. "Henry, everyone knows that."

"Heh, yeah, I guess so." He took a bite of his own sandwich and savored the flavors as he thought out his words. "I had this manager, Jordie Heathrow, and he made sure I got to my gigs, got paid, and socialized. The problem was, he liked the socializin' a lot more than I did. Part of the reason I left was because the partyin' wasn't for me anymore. But I think it was Jordie's favorite part."

Trip raised an eyebrow. "I thought young guys loved that sort of stuff."

"Yeah, most of 'em do, but it just got to be a waste of time for me." Henry rubbed the back of his neck. "And it killed the music in me."

"What?" Trip sat back in his chair.

"Yeah. I couldn't find the music anymore. Nothin' was comin' to me. You're only as good as your next album, and the way things were goin', I wasn't any good."

"That's horseshit."

"Maybe, but I wasn't inspired to write songs or play." Henry tried to smile around his loss, but it still stuck in his gut like a lead weight. "So, I had to find somethin' else to do and came home to Wyoming. A couple of days ago, Ransom tells me Jordie is lookin' for me, so I called him back today and he says he's comin' out here."

Trip nodded as he continued eating. "Did he say why?"

"He's tryin' to get me back into the music scene." Henry scowled at his fries. "I told him it was a done deal and I didn't want to go back to it, but he said the music execs wanted me back and I should give him a chance to explain as a friend."

Trip snorted. "One of the things I've learned is real friends don't manipulate their friend into something he doesn't wanna do."

"Yeah, I told him not to come, but he sent me his itinerary, so he's comin'." Henry took another sip of the mead, but the frustration remained. "I've decided I won't let him come to the ranch. I don't want him here ruinin' the energy of the place."

"Where you gonna meet him?"

"Fort Collins. I figure that's close enough to Wyoming." He shook his head. "Too close if you ask me. I liked it better when he was in Tennessee and didn't know where I was."

Trip nodded and his brows came down. "He's not an

ex-boyfriend, is he?" When Henry raised his own eyebrows, Trip shrugged. "I know I'm not used to bein' in a relationship and all, but I really like you, Henry, and I don't think I can compete with an ex of yours who wants to get back together."

"Aw hell, no, Jordie's not an ex. He was just my manager, and he used to be a friend." Henry reached out and grasped Trip's wrist as he met his gaze. "I swear, it was never like that between us, and I never wanted it to be."

Trip nodded again and took his hand back, his shoulders tightening. "Aw hell, I'm worried I'm just too damn old for you. You're young, a good lookin' man, and you can have anyone—"

"Can I have you?" Henry wanted to nip that in the bud quick.

"Well, yeah, but—"

"Ain't no buts about it. You're the man I want. Jordie's old news. When he doesn't get what he wants, he'll get bored and head home." Henry shrugged. "I'm serious. Jordie's into all that partyin' and drugs and shit. It ain't my thing. I came home to Wyoming because I wanted somethin' real. I just lucked across you. I swear to you I don't want what Jordie's offerin'."

"You sure about that?"

Henry rose from his chair and came around the table to kneel in front of Trip, his gaze on the gray-blue eyes of his lover. He dropped his hands on Trip's thighs. "I'm sure, Trip. You're just the speed I like to go."

"And what speed's that?"

Henry kneeled up and brushed his lips along Trip's collar, inhaling his scent before dropping a kiss on the sensitive skin below his ear. "Sexy, sultry, and hot cowboy."

Trip moaned and tilted his head to allow Henry better access. Henry cupped the back of Trip's head with one hand and fisted his shirt with the other as he nip-kissed the skin. His cock solidified in his fleece pants with every one of Trip's moans. *Damn, can the man be any sexier?*

Henry dropped his hand to Trip's groin and palmed the hard ridge of warm flesh encased in denim. He remembered having the thick, curved cock in his mouth and he swallowed hard at the idea of riding such a lovely toy.

"I think this needs to come out to play." He rubbed the heated denim harder.

"Now? Ain't you hungry?"

"More than you know, Trip." He unclipped the belt buckle and pushed the button through the hole until he could reach the zipper on Trip's jeans. "May I?"

Trip groaned. "I can already tell I'm not going to be able to say no to you much."

"So that's a yes?" Henry raised his eyebrows, allowing his fingers to massage the sides of the growing bulge.

"Aw hell, yeah, it is."

Pleasure zinged through Henry at the tight excitement in Trip's voice. *Aw yeah.* He yanked the zipper down and reached into the tight space behind Trip's fly. Hot, hard flesh pressed against the cotton of his briefs. Henry's mouth watered as he pulled Trip's cock out and stroked the warm, smooth skin.

"Aw glory, Henry. That's so fuckin' good."

Henry raised his gaze. Trip had his head thrown back and he swallowed hard as Henry ran his thumb over the cockhead. *I'm gonna suck this cock until he explodes.* Trip's hands tightened on the edges of the chair's seat as Henry leaned forward to take his cock in his mouth.

Trip moaned and Henry mirrored it as the spicy, tangy flavor of Trip's pre-cum hit his tongue. Damn, the man tasted good. Henry pushed the edges of the jeans wider and fondled Trip's balls as he slid down on his shaft. He loved the sensation of the wide head against his tongue and massaged the crown as he pulled off.

"Fuuuuuccccckkk..."

Trip's groan echoed Henry's desire. He definitely wanted to fuck Trip, but he wanted to savor the cock in his mouth some more. Henry hummed as he lapped up his delicious treat, tilting his head to get a deeper angle. He strummed his tongue over the head then dipped the tip into the slit.

"Good glory, Henry..."

Encouraged by Trip's pleasure, Henry tickled the slit in the head and reached into the briefs to massage Trip's balls. The older man moaned and spread his legs, giving Henry as much play in his tight jeans as possible. Henry licked and sucked the thick shaft, raking his teeth over the flared crown.

"Okay, enough." Trip's warm hands gripped Henry's head and gently pulled him off the tempting cock.

"What? But I was just getting started." Damn, he sounded petulant to his own ears.

"Oh, I know you were, but if you suck me off now, I ain't gonna be much use to you later." Trip pulled him up and leaned down to kiss Henry's lips, swiping his tongue into Henry's mouth.

Pleasure and lust surged in Henry's chest, and he moaned as he gave as good as he got with the kiss. *Shit-oh-dear, Trip can kiss.* His cock threatened the seams on his fleece pants, and he wished he could rub it against Trip's. But the older man ended the kiss too soon and tucked his rigid cock back into his briefs. He left his jeans undone just to tease, Henry was sure.

"Let's finish our dinner before we eat dessert." Trip winked.

Henry rose, anticipation sparking in his chest. "So, there's a chance for dessert?" He waggled his eyebrows.

Trip gave him a lazy, sultry smile. "That's what I was plannin' on."

"Hot damn." Henry sat back down in his chair. "I guess I can wait, then." He stuffed a fry into his mouth.

"You said your day wasn't great, either. What made it so rough?"

Trip shrugged. "It wasn't rough so much as an emotional wringer. I, uh, I went to see my shrink, Dr. Emily."

Henry swallowed the fry and sipped his mead to give him time. "I didn't know you had a shrink."

Trip cleared his throat and nodded. "Yeah, ever since Tom got me started on the ranch, I had to have a shrink to help with my PTSD." He rubbed the back of his neck, and Henry tried to listen rather than react. "She's helped me a lot over the years, but uh learnin' that I was interested in you has given me a lot to think about."

Henry stuffed more food in his mouth to keep from saying anything stupid, but his gut cramped in concern. Had Trip decided something? *Just wait, son, and don't jump to conclusions yet.*

"She told me today my sexuality is my own business, which is true, but I needed to make it clear to my friends and family."

The lead ball in Henry's stomach rose up to his throat and he wasn't sure he could swallow it down. Coming out was never easy and many families couldn't handle it. His own mother had been supportive of his sexuality, but he'd lost friends who'd been disgusted at his interest in guys. *And I left them all in the dirt of Casper.*

"I told Tom and his fiancée Amber last night."

And there goes my job. The food turned to dust in Henry's mouth and his hard-on died.

"Oh?" He cleared his throat. "What did they say?" *Start packin' your bags, son.*

"They told me they were happy for me."

Henry waited, but Trip stopped speaking. "That's it?"

Trip shrugged. "Tom said he'd have to get used to it."

"Uh, yeah." Henry sat back in his chair, trying to focus on his food.

"I also talked to Byron Abernathy today, the vet who broke his leg."

Aw shit, here it comes. "Yeah, how's he doin'?" He lost his appetite completely.

"Good. Healin' up with the help of his daughter." Trip nodded. "He should be able to get back to work in about seven weeks or so."

"So, I have seven weeks until I need a new job." That wasn't much time. Henry had hoped he'd have a little longer to spend with Trip, but it seemed the relationship was dead in the water. *Aw hell, better to nip it in the bud now than let it go longer when I get in too deep.*

"What?" Trip's head came up and his eyes widened. "Aw hell, you think Tom's gonna fire you, don't you?"

"Well, yeah. What the hell do you need two vets for? And Byron's been here longer. I can't take his job from him." Henry shook his head and took his dishes into the kitchen, no longer hungry. In fact, his stomach cramped with something that felt suspiciously like grief. "I'll call Ransom tomorrow and see if he knows of any other ranches lookin' for a live-in vet."

"The hell you will." Trip snapped the statement, rising to his feet. "No one's gettin' fired. I'll tell you what I told Byron. It'll be good to have two vets onsite because you can spell each other. You can benefit from his knowledge and experience, particularly with the animals at the Triple Star, and he can benefit from your strength, youth, and the newer breakthroughs in veterinary medicine." Trip frowned as he braced his hands on the table. "This is a win-win situation for you both, and it's always good to have backup."

"You're not gonna fire me?"

"Nope, not while I have a say."

Some of Henry's unease settled. "Does Byron know who I am?"

Trip chuckled, nodding. "Yeah, his daughter listens to

all your albums."

"Heh." Henry rubbed the back of his neck. "Good to know. Does he know I'm gay?"

"Yeah, he does. And he knows I'm interested in you more than just a friend." Trip settled back in his chair. "I can't tell you the reason behind it 'cause it ain't my story, but he's okay with us bein' more than friends." He paused, meeting Henry's gaze with what looked like hope. "I'd really like to be friends and more, and family's good with it. What do you say?"

Henry swallowed the last of his food. "I say I'm ready for dessert."

A sultry smile curled Trip's lips and Henry's cock flexed. "I'm okay with that."

CHAPTER TWELVE

Trip's cock threatened to erupt out of his jeans with Henry's words, but he swallowed against his rising excitement and nodded. "Want me to help clean up?"

"Why don't we leave it until after dessert?"

Trip cleared his throat. "Uh, yeah, we could do that."

Henry rose and took his hand, meeting his gaze. "Are you nervous?"

"Hell yeah, I'm nervous. The last time I had sex with another person, Tom was still in training pants." He rubbed the back of his neck, but didn't let go of Henry's hand.

Henry paused and looked him over, surprise etched in every line of his body. "No sex? In over two decades?"

Chagrin pulled the edges of his Trip's mouth down. "No, none."

The younger man whistled, but a sweet smile curled his lips. "I'll just have to work harder to make it good for you, then. Come on into the bedroom. We'll start slow."

Henry pulled Trip into the bedroom and turned on the two beside lamps. "Let me undress you."

"What about you?" He'd never had someone undress him before.

"We'll get to me." Henry gave him a sultry smile as he

stopped in front of Trip. "Tonight is about reintroducing you to pleasure."

"Should I pull off my boots now?" Anything to give him a little more time. He swallowed as Henry's gaze dropped to his feet.

"Yeah, might be a good idea. Want me to help?"

"Nah, I got this." Trip sat down, very aware of Henry's proximity and the erection straining the front of his sweats. He focused on the boots, but he couldn't keep the blush from staining his cheeks with the ideas running through his head. *What will sex with a man be like?*

Once the boots were off, he rose to set them aside then turned back to Henry. The younger man had stripped to the waist and Trip lost the ability to speak at the beauty of Henry's physique. While he wasn't ripped like a body builder, Henry didn't wear much extra fat and the lines of his abs etched the skin of his belly. A slender trail of hair disappeared down into his sweats and Trip's gut tightened with anticipation.

"Damn, Henry. That's a helluva view."

The younger man smiled, and Trip's cock flexed in his jeans. "Thank you, Trip. I'm lookin' forward to your version." He pulled Trip back to the bed. "Let me get started on that."

Trip stood spellbound as Henry took his time unbuttoning his shirt in a seductive dance. The younger man opened it completely and pulled the tails from Trip's jeans before he leaned in and pressed his nose to Trip's chest, inhaling.

"Damn, you smell so fuckin' good." He slid his hands up Trip's ribs as he rubbed his face in Trip's chest hair, groaning softly. His thumbs strummed Trip's nipples with enough pressure to send erotic sensation straight to his dick. "I want to suck on these nipples so much." He raised his head to meet Trip's gaze. "Would you let me?"

He'd never had anyone suck on his nipples, but he

shivered at the thought. "Yeah."

"Fuck, yeah."

Henry lowered his head and dragged his tongue over one nipple. Trip saw stars. Hot, wet pleasure zinged straight to Trip's cock, and he couldn't hold back the moan wrung from his throat. Henry hummed as he suckled the nipple, one thumb massaging the other, and Trip lost himself in the eroticism. *Why the hell didn't I know that was sexy?* Livvy hadn't sucked on his nipples, but then they hadn't experimented much with sex in their marriage. *I'm sorry, Livvy. We should've done more.*

Trip yanked his attention away from the past to focus on the present. Henry switched to the other nipple, and they both moaned at the same time.

"Damn, you're fuckin' responsive. I could suck on these all night." Henry grinned as he backed away with a mischievous smile. "But I ain't gonna do that. There's too much more I want to do to you tonight. Let's get these jeans off your hot ass."

Trip unbuttoned his pants, but grabbed Henry's hands and held them still for a moment, meeting the glorious hazel eyes of the younger man. "I know I'm old and been around for a long time, but you're gonna have to baby me a little. I, uh, I ain't never done this before. Not even with my late wife. We weren't that adventurous in bed so we never tried anal sex." He hitched a shoulder, hating to admit his inexperience. "I don't wanna disappoint you."

Compassion and something sweeter filled Henry's face. "I'm glad you told me, though I kinda expected that. I promise, we'll go slow and easy, Trip. We'll take it at your pace." He stroked Trip's cheek with one callused hand. "Tonight it's about sweet, sexy pleasure, and I'll show you how it's done."

"You ain't disappointed?"

Henry raised his eyebrows as he shoved the jeans and underwear off Trip's hips. "With this sexy ass? Never." He dropped with the jeans and buried his nose in Trip's scrotum. "Glory, you smell so damn good down here." Trip's cock responded to the compliments and the caresses of Henry's clever fingers. "And so damn responsive. I can't get enough of you."

Trip wasn't much for talking during sex, but Henry's words jacked his arousal up. *I can't get enough of you, either.* For some reason, Trip couldn't say it aloud, but he hoped his body and his expression would translate.

"Oh, glory, okay, on the bed with you. I want to spend some time lovin' this body of yours." Henry pointed at the bed and Trip had the oddest feeling his younger lover might be more dominant. The thought didn't scare him as much as it would have with anyone else.

Trip settled on the bed and scooted back to the headboard, his cock straining toward his belly from a nest of salt-and-pepper curls. He hadn't "manscaped", a term he'd read on the internet lately, and he hoped it wouldn't turn Henry off. He'd never considered trimming or sculpting his body hair without a partner to see it. Would Henry prefer him with less hair? His cock drooped at the train of his thoughts.

"Hey, now, what are you thinkin' about? You lost your smile and your focus." Henry crawled up beside Trip, entirely naked. His own body hair consisted of a "treasure trail" from belly to cock and a thick thatch of dark curls around his balls.

"I was just worried about my body bein' sexy enough for you." Trip shrugged, the edges of his mouth pulling down. "It's been so long that I've had to worry about what a partner thinks…"

Henry settled beside Trip's and ran his fingers over his chest and belly. Tickling sensations followed in their wake.

"I love your body as it is, Trip. It's beautiful, masculine, especially with all this hair." Henry sighed with pleasure. "I love the feelin' of it under my hands, and I'm

gonna love it against my own body, too. And this cock."
Henry grasped Trip's shaft and stroked, stoking the arousal
already simmering in Trip's gut. "I'm gonna show you how
to use this to give us both pleasure."

"Aw hell, if you keep strokin' like that, I'm gonna
come like a teenager watchin' his first porn."

"Not tonight. I'll teach you the pleasures of holding
back." Henry winked before he rolled over on top of Trip
and slid down until his shoulders pushed Trip's thighs
apart. "I have plenty of condoms and lube, and we're going
to take our time."

"You came prepared, eh?" Trip chuckled.

"Oh, hell yeah. I've been lookin' forward to this all
day." And he sealed his lips around Trip's cockhead.

"Holy fuckin' glory." Trip threw his head back as his
pleasure ramped up to a screaming pitch. *And he's only put
my cock in his mouth.*

He'd never been so sensitive or quick to come, but the
sight and scent of Henry's hair pooled around his groin
turned him on more than he'd ever experienced before. And
the hot, wet suction on his shaft and cockhead drove him
insane with pleasure.

Henry hummed against his taut flesh and Trip hissed,
tightening his hands into fists in the bedclothes. His arousal
built with each swipe of Henry's tongue on his shaft, and
when the younger man bobbed his head, sucking hard, he
lost his grip on his orgasm.

"Oh, fuck, I'm gonna come. I can't hold back. Sweet
Jesus…"

"Oh, no you don't." He pulled of Trip's cock with a sly
smile and a firm grip at the base. "Not until I'm ready to let
you come. Hold it back until I say, braveheart."

The endearment would've sounded odd from anyone
else, but the confidence and warmth in Henry's voice sank
into Trip's heart and scrubbed away some of the darkness
residing there. He wanted to do as he asked and wanted

more of those endearments. He wanted to please his younger lover, serve him to the best of his ability, and bring them both pleasure while doing it.

"That's it, good man." Henry held tight until the arousal settled to a manageable level in Trip and his hands released the bed. "Now, normally I top, which means I would shove my cock into your hot ass and ride you for the hills. But because you've never had this experience, I'm gonna let you fuck me. It'll be slow and easy so you can get the idea. That sound good?"

Fuck, anything he does to me sounds good. "Yeah, that sounds fine."

"Good." Henry let go of Trip's cock and scooted off the bed. "I'm gonna grab the lube and condoms, and we'll see how far we can push you tonight."

Trip swallowed hard as his stomach clenched, but he wasn't sure if it was from excitement or anxiety. Everything with Henry was new, uncharted territory, and part of him wanted more, but another part shied away. Everything he'd ever been taught about homosexuality and male-male relations said this was wrong. But being with Henry warmed his lonely heart, and everything they'd shared felt good.

"Now, don't go thinkin' too much. I want that cock good and hard when you shove it into my ass." Henry's mildly chiding voice dragged him out of his thoughts. "I need you to focus on me in the here and now. We ain't got time for past distractions." The younger man paused and his brows came down. "Unless you're havin' second thoughts. You still okay with everythin' we're doin'?"

Trip cleared his throat as the fear of pissing Henry off closed it. "Yeah, I'm still okay. I'm workin' through the things I was taught about sex with men and what I'm feelin' right now."

"Well, let's talk about that." Henry set down the foiled wrapped package and the bottle of lube as he returned to

140

the bed. "I don't want anythin' to ruin tonight, but I know those long-taught beliefs fuck things up for lots of people, especially those who've just discovered their interest in the same gender." He rubbed his chin. "Tell me what you feel when I touch you. Is it disgust, fear, soul-deep unease?"

Trip shook his head, suddenly feeling all those things with the thought that Henry would stop pleasuring him. "No, I don't feel any of them while you're touchin' me. I don't feel wrong or scared or uneasy. I don't wanna get sucked into those backwards social beliefs that fuck people up, and I don't wanna let you down. But I'm an old dog. Sometimes it's hard for me to learn new tricks."

"Oh, braveheart, you couldn't let me down." Henry stroked his chest, trailing his fingers down his belly to tangle in the curls around his cock. "Tellin' me how you're feelin' is the most important, here. Sex really ain't fun unless we're both enjoyin' it."

When Trip raised an eyebrow, Henry nodded, idly stroking Trip's cock back to fullness. "It's true. I don't like sex if my partner isn't havin' fun. It ain't my thing."

"Yeah, I agree with that."

"Yeah, so that's what I mean when I say I wanna know how you're feelin' about it when we make love. I know this is new for you, but I want it to be good." Henry gave him a sultry smile. "I want it to be so good you can't think of nothin' else for days."

Trip's cock flexed as those thoughts filtered through him. "Yes, sir, that sounds fine to me."

"Good. Before I get to pleasurin' this hot body of yours, let's pick some words that make it real clear how you're feelin'." Henry reached for the lube tube and held it in his hands. "Most folks use the stoplights because they're easy to remember. Green means everythin's fine, yellow means things are startin' to cause pain or discomfort and need to change, and red means, holy shit, fuckin' stop."

The younger man grinned when Trip chuckled. "Get

the picture?"

"Yeah, vividly." Trip nodded.

"Would that terminology work for you?"

"I think so. Can't think of any other time I'd use it."

"Good. We'll stick with that unless somethin' changes." Henry leaned over and kissed Trip's lips with a sultry swipe of his tongue. "Anythin' else you wanna talk about? I wanna make sure you're all right with this."

"I am, I'm just nervous, is all." Trip tried to find his smile.

"Yeah, I can tell, but I promise we won't do anythin' you don't want. Your pleasure's important to me, and I'll only do as much or as little as you choose."

Trip frowned. "Really? How is that pleasurable for you?"

"Because bringin' you the best pleasure and only as much as you want is a goal of mine." Henry stroked Trip's cock with sure fingers. "If you're not havin' fun, my mind can't engage and it's an empty orgasm. Yeah, I could get my rocks off, but it's like the difference between an excellent meal and a quick snack of junk food. Both are tasty, but only one sticks with you." He kissed Trip's shoulder. "And I don't really care for junk food."

"Yeah, I don't, either." Trip moaned as Henry's grip on his cock tightened. "Oh, glory, Henry. That feels so damn good."

"It's gonna feel even better in a few. Let's put a condom on this weapon and get ready to use it." Henry handed Trip the foil package and watched as he tore it open. "Roll it on slow. I want to see your cock stretch the latex."

Fuck, that's sexy. Trip shivered as he rolled on the condom, the avid pleasure in Henry's face making his cock jerk. He'd never thought condoms could be sexy, but Henry's attention made it more than just protection.

"Damn, you're so fuckin' sexy it makes my balls

tight." Henry rolled onto his back beside him and handed him the lube. "Now here's where things are different with men and women. You're gonna have to prepare me for that thick shaft of yours because while I'm looking forward to you fuckin' me, I want it to be good for both of us, and you're a big boy."

Trip frowned. "Am I? It's the only dick I've really paid attention to and it never occurred to me if the size was anythin' special."

"I wouldn't say you're porn-star big, but you definitely have some heft and girth." Henry shivered and grinned. "And I'm gonna enjoy it. But first, you gotta get my hole ready. Put some lube on your fingers and start massagin' my anus."

Trip paused. "You sure?"

"Yeah, I'm sure. Just think of it as massassin' a tight muscle to get it to relax. Same principle."

Trip took a deep breath and squirted some lube on his fingers. "You ready?"

"Yup."

He nodded and slowly reached between Henry's legs beneath his balls to find his ass. Henry smiled and opened his legs wide to allow Trip a better view. Trip thought it would be awkward, but Henry's cock flexed each time he rubbed over the puckered skin and he moaned a little.

"That feel good?"

"Yeah, it does." Henry nodded. "Now, get a little more lube and push a finger inside my ass. But just one and go slow."

"All right." Trip swallowed hard and did as he asked.

"Oh, yeah. Rub my ass." Henry's voice filled with lust, and he threw his head back as Trip pushed a finger inside. *God, it's so tight and hot.* The lube allowed him to slide, and he worked the ring of muscles gently.

"Good. Oh, fuck, that's good. Now add a second finger. And when you think I'm ready, a third." Henry gave

Trip a sultry smile. "You're big so I want to be properly stretched to take you."

The conversation was both more erotic and more surreal than any Trip had ever had, but he found himself willing to listen and learn from his younger lover any way he could. He wanted to please Henry, and he wanted to be good in bed for him. He'd never wanted anything so much in his life. By the time he'd added the third finger and rubbed the inside of Henry's channel, his own cock flexed and his balls drew up tight with each moan.

"Now, rub some lube on your big cock and push it into my aching hole. I want to make love with you." Henry opened his arms, urging Trip to crawl over him.

"How?" Trip swallowed hard, but followed directions before kneeling between Henry's legs.

"Line your cock up with my hole and slowly push in. Real slow."

He lifted Henry's balls and lined his cock up with his ass. He took another deep breath before he pushed against the tight ring of muscle below. Sweet erotic pleasure slowly built as he hesitantly pressed forward. *Oh, sweet glory.* Henry moaned low and guttural as Trip entered his body in a long, slow glide until Henry's balls rested against his groin.

"Oh, shit, you're so thick and I'm so full." Henry moaned, his face suffused with pleasure.

"That's good, right?" Trip could barely find coherence with the tight heat of Henry's body pressing on his cock.

"That's real fuckin' good. Now I need you to move." And he punctuated the statement with a squeeze of his inner muscles.

Trip's brain short-circuited. *Hot. Tight. Fuck.*

It had been so long since he'd had his cock surrounded by another person, he'd forgotten the overwhelming pleasure. He closed his eyes and reveled in the sensations flooding through him.

"Move, Trip."

Oh, right. He was supposed to make love with Henry, not just bask in the pleasure. He opened his eyes and pulled his hips back, scraping the head of his cock along the walls of Henry's channel. They both moaned, and Trip couldn't stop himself from reversing the action and sliding back into Henry.

"Oh, glory. Yeah, that's it. Nice and slow, just like that." Henry met his gaze as they moved together. "See my cock just gettin' harder and harder? You're doin' that, braveheart. You're makin' me see stars every time you seat that big cock in my ass."

Henry's erotic words ramped up his pleasure, and he shifted into a slow, regular rhythm. Henry moved with him, but grabbed his own cock and pumped it in time with his strokes. He watched, riveted as Henry's cock grew harder.

"Oh, glory, Henry. I'm gettin' close." Trip tried to fight the oncoming release, but his body was too turned on to turn back.

"Just a little longer. Fuck me with your big cock. Fill me with your thick shaft."

Trip whimpered and increased his pace a little because he couldn't hold back. Henry grinned at him, his eyes blazing with arousal and something else Trip couldn't identify. He wanted to kiss the younger man, but when he tightened those inner muscles, Trip was lost.

"Oh fuck, I'm gonna cooommmmeee!"

"Oh, yeah, Trip. Come for me, braveheart. Yeah, just come." Henry jerked his own shaft until thick ropes of white cum decorated his chest and hand.

Trip lost focus on everything as his own orgasm shot him into a space of sublime pleasure and peace. Hot jets of cum spurted into the condom, giving him a sense of home. He'd found his partner and the place he always wanted to be. Henry was more than just a quick weekend fuck. This was the man he'd been searching for after the death of his wife.

He almost whispered, "I love you" when he collapsed on the younger man but held back for fear it would ruin the lovely intimacy they'd created. But he knew, as he settled on Henry's chest, that he never wanted to be without him in his life.

****

Henry cradled Trip to his chest and stroked his head and back with his hands. That had been the best sex he'd experienced in years, and he hadn't even topped. But the way Trip had fucked him so slow and sweet warmed his heart. For just a brief moment, he entertained the idea of living with and loving Trip full time, like an old married couple, and his heart had swelled with desperate need. He wanted to tell Trip how much he loved him.

Hold on. Love?

The word seemed foreign to him, unable to encompass the entirety of the emotions swirling within his chest. Besides, it was way too early to succumb to the Big L Word. *Isn't it?* He'd never felt like this for anyone before, even when he'd had a boyfriend.

He tightened his arms around the older man and inhaled his masculine scent. Surprise hit him when he realized he was content. He didn't want to go anywhere or do anything or be anyone else. Happiness lay in his arms, and he wanted to hold it forever.

I'm growin' sappy.

Trip groaned and lifted himself off Henry's body, but his motions were languid and his expression held relaxed satisfaction. *Damn, I wanna see that on his face all the time.* Trip reached down and gently pulled out of Henry's body, grasping the condom before it made a mess.

"I'm gonna go clean up a bit." He paused as if he wanted to say something more, but took his leave and disappeared into the bathroom.

Henry rearranged his body to wait for Trip to return, his emotions and thoughts rioting in his head. He wanted more with Trip than he'd ever wanted with anyone else, but he understood that making a move too early would kill anything that could be. He needed to spend time with Trip and solidify their relationship because he'd never given up on anything, and he wouldn't give up on this.

Trip returned, naked, handsome, and sexy, with a wet washcloth in his hands. "Do you want me to clean you up or would you prefer to do it yourself?"

"You may clean me." Henry hadn't had anyone do that for him in a long time.

He expected Trip to be perfunctory and efficient, but the older man took his time wiping the warm rag around Henry's balls and along his crack. His touches were sure, but gentle and Henry would happily accept his ministrations again.

When he finished, Trip took the cloth back to the bathroom before he returned to the bedroom and gathered his clothes.

"What are you doing?" Henry propped himself up on his elbows.

"Gettin' dressed so I can head home." Trip reached for his underwear.

Henry's sublime pleasure dropped. "Home? You ain't plannin' to stay tonight?"

Trip paused as he settled his briefs over his hips. "I wasn't. I didn't think you'd want me to and I got chores in the mornin', pretty early."

"Yeah, I got chores, too." Henry nodded, desperate to find a way to keep Trip in bed with him. "But I figured we could get up and do them together. You know, twice as many hands makes half the work?"

Trip tilted his head and chewed on his bottom lip. *Hey, that's my job.*

147

"What are you really askin', Henry?"

"I guess I'm really askin' if you'd be willin' to stay with me tonight." Henry swallowed hard. He'd never had to request before. "I'd like you to sleep with me, and I do mean sleep, though morning sex isn't out of the question."

"You really want me to stay?" Trip raised his eyebrows.

"Hell yeah, I want you to stay." Henry patted the bed beside him. "I even promise not to hog the covers."

Trip laughed and dropped his pants, adding the briefs after a moment. "Don't worry about that. I keep pretty warm. Livvy used to say I had my own internal furnace."

While the mention of Trip's late wife made unease ping in Henry's mind, he liked it when Trip settled into the bed beside him.

"Good to know if I ever get cold I can cuddle up to you."

"Yeah, I'd like that." Trip turned on his side to face Henry, his big cock lying against his thigh. "I, uh, think I'd like to hold you. If, uh, if that'd be okay."

Henry cursed the hesitancy he heard in Trip's voice. "Hell yeah, it's okay. I'm gonna turn off the lights."

"I can do that—"

"Nah, I gotta use the john anyway. I'll be back in a bit."

Henry headed for the bathroom, excited. Trip would sleep with him. *Now if I can just keep him all weekend.* That was his plan. He used the toilet and washed the drying cum off his chest, the excitement threatening to burst into laughter. Instead, he took deep breaths while he dried his body and returned to the bedroom, switching off the light as he passed.

Despite the darkness, Henry could see Trip under the covers of his bed and pleasure zipped down his back. He had someone to cuddle all night long. He settled beside his sexy lover and drew Trip's arm over his body. *Now, I just have to figure out a way to make him stay forever.* The thought followed him down into sleep.

CHAPTER THIRTEEN

Henry spent the best weekend he'd ever had with Trip. Between sharing the chores of the ranch and making meals together, it felt exactly like a romantic vacation. In between the meals and chores, they spent their time in bed, touching and talking about intimate matters. The external world fell away and he allowed himself to revel in the fantasy of sharing his life with his sexy, mature cowboy.

When they weren't doing chores or being intimate, they shared life stories with each other, and Trip managed to convince Henry to play the guitar. He hadn't felt up to the challenge, but Trip's gentle persistence had worn him down, and he'd played a few of his earlier songs.

"Damn, son, you have a shit-ton of talent there." Trip gaped at him, his eyes full of wonder. "Tell me again why you still don't do that for a livin'?"

Henry sighed and set the guitar aside. "Because it was the 'music industry', not bringin' music to people. It became a production, rather than fun. And there was no quiet like here." He stood and headed for the kitchen. "I'm gonna make some coffee before I check on the animals."

Trip rose and caught up to him, gripping his shoulder. "Hey, I'm sorry. I didn't mean to make light of your decision. It's just that you really do have talent."

Henry nodded, but didn't turn. "Thanks."

"No, I mean it. Even if you don't go back into the professional side of music, you should still play." Trip paused and shrugged, a half-smile curling his lips. "I really like to hear you play."

Henry looked over his shoulder. "Do you?"

"Hell yeah. If you don't play for crowds again, I hope you'll play for me."

Gratitude and warmth suffused Henry's chest, and he grabbed Trip's shirt, dragging him closer before he slanted his mouth over his lips. The man moaned and kissed Henry back, his roughed hands grasping Henry's ass through his jeans. When they broke apart, Henry grinned.

"I'm happy to play for you, braveheart."

Trip grinned back at him, and they went on with their day. The whole weekend seemed like a fantasy come true for Henry. He got to play guitar for fun, helped animals with his expertise, and made love to his hot lover each night. In fact, at one point, Trip pinned him against a wall and ploughed his ass while fondling his nipples, and Henry had never felt so loved.

The only fly in the ointment consisted of several texts from Jordie, constantly asking what Henry was doing and if he'd be there to see him. Henry refused to answer and ruin his weekend with Trip.

On Sunday night, they sat in Trip's living room drinking coffee and watching the snow fall outside. Henry liked being in his home even more than being in the bungalow, but having sex where Mrs. Guthrie could stumble in upon them wasn't conducive to easy connection. Still, he wished he could live with Trip full time.

"I'm not ready for tomorrow." Henry sipped his coffee to swallow down the disappointment of the ending to their romantic weekend.

"No? Somethin' come up at the clinic?" Trip shot him

a concerned look.

"Nah, it's just that I have to go back to work and don't get to spend my time with you."

"I won't be far. I'm here most of the time."

Henry nodded. "But I'm gonna be sleepin' alone."

Trip nodded as well, and rubbed his chin as they lapsed into silence. Henry's gut clenched as the silence stretched, and he thanked his lucky stars he hadn't told Trip he loved him. *Dammit, it's too early for love.* Too bad his heart hadn't gotten the memo.

"Speakin' of sleepin' alone, I'd best get to it." Henry didn't wait for Trip to say anything. His heart hurt too much to drag it out. "Thanks for the great weekend. Best one I've had in a long time." He headed for the hat tree to retrieve is coat, scarf, hat, and gloves.

"It's early yet and the snow's comin' hard. Don't you think you should stay a bit more?"

"Nah, I got an early day tomorrow." It wasn't true, or not completely. All his days started early, but he couldn't face the emotions and Trip's apparent indifference.

"Let me give you ride back to your place so you don't have to walk in it."

"I brought my truck today, remember?" Henry tried to smile but he ached all the way to his bones. "I'll see you in the barn tomorrow."

"Oh, right. Yeah. Tomorrow." Trip nodded, his gray-blue eyes filled with something, but whatever it was, he didn't speak it.

"Okay. Have a good night, Trip." Henry plopped his hat on his head and stepped out the door of Trip's apartment, feeling cold even before he reached the outer doors of the lodge. *I don't want to sleep alone anymore.*

Damn, the man was addictive.

He sighed and stared out at the blowing snow in the lights from the porch. Everyone else was bedded down for the night, even the horses. *I'm the only idiot drivin' around in a snowstorm.* He wished he could change his mind and head back into Trip's place. But the real world started in the morning, and he had no idea how Trip would be when faced with employees and family around him.

Henry zipped up his coat and pushed out into the night. He hoped Trip would treat him the same as he had during the weekend. *Best not to count on it.* His breath plumed in the frozen air, and he willed his heart not to freeze with it.

****

Trip let his gaze unfocus on snow-shrouded windows as the door to his home clicked shut. The sound seemed to echo louder than he remembered, and he wondered if he needed to check the hinges. The house grew quiet, and he settled back in his chair, trying to find the peace that usually came with the silence. But instead of peaceful, it felt empty and lonely.

That's because Livvy's not here.

Don't be a fool and a half, Trip. You know it's not me you're missin'. His wife leaned against the back of the other armchair, the one in which Henry had been sitting.

"I always miss you, Livvy."

Horseshit. You're missin' Henry, and you know it. She shook her head and gave him her best exasperated look. *Why didn't you ask him to stay?*

Trip sighed and stared out at the falling snow, despising the clench in his gut. "I'm worried about Estelle. She doesn't like Henry bein' with me."

Livvy nodded, her expression shifting into solemnity. *Yeah, I always thought she had a sweet spot for you.*

"Really?" When she nodded again, he shook his head. "I never saw it, I swear, darlin'. It was always you and no one else."

Until Henry.

"Yeah, until Henry." He shot her a guilty look. "That's

okay, right?"

Trip, I'm dead. She said it so matter-of-factly he couldn't help but smile. *But you're not, and there's no reason for you to be alone and celibate just because you once married me.*

Trip nodded again, swallowing hard. "He lights my campfire. Just like you did when you were alive."

I know. And I think you should pursue it. Just don't give up on him, all right? Remember he's young.

That sounded like a warning of things to come. "What the hell does that mean?"

But Livvy had faded from view and he was left to puzzle out her statement until his eyes grew too heavy to keep open.

CHAPTER FOURTEEN

Henry tried to focus on his work to keep his mind from wandering to concerns and worries about Trip, but when Tom Colton showed up in the clinic, he figured the proverbial other shoe was about to drop. Despite his concerns, he waved as Tom stepped in the door.

"Good afternoon, Mr. Colton. What can I do for you?" Henry tried to smile.

"You got a minute? I'd like to talk to you about somethin'." Tom didn't smile. His voice remained reserved and Henry swallowed back the unease.

"Sure. Come into the office. We can talk there."

He led the way to the vet's office where they could shut the door and tried not to borrow trouble. Tom could be there to discuss veterinary issues. *Yeah, and I'm secretly attracted to women.* He sat in the office chair and gestured to Tom to sit in the guests' chairs across from him.

"What's up?"

"Is it true you're in a relationship with my father?"

Well, at least I know he doesn't pussyfoot around. Henry took a deep breath. "Before I answer that, have you asked Trip about it yet?"

Tom nodded. "He told me."

He let his brows lower a little. "If he told you, why are you askin' me?"

"Because I want to know what your intentions are."

Henry couldn't hold in the bark of laughter. "You can't be here askin' me that, seriously? What is this, the 1950s when a man was expected to ask a woman's father if he could date her? Trip is neither your son nor a woman."

"Just answer the question."

"You didn't ask one. But since I value my job here, and I value the good graces of Trip's family, I'll let you know. I like him a lot. I respect him and you." Henry kept his voice even despite the building anger. "I'm not seducin' him, I'm not trickin' him, and I'm not takin' advantage of him. And I don't want his money. That about clear it up?"

Tom's jaw bunched as he stared, but Henry didn't back or look down. He wasn't going to make excuses and anything he and Trip did was between them.

"We hired you to be a vet."

"I am a vet. My certification has nothing to do with whom I'm in a relationship."

"You're sleepin' with the boss." Tom scowled and crossed his arms over his chest. Henry resisted the urge to mirror his pose.

Instead, he sighed and leaned forward, resting his elbows on the desk. "I'm not, Tom. You hired me. But that said, it was still Trip's decision. I wasn't going to act on anythin' until he chose to do something." He rubbed his chin. "What do you really want to know? If your dad told you about this already, why are you comin' to me?"

Tom dropped his chin. "I dunno. I think I was just tryin' to understand how my dad could love and be with my mom all those years ago and now he's interested in bein' with you. How does that make any sense?"

That question burned in the back of Henry's mind, too, but he shoved it aside. *It doesn't matter. What matters is Trip wants to be with me now.*

"That's somethin' you'll have to talk to your dad about. I can't give you that answer. But what I can say is I'm hopin' your issue isn't with me being gay."

Tom shook his head. "Nope. That doesn't bother me."

"You sure? 'Cause you came in here all but demandin' what the hell I was doin' with your dad. Are you sure you're not tellin' me what I can and can't be?"

"Here's how I'm lookin' at this." Tom frowned as he rubbed his chin. "I want my dad to be happy, and it's been thirty years since my mom died. He says he's found happiness with you and he wants to keep goin' with this relationship. I'm not one to shit on anyone's dreams, but if you hurt him, I'll run you outta here."

"And what if he hurts me? This ain't one-sided."

"I don't know you well enough. My dad's my priority."

"I understand that. But just keep in mind, it also ain't really your business what goes on between me and Trip unless it affects my work, bein' your employee and all." Henry stared Tom down. "I respect you, Tom, and what you do here, and the animals I look after. But give the same respect to your dad and who he chooses to be with."

"That bein' you?"

"Yeah, for now, it's me." Henry held up his hand to forestall Tom's response. "Look, I know you're worried about your dad, but he's old enough and savvy enough to know what he wants. You're not losin' an inheritance, hell you're not even losin' your dad. What's really botherin' you?"

Tom opened his mouth, but closed it a moment later. "I dunno. It's seems real sudden. I knew you were gay when we hired you, but I didn't expect you to hit on my father."

"I didn't hit on him. He asked me if I'd like to date him." Henry nodded at Tom's dropped jaw. "That's right. I thought your dad was handsome, but I wasn't gonna do a damn thing about it. I don't mess around with het guys or married men. But your dad wanted to see if there was more between us than just attraction. I followed his lead."

"Are you tellin' me he asked you out?"

"Yes, sir, I am. He made the first move."

If Tom's jaw could've unhinged and hit the floor, Henry figured it would have. The man resembled a big-mouthed catfish he'd seen while living in Tennessee.

"The hell you say."

Henry shrugged. "It's true. I didn't try to convince him. He convinced me."

"That's not possible." Tom shook his head.

"If you don't believe me, take it up with him." Henry kept his voice even. "The point is, he wanted to give it a try, and I agreed to it. He's not my direct superior, so there's no ethics issues. The question I have is are you gonna be okay with it?"

"I dunno."

At least he's honest about it.

"Would it have made a difference if I was a woman?"

Tom lapsed into silence his gaze on Henry's face. "Maybe. Then I would've been worried about the gold-digger aspect."

Henry snorted. "You don't have to worry about that. I got my own money."

"So why are you with Trip if not for his money or his ranch land?"

Henry shrugged again and offered him a half smile. "Because I like him." He hadn't told Trip his feelings yet, and there was no way in hell he'd mention them to Tom first. *Besides, I'd bet my truck Tom doesn't believe in love so early in a relationship.* Hell, he wasn't sure he believed it himself.

Tom sighed and rubbed his forehead. "Does he light your campfire?"

"What?" Henry raised his eyebrows.

"Light your campfire. Warm your heart. Make you

smile, shit like that?"

Henry had never heard it put that way, but he had to agree the imagery suited. "Yup. I'd say that's accurate."

"She-it." Tom nodded and shot a rueful smile at him. "Yeah, that's what Trip said, too."

Henry blinked and tried not to let the news of Trip's interest warm his chest too much. "Really?"

"Yeah." Tom sighed. "He said—" He cut himself off. "You know what? I think I better let him tell you that. It ain't my story to share."

Henry throttled back the urge to growl.

"Let's just leave it at I care a lot about my dad, and I don't want to see him hurt. But he's his own man and he can make decisions about who he wants around him." Tom grimaced. "Right now, that seems to be you."

"For what it's worth, I want to be around him, too."

"Yeah, I hear that." Tom nodded. "I guess I got nothin' else really to say. Well, that isn't true, but nothin' useful, so I'll let you get back to your afternoon."

"Thanks for stoppin' in, Tom." He stopped himself from saying more, feeling a mixture of relief and indignation. He rose from the chair and escorted Tom out into the clinic.

"Yeah. Thanks for talkin' to me. You have a good evenin'."

Henry nodded as Tom left. *I guess that's good.* Henry hoped he'd cleared the air, but relationships like this were always tricky, especially where family was concerned. Henry had never been with an older man, especially one with adult kids. And he suspected Tom had a couple years on him. *Aw hell, I'm probably the age of his younger brother if he had one.*

Age always made people get a bit twitchy. The pervasive belief in folks about the same age getting together was a long-held bias. But he'd meant what he said when he told Trip age was just a number. Attraction didn't check birth certificates.

His phone pinged with a text, and he absently pulled it out to check.

Tomorrow's the day. My flight gets in around 2:30. See you in Fort Collins!

Jordie's text ended with several cutsie emojis, and Henry dropped his chin to his chest. Fuck. He'd have to deal with that in the new day. He rubbed his face with his hands. He didn't want to go back to that world. He liked it in Wyoming with the quiet, the animals he cared for, and the Triple Star Ranch. He didn't want Jordie polluting the new peace he'd found.

And I don't want him to know about Trip.

Why he needed to protect Trip *from* Jordie wasn't clear, but it sat in his gut and screamed warnings. He set the phone aside and headed back into the barn to continue his duties without answering Jordie. He'd deal with the problem tomorrow.

****

Tuesday came before Henry was ready, but like taxes, it arrived inexorably. His phone had blown up with texts and emails from Jordie from the moment the guy must have woken up until he'd boarded his flight. Henry wanted to thank the airline for requiring people to shut off their phones just for the respite.

It didn't help that his mind kept going to the conversation he'd had with Tom. He hadn't been able to talk to Trip about it, but he hoped it had changed the way Tom looked at Henry's relationship with his father. He didn't want to cause friction between the Coltons, but he wouldn't hide how he felt about Trip.

As soon as Jordie's plane landed, the texts and calls started again, and Henry made a mental note to change his phone number. Out of sheer self-defense, he promised to meet Jordie in Fort Collins for dinner. That seemed to mollify the other man enough to silence Henry's phone, and he was able to get some of his work done. Henry didn't want to see Jordie at all, but this would allow him to set the record straight, and Jordie could go back to his life in Nashville.

Trip texted him a few times, touching base and asking Henry how he was doing. It warmed Henry's heart and he responded in kind, but kept the phone on silent. He had no interest in letting Jordie know about Trip.

Henry texted Trip about going to Fort Collins before he left, but Trip hadn't answered by the time he got on the road. Despite the lack of precipitation, the wind howled out of the west and kept the evening cold as the sun set. The closer he got to Fort Collins, the tighter his gut clenched. Jordie was a smooth, wheedling man, excellent as a manager for getting his way. Henry damn near turned around to head back to Wyoming twice, but he finally made it into Fort Collins and followed Jordie's directions to a small diner up close to the foothills of the mountains.

It's gonna be fine. You'll have a drink or a meal with him and be done.

Henry hoped it would be the case as he stepped out of his truck and locked the doors. The wind wasn't as sharp in Fort Collins, but he kept his coat zipped despite the relative warmth. *Too bad I'm not with Trip. Then the cold wouldn't matter.* The man warmed him inside and out. He'd even received a text from Trip wishing him a safe drive.

Stepping inside the rather chic café Jordie had directed him to, Henry spotted the other man in a booth against the wall. Henry nodded to the hostess and strode for the booth, hoping his expression didn't give away his lack of interest. The other man's face had become gaunt and more lines bracketed his eyes and mouth than when Henry had last seen him, but a wide grin appeared when Jordie saw him. The other man waved and beckoned him over.

"Oh, shit, it's good to see you, Henry." Jordie rose and made a move to hug Henry until he glanced around at the other patrons and stopped. "Have a seat. I'm so glad you came." He settled again and gestured for Henry to join him.

Henry nodded, sealing his lips over any happy words of greeting. "What can I do for you, Jordie?"

"What, no greeting? No good to see you?"

Henry raised his eyebrow. "Glad you're doin' okay. Now, what all do you want?"

Disappointment settled over Jordie's expression and he ran a hand through his short hair. "I wanted to see you and talk to you face to face. You took off so fast in Tennessee, I didn't get a chance to say goodbye." He pouted, and Henry resisted the urge to roll his eyes.

He could just imagine that "goodbye". It would have come with a lot of petulance, manipulation, and whining, and Henry had wanted to forego the experience. *Looks like I'll be gettin' my fair share of it now.*

"That's what this is about? You wanted me to drive all the way to Fort Collins just to say goodbye?" Henry gathered himself to stand. "In that case, goodbye, Jordie."

Jordie's hand slapped against his arm and his face tightened up with anxiety. "Wait, Henry. Please. Stay a moment. Shit, can't you give me at least one dinner to catch up? It's been ages."

Henry narrowed his eyes at the manipulation. "I'm done with your world, Jordie. I'm not going back to the music industry. I told you that on the phone."

"I know, I know. Just sit down, will you? Everyone's staring."

Henry didn't much care if people stared. He'd lived his life in the spotlight for years and staring didn't amount to much. But he settled back into the other bench seat and waited for Jordie to go on. The other man's brown gaze flickered around the room a few moments before settling back on Henry and a smarmy smile curled his lips.

"You're looking good. I guess Wyoming is good for you." He shrugged. "Of course, you were always good-looking, which is why your records sold so well."

"My records sold so well because I'm a damn good musician, Jordie. Get to the point. Why are you really here in Colorado?" Henry kept his voice even.

"I wanted to see you and hear your voice. I missed you when you left so suddenly and didn't take your phone. Why did you leave it behind?" Jordie frowned.

"It wasn't really mine. The label paid for it. I didn't want to take anythin' from them."

"It made it hard to find you."

That was the idea. "I suppose so. I didn't figure anyone'd be lookin'. I gave back the advance money and terminated the contract. What more was there to do?"

"You could've told me. I got in big trouble with Lariat Records because of it. You could've given me some warning."

Henry frowned. *Why had they been pissed with Jordie?* And he'd been unsatisfied with the party life for months, telling Jordie in small ways he was done, but the other man hadn't listened. *He's never really listened once I hit it big.* That was the difference between Jordie and Trip. Trip listened and took his words seriously despite their age differences. Jordie ignored Henry and made decisions for both of them that didn't suit.

"I guess I could've made it more clear I was done, but you didn't seem to hear me. So, I took the opportunity to leave." Henry nodded, not giving an inch. "You really didn't need to come all the way out here to have me tell you to your face. I could've done that on the phone. Why are you really here?"

Before Jordie could answer, the perky waitress sauntered over to their table with a big smile and asked for their order. Jordie ordered a roast beef sandwich and steak fries. The waitress turned to Henry.

"And for you?"

"Just coffee for me, thanks." He gave her a polite, vague smile.

"Aw, come on, Henry. Have dinner. My treat." Jordie gave him the coy smile.

Henry met the woman's gaze. "Just coffee. Thanks."

"Cream or sugar?"

"Black."

"Will do. Comin' right up." She sauntered away and Henry met Jordie's scowl, but it quickly morphed into a grimace.

"What?"

"Why won't you have dinner with me?" Henry had forgotten how well Jordie could whine.

"Because I'm not going to do this with you, Jordie." Henry sighed and stopped waiting for the other man to get to the point. "I'm not coming back to the music scene. I like my life here in the west, and I like my job."

"Job?" Jordie sneered. "You mean as a veterinarian?"

"Yeah, that's it." Henry sat back against the bench seat. "It's a good job, and I like the people I work for. They're doin' something good for the community. It's what I want to do."

"Yeah, but you don't make nearly as much money and you're in Wyoming, for god's sake." Jordie shook his head. "You were at the top of your career as an entertainer, bringing in money hand over fist. Why the hell would you give that up? We were living the high life. It's the goddamn American dream."

"Whose American dream was it? 'Cause it wasn't mine." Henry shook his head. "I wasn't into the party scene."

"Yes, you were. I can't even count how many lovers you had." Jordie frowned as the waitress returned with Henry's coffee. "It was honestly obscene."

Henry laughed, agreeing with him. "Yeah, it was, and

you were right there with me. You had your fair share."

"See?" Jordie grinned. "It was good, right? And we can do it again. I just need to make a couple of phone calls and the execs will take you back, no questions asked. Frankly, they'd be overjoyed you're coming around. You leaving was a huge loss."

Henry lost his smile. He didn't believe the execs cared one way or another. Oh yeah, they'd love it if he came crawling back to make them more money, but as long as they didn't lose anything, they wouldn't give a rat's ass whether he strummed guitar for them or not.

"It wasn't that much of a loss to them, and I ain't goin' back. I thought I made myself pretty clear." He sighed as Jordie's expression morphed into determined anger. "Look, I know you don't like it and I know you can't understand it, but I've moved on. I don't even have more music in me. I haven't written a single song since I left. Hell, I haven't played my guitar. There wouldn't be anythin' to sell if I went back. You know how the biz works."

Jordie waved his hand. "I'm sure you just need a little inspiration. God knows you won't get it in bum-fuck Wyoming."

Henry refrained from reminding him Wyoming's inspiration was what had made him famous in the first place. "No, it's not about inspiration. It's about heart. My heart's not in it and I don't want to do it anymore. I'm sorry you had to come all this way to hear it, but that's my decision." He patted the table. "Thanks for the dinner invite, but I'm headed home now."

"What's your hurry? You got someone waiting for you?" Jordie's lip twisted as if he couldn't believe anyone in a small state like Wyoming would be worth the time.

That's the thing. Trip's worth all my time. "Would it matter if there was?" Henry shook his head and threw a five-dollar bill on the table for his coffee. God knew he didn't want to owe Jordie anything. "I'd like to say it was good seein' you, but that wouldn't be the truth. You take care, now."

He rose just as the waitress came back to serve Jordie's food.

"You heading out, sir?"

"Yup. Gotta get home before the weather turns on me." Henry gave her a vague smile.

"You want me to put your coffee in a to-go cup?"

"Sure, that'd be fine." Henry shot a look at Jordie and caught a look of calculation on his face before it shifted into hurt.

"Seriously? You're really gonna leave me here to eat alone?" Jordie pouted.

Glory, I hate that voice and look.

"It's a forty-mile drive to Cheyenne and they might shut down I-25." He smiled as the waitress brought him a cardboard to-go cup. "Thanks. I appreciate it."

She beamed at him and tilted her head coyly. "Sure, anytime."

He nodded to her then to Jordie. "See you." He didn't wait to see if the other man would respond as he took his coffee and headed out the door.

Anger simmered in his gut at Jordie's insistence about him returning to the music industry. And the American dream statement? When had Jordie ever worked his ass off to do anything for his own American dream? Henry growled as he unlocked his truck and slid behind the wheel. His phone pinged and he checked the screen to see if Jordie had had the nerve to text him so soon, but it was just an email from the record label reporting the deposit of his monthly earnings.

He started the truck and shoved it into gear as some of his anger cooled. At least he still had the passive income from his record sales and a steady job at the Triple Star Ranch to keep him solvent. He didn't need to go crawling back to Lariat Records for a job.

The sky opened up with snow when he hit the Wyoming state line, and he thanked anyone listening he was almost home. Home. That's what the Triple Star had become to him in the short time he'd been there. He was needed and wanted there, and he would strive to stay there permanently.

The snow continued steadily until he turned off I-25 onto Route 224. His phone pinged a few more times, but he kept his eyes on the road. Despite his focus, his mind kept running to Trip and how much he enjoyed being with the older man. The age gap between them didn't seem to matter. Their connection reached deeper than mere generations, and the differences between them made their relationship more interesting. Trip had experience and understanding most men Henry's age couldn't dream of.

The snow stuck to the ground beside the road, but the pavement remained clear and Henry soon reached the gate to the Triple Star. He wanted to see Trip tonight as he pulled up to the front of the Lodge. The sun had set long ago, but it wasn't very late, and he hoped Trip wouldn't mind a visit.

Opening his truck door took some effort with the wind ripping off the western plains, but he shoved his way out into the snow and hurried for the Lodge's front doors. Stepping inside from the bitter cold resembled hitting a warm wall and he sighed with relief.

Andrew, the redheaded young man who worked the reception desk, looked up and smiled. "Hey there, Doc Bright. How are ya?"

"Good. Damn glad to be inside tonight. That wind out there is bitter cold." He shook his head as he stopped at the desk. "I'd forgotten how damn cold it gets here."

"Yeah, it's a lot different than bein' in Nashville, I'm sure."

Henry blinked in surprise. "How'd you know I'm from there?"

Andrew grinned. "I overheard Tom Colton talkin' to Miss Amber about you and looked you up. I should've recognized you as Henry Bright, the Kick-ass Cowboy of Nashville back when you first arrived. I've listened to your music since it first came out. It's damn good."

Henry huffed a surprised laugh. "Yeah? Thanks. I'm glad you enjoyed it."

"Are you kiddin' me? It's the best." Andrew grinned. "Right up there with Keith Urban, and Big & Rich with a side of Lady Antebellum."

He'd never heard those comparisons, but he wouldn't turn them down. "Thanks a lot. That's kindly said." He waved toward Trip's apartment. "Is Mr. Colton in tonight?"

"Yeah, I think so. Hey, if you wouldn't mind, would you sign my copy of "Hard Row to Hoe"? It's your best album in my opinion."

"Yeah?" Henry smiled, though his heart ached a bit. It had been a good one for him to record, too, but everything had soured about it after it was released. "Sure. Pull it out and I'll sign the insert."

"Hey, thanks a lot." Andrew reached under the counter and pulled out the CD case. It sat empty, but he'd heard the familiar sounds of his work over the PA system a few times. "Can you sign it 'To Andrew'? I'd really appreciate it."

Henry nodded. *To Andrew. Keep on keepin' on. It's a Hard Row to Hoe. Henry Bright.* He passed the case back to Andrew and patted the counter. "Thanks for the compliments. I'm gonna stop in to see Mr. Colton."

"Sure thing. And thanks for the autograph. I'm sure glad you're workin' here."

Henry waved and headed for Trip's place, but a smile curled his lips. Nothin' better than meeting a fan to raise his spirits. *So much better than spendin' time with Jordie.*

His mood plummeted, but he shoved the sour thoughts aside and reached to knock on the door. But the sounds coming from inside stopped him and he froze. *Is that my music?* He listened hard. After a few seconds, he realized it wasn't his, or rather it wasn't him playing it. Someone else played his songs on an acoustic guitar.

As much as he loathed interrupting whoever played, he couldn't walk in unannounced so he turned his back and sank to the floor, listening. The guitar player had skill and talent, and Henry closed his eyes, enjoying his music for the first time in months.

Listening brought back memories of where he'd been when he wrote the songs and how he'd felt. That last album had been pulled from the depths of his soul, each song composed of blood, sweat, tears, and yearning for home. He'd hoped the fans would like it, but the music had been a bear to write, as if he'd touched on the true meaning but fell short. He remembered the dread filling him as he'd finished recording, knowing he'd be required to do the parties and photo shoots.

To his surprise, tears cascaded down his cheeks as he listened. The music flowed from the apartment behind the door and dragged out all the loneliness and desperation he'd experienced in the writing. Henry wept all the pent-up emotions. The fear, the insecurity, the loneliness, the dread, the loss of the voices who told him the notes to put down along with the lyrics. Even his anger at Jordie and his insistence to return. All of it flooded out of his eyes to drip on his chest.

He was so lost in his emotions, he didn't notice when the playing stopped. But he heard the sound of footsteps coming toward the door and he scrambled to his feet, hurriedly wiping away the tears.

"Henry? What are you doin' here?" Trip blinked at him as he stood in the doorway, his expression laced with concern. "Are you all right?"

Aw hell.

"Yeah, yeah, I'm fine." He wiped his nose with his

hand and swiped his jeans. "I, uh, just stopped by to see if you'd mind some company. I could really use some tonight."

Trip gazed at him a few moments, his expression pensive. "Yeah, come on in. I was gonna go get some of Estelle's sweet rolls, but I can do that later."

Henry sniffed and nodded as he stepped through the doorway. Trip closed it behind them and reached for Henry's coat.

"Here, let me take that. You want some coffee or somethin'?" Trip took Henry's coat and hat and hung them on the hat tree before heading for the kitchen.

"Yeah, coffee and maybe somethin' to eat. I haven't had supper yet." Henry nodded as he sat down at the kitchen table.

"What the hell do you mean you haven't had supper yet? Work ended hours ago." Trip shook his head as he started coffee in the coffeemaker. "Let me make you a sandwich. Turkey cold cuts all right?"

"Yeah, they're fine." Henry scrubbed his face, hoping the evidence of tears was gone. "Were you in here playin' a guitar?"

Trip hitched a shoulder as he got out the sandwich fixings. "Yeah, well, I don't know if I'd call it playin' so much as pluckin'. I'm not as good at it as you are, of course, but I like to strum now and then."

"It was nice to listen to it played by someone else. It reminded me of when I loved playin' music." He stopped before he said more and the tears started flowing again.

Trip didn't say anything for a few moments as he finished the sandwich and Henry wondered if he'd said too much. Not all men, particularly in Trip's generation, could handle expressed emotion. Henry let himself cry, but only when alone. But somehow, he couldn't seem to stop showing Trip.

Trip set the plate with a turkey sandwich down in front

of Henry and settled into the chair opposite him. "You don't love playin' music anymore?"

The lump in Henry's throat grew bigger and he had to take a bite of the sandwich to dislodge it so he could speak. "Not for a long time now. When it was all for the next paycheck and release party, it wasn't fun anymore. It's why I left Nashville." He stuffed the sandwich into his mouth again and made himself eat. He didn't think Trip would think kindly of him if he fell into a bundle of tears on his table. *And what the fuck's wrong with me?*

Trip nodded, his steel-blue gaze assessing everything. Henry had met a lot of men in his life and knew how to read them pretty well. Most in the music industry had looked at him with calculation, either for financial or sexual potential. He'd learned how to see what they wanted before they'd made the first move.

But Trip's assessment seemed more intimate and health related rather than what kind of benefits Henry could be to him. He waited for Henry to finish eating before he rose to bring him a cup of black coffee and a slice of pie.

"It's apple. Great for digestion as well as tasty as hell." Trip nodded to the pie. "You want some ice cream with it?"

"Nah, this is good enough."

Trip nodded again. "You wanna tell me what's really goin' on? You're worked up about somethin', and I suspect it has to do with music, but why don't you tell me and we'll work it out, together?"

Henry swallowed and shoved the anger and frustration at Jordie away. "You really wanna know? 'Cause it's just stuff left over from when I left Nashville."

"No man ever solved everythin' by himself. What are friends for if not to help you work shit out?"

"Is that what we are, Trip? Friends?" God almighty, Henry wanted to be so much more than friends.

"I hope at the very least we're friends, Henry. But I have to say I'd prefer if we were more than that." Trip met his gaze steadily, no flinching or squirming.

Glory, I wish I had his confidence.

"I'd like that, too." Henry tried to find his smile. "I drove down to Fort Collins tonight to meet with Jordie Heathrow 'cause he flew in from Nashville today."

Trip nodded slowly. "Why'd he come to Fort Collins?"

"He wanted to meet to try to convince me to get back into the music scene." Henry scowled and shook his head. "He kept tellin' me I was throwin' away everything, includin' the American Dream. But I don't want whatever American Dream he's goin' on about. It wasn't worth it. It was all empty shit." He tightened his hands into fists to keep from hitting something. "None of it was real and the music dried up inside me, killed by the emptiness."

"He wanted you to come back to the music industry?"

"Yeah, and he kept whinin' and wheedlin', and it just pissed me off. I told him my heart's not in it anymore and I'm not goin' back." He shook his head. "That's when he insulted Wyomin', and I was just done." He didn't mention Jordie's insinuation about Henry having someone waiting on him. *Because Jordie might be right.*

Trip snorted with a half-smile curling his lips. "Them's fightin' words right there."

Despite his anger, Henry laughed. "Damn straight."

"I'm sorry to hear he just wouldn't take no for an answer." Trip shrugged. "Sounds like the guy's got a hard-on for that life and he thought of you as his golden ticket. I gotta say I'm damn relieved you don't wanna go back to Nashville."

"Oh, yeah?" Some of Henry's anger slid away.

"Yeah. Where'd I find another vet on short notice?"

"Oh, right." Henry's humor died. "Yeah, that's right."

"Whoa, back, son. I think you didn't get my joke." Trip reached out and grasped Henry's forearm. "That's only one reason I don't want you to go. I have too many others that complicate things, but are no less valid. Most importantly, I love…bein' with you and sharin' my space. Last weekend was the best I've had in a long time, and it's all because of you."

I guess that answer's the question of if someone's waitin' on me.

Henry cleared his throat. "I feel the same. I didn't want it to end."

Trip nodded with a grimace. "It damn near gutted me when you walked out my door Sunday night. Worst feeling I've experienced since my wife died."

"Really?" Glory, could he sound any more pitiful?

"Yeah." Trip rubbed his chin. "I didn't like it at all. And I'd like to avoid it as much as possible in the future. What do you say?"

Henry blinked. "I, uh, I'm not sure what to say. What exactly are you askin' me? Or are you askin' anything?"

Trip moved his hand to the back of his head and rubbed the nape of his neck. *Hey, that's my job.* Henry waited in tense silence, willing Trip to come out and ask him to stay forever.

"I guess I'm askin' if you'd spend more nights here at my place." Pink tinged Trip's cheeks, but he met Henry's gaze. "I'd like you to spend more nights here with me. I'd like to share meals and stories and music with you, even if it's only me playin' to you. You think that might work?"

Henry couldn't speak for several moments because the damn lump was back in his throat. And the tears threatened to overflow his eyes again. *Fuck, I'm gonna make him think I'm an emotional sap.* When it came to love, Henry definitely felt emotions.

When he didn't say anything, Trip cleared his throat. "We're both adults, and I ain't hidin' my relationship with you from anyone. The important people already know so there doesn't seem to be a reason to keep you from spendin' time here." He clenched his jaw and rubbed his head again. "Please, Henry? The lodge is a helluva lot closer to the barn than your bungalow and winter's fixin' to set in. What do you say?"

"Give me a minute." Henry swallowed hard a couple of times before he could make sure he wouldn't embarrass Trip the moment he answered. "I want to make sure I'm hearin' you right. Are you askin' me to move in with you, Trip?"

Trip shrugged, biting his lip. "Maybe not fully move in, but definitely give you some space here so you don't always have to head off to the bungalow each night. I, uh, well, I've never lived with anyone else in this apartment, but it's big enough." He shot Henry a rueful smile. "Tom insisted it have two bedrooms even though it was just me livin' here. He said in case I wanted a 'man-cave'."

Henry tried to laugh, but it came out a choked sob. "You want me in your man-cave?"

Trip grinned. "Hell yeah. What else do you keep there if not a hot man?"

They both froze a moment and Trip swallowed hard. "Not that I'm keepin' you, or that you're a kept man, or...aw hell." A blush worked its way up his cheeks.

He's fuckin' adorable.

Henry rose and stumbled around the table to grab Trip's face. "Damn, you're the sexiest man I know." Then he kissed him with every bit of love in his heart. "I'd be happy to bunk in your man-cave."

The blush remained on Trip's cheeks, but he grinned and kissed Henry back. Their tongues dueled for supremacy, sliding against each other with erotic abandon. Henry's cock rose to tighten in his jeans and he ached to feel Trip skin to skin. He pulled back and met Trip's lustful gaze.

"I can't move in tonight, but I'll stay until mornin'."

"That sounds fine to me."

Henry's heart swelled with excitement and joy, things he hadn't felt since he received his first contract with Lariat

Records. He kissed Trip again as his heart pounded in his chest.

I love him.

Henry pushed through the surprise to keep kissing Trip, but he couldn't deny the truth. It didn't matter that it had only been a couple of weeks. He'd fallen for Trip Colton, hook, line, and sinker. He'd never felt this way about anyone before. None of the men with whom he'd had flings or relationships had come close to engendering the emotions ricocheting through him with every one of Trip's smiles.

"Trip, I need..." Words failed him with a rise in insecurity. What if Trip laughed at him or turned him down? Henry swallowed hard, took a deep breath, and met Trip's gaze. "I need to make love with you."

Trip studied him for a while, one hand cupping Henry's cheek. "You wanna make love?"

"Yeah...yes, I do. With you." Henry nodded to support his breathless agreement.

"I think that's a fine idea." Trip smiled and pulled Henry down for another intoxicating kiss that left them both breathless. "Help me clean up and we'll go to bed directly."

"Yes, sir." Henry grinned as he backed away then held out a hand to help Trip to his feet. "I'll rinse the dishes and put 'em in the dishwasher."

Trip laughed as he ambled toward the front door. "I'll lock the front door."

"You don't usually?" Henry called as he worked on the dishes.

"I didn't at first." Henry heard the lock click. "But the more people we housed for the therapy, the more we needed to protect them and us from the night terrors." Trip reappeared and worked on packaging up the food while Henry cleaned the counters. "And now I have a certain preference for privacy." He shot Henry a smile. "I don't mind folks knowin' that I'm involved with you, but I'd rather keep our lovin' private."

"I can't argue with that."

They finished cleaning up and Henry had the oddest feeling of déjà vu, as if he'd done this hundreds of times with Trip before. It felt easy, comfortable, and perfect, as if it was meant for him to be here, being domestic, with his lover and husband.

Whoa, wait. Husband?

Wyoming didn't support marriage equality, no matter what the Supreme Court said. Hell, there were still laws on the State books that allowed employers to fire someone because they were gay. Why the hell was he thinking about marriage? Henry mentally shook his head to clear out the fantastical thoughts and followed Trip into his bedroom.

"I think there's a fresh toothbrush under the sink if you wanna brush your teeth." Trip headed for the bathroom while Henry sat on the bed and removed his boots and socks. "I gotta take my meds before I forget."

"Meds?" Henry unbuttoned his flannel overshirt and peeled it off his shoulders.

"Yeah, blood pressure meds to keep the blood flowin'. Vitamins to keep me functionin' right. Glucosamine to make sure my joints don't lock up." Trip shook his head as he headed for the bathroom. "Good thing I ain't fallin' apart."

Henry laughed and reminded himself to learn what all Trip needed to take on a regular basis. *It's what spouses do.* There was that connection to marriage again. He laid his shirt on the nearby chair and pulled off his undershirt before ambling to the bath to search for the toothbrush.

Henry paused at the doorway and took in Trip's strong form. Yes, he had silver in his hair and lines on his face. His skin wasn't as taut as a younger man's and he had a bit of a limp, but he wore his experience with grace and honor, and it was sexy as hell.

"What you grinnin' at?" Trip met his gaze in the mirror.

"You and your sexy ass. I'm just countin' my blessings for such havin' such a hot man in my life." Henry strode into the bathroom and wrapped his arms around Trip from behind, his chest against his back. He inhaled Trip's masculine scent and let his heat seep into him.

"Flatterer." Trip chuckled, the sound rumbling through Henry's chest.

"Doesn't mean it ain't true." Henry squeezed him before pulling back. "Where's that extra toothbrush?"

Trip grunted with amusement and bent to open the cupboard below the sink. Henry enjoyed the view of his jeans growing tight over Trip's ass. *Damn, I'd like to fuck that ass.* Trip wasn't ready for that. He might never be ready for it, but the fantasy settled in the back of Henry's mind.

"Here. Turns out I got a couple of them. Estelle must've done some shopping." Trip held out the toothbrush and Henry took it, leaning in for a kiss to banish the thought of the woman who didn't approve of their connection.

"Thanks. I wanna make sure my mouth is clean when I kiss and blow you."

Trip's eyes sparked with arousal. "You plannin' on blowin' me tonight?"

"Yes, sir." Henry peeled open the package and tossed it. "Just give me a minute or two and I'll be ready for bed."

He stuck the toothbrush under the running water as Trip grabbed his ass, squeezing one cheek.

"Don't take too long. I've a mind to suck on that cock of yours tonight, too." He winked at Henry in the mirror and retreated to the bedroom. Henry gaped after his lover, the toothbrush all but forgotten.

CHAPTER FIFTEEN

Trip had never been so bold in his life, but the idea of having Henry's cock in his mouth turned his own dick to stone. He wanted to run his tongue over Henry's hard shaft and suck on it like one of those red, white, and blue popsicles the kids used to get from the ice cream trucks. Glory be, the thought made him groan with delicious torture. He jerked his shirt over his head and threw it in the closet, too excited to hang anything up.

He wanted to feel Henry's body against him every night. *I want him here with me.* He hadn't expected to ask Henry to move in after knowing him such a short time, but the request had slipped out and felt right. He was too old to pussyfoot around and wait for the right time, some prescribed set of weeks or months until it was acceptable to ask for Henry's company. He didn't want to waste time and winter approached. Living in the lodge with Trip made more logistical sense.

He wanted as much time with Henry as he could get. Trip unbuttoned his jeans and pushed them off his hips along with his briefs. His semi-hard dick made it tricky to get undressed without making him groan. Or imagining Henry with his lips stretched around his girth. *Or in my ass.*

The last thought took him by surprise and his gut tightened with unease. He'd never had anal sex himself, though he'd enjoyed giving it to Henry, and old social mores about it rose up in his mind. Henry said there was a little pain, but when done right, the pain changed into pleasure and felt amazing. Was he really considering having Henry fuck him?

He mulled it over as he threw his clothes in his closet. Henry finished in the bathroom and returned to the bedroom, his jeans unbuttoned. Trip's mouth watered at the sight of his open fly. *Glory be, I want him.*

"I'm sure a lot of folks have told you you're a handsome man, Henry, but I gotta say, you definitely trip my trigger." Trip met his gaze as he slid into his bed.

A goofy smile curled Henry's lips. "Yeah, a few folks have mentioned that. But it's never meant as much as it does comin' from you." He slipped his jeans and briefs off and Trip swallowed hard.

"Damn, I wanna suck on that cock of yours."

Henry paused and swallowed hard, his Adam's apple rising in his throat. "You do?"

"Hell yeah. Come to bed and bring me that dick."

Henry grinned. "Damn, Trip. I like you bold and demandin'." He slid into the bed and snuggled up to Trip, pressing himself to his chest. He ran one hand down Trip's belly until it came to rest at the base of his dick and he stroked his shaft toward hardness. "I also like your cock in my hand."

Exquisite pleasure from Henry's callused hands flooded through Trip and he threw his head back to moan. Henry knew just the right pressure and motion to stiffen his dick and Trip relaxed into it.

"Yeah, well, I'd like your cock in my mouth." He sat up and gave Henry what he hoped was a sultry smile.

"I think I can oblige." Henry grinned. "But I want the same. What do you say to some sixty-nine?"

For a moment, Trip couldn't say anything. But his cock flexed as more blood headed south. *Yeah, that's a good idea.* Instead, he grabbed Henry and pulled him against his chest until they lay nose to nose. "I think that's a damn fine idea."

Henry closed the distance between them and kissed him, his tongue tangling with Trip's. Trip's heart thundered in his chest as his dick strained with heavy arousal and he reached down to stroke Henry's matching shaft. He loved the length and girth of Henry's cock. It was more slender than his own, but longer and straight. Trip wondered what it would feel like to have Henry fuck him.

"Good." Henry pushed the blankets back on the bed and angled his feet toward the headboard as he scooted closer to Trip's body. "I've been thinkin' about gettin' close to this cock all day today."

"Have you now?" Pleasure and excitement built in Trip's chest. "You don't have to wait any longer, then."

He lifted one of his legs as he turned his head toward Henry's groin. His shaft rose out of thick, dark hair resting in short arcs like feathers. Trip grasped Henry's cock and held it while he nuzzled the round testicles growing taut under his hands. They smelled of musky man and heat, and Trip inhaled deeply. *Glory, I love the scent of my man.*

The thought surprised him enough to pause, but his thoughts shattered when Henry grabbed his dick and wrapped his lips around it. *Holy God in Heaven, that's so damn good.* Wet heat surrounded his cockhead and he lost track of what he was doing. When Henry rolled Trip's balls in his fingers, Trip forgot how to breathe.

Henry hummed around Trip's shaft and it reminded him to get to his own work of sucking on the younger man. *I won't let him show me up.* But instead of grabbing Henry's stiff cock and shoving it into his mouth, he licked the long vein on the underside. Henry moaned and Trip hid a grin as he continued to enjoy his treat.

"Fuck, Trip. You're so damn good at that." Henry moaned as Trip sucked him harder, rubbing Henry's balls with his fingers.

Trip raked his teeth over the edges of Henry's cockhead and followed with his tongue to soothe the sting. Henry's hips flexed, driving his dick deeper into Trip's mouth, and he whimpered with pleasure.

"Shit-oh-dear, it feels so fuckin' good."

Pleasure and pride filled Trip, and he kept licking and sucking Henry's delectable cock. He pulled off his shaft and dropped his head to lick the taut skin on his balls. Henry groaned and his hands tightened on Trip's thighs.

"So that's how it's gonna be, huh? Alrighty then." Henry's growled comment made Trip's cock flex.

Henry grasped his shaft and stroked his tongue over the sensitive head, tickling the slit. Trip maoned and tightened his lips over Henry's cock, but the younger man was merciless in his sensual onslaught. Henry squeezed Trip's shaft with his hand as his tongue painted erotic designs on his flesh.

Glory be, the man is diabolical.

But Henry didn't stop. He sucked on Trip's cockhead and squeezed his shaft with one hand while he massaged Trip's scrotum with the other. Trip tried to keep his attention on the straight dick in his mouth, but Henry kept distracting him with his touches. His focus slowly deteriorated with Henry's determined attention, but he damn near came when Henry scraped his teeth over the edge of the glans.

Arousal built in Trip's balls, coiling at the base of his spine like a snake ready to strike. He moaned and rocked his hips, trying to get his cock deeper into Henry's hot mouth. But Henry pulled back and used his tongue to press the divot on the bottom side of the head.

"Oh, fuck, Henry. I'm gonna come."

Henry hummed with what sounded like approval and

tightened his grip, igniting Trip's orgasm. It flared from his balls straight through his body to shoot his awareness out among the stars. Fireworks exploded behind his eyes and he couldn't do more than hold Henry's cock in his mouth and moan.

Henry swallowed down everything he had to give, licking and massaging Trip's cock until he whimpered and writhed from overstimulation. Henry let him go with a chuckle that turned into a groan as Trip retrieved his awareness from the euphoric abyss.

Suck me until I'm incoherent, will he? We'll see about that.

Trip turned his attention away from Henry's smug grin to his straining cock. He slid the head to the back of his throat and swallowed, tightening his lips on the shaft. Henry moaned and rocked his hips, grabbing Trip's ass as if to anchor himself. But Trip wasn't giving up. He sucked and massaged the cockhead with his tongue as he stroked his fingers over Henry's balls. When his fingers drifted down behind Henry's testicles to the soft skin between them and his anus, Henry threw his head back.

"Oh, fuck, yeah. Fuckin' suck my cock hard, braveheart."

Trip didn't need to be told twice. He set up a slow, steady rhythm, squeezing and jerking Henry's shaft with his hand while he suckled on the head. Henry's body grew taut and he flexed his hips, trying to closer to or farther from Trip's mouth. His whimpers grew louder and his cock grew harder as he neared his peak.

"Oh shit. Oh my god, I'm gonna come. Suck me. Suck me hard!"

Trip focused on drawing out Henry's release and was rewarded in a few short strokes.

"Fuuuuccccckkk!" Hot jets of cum erupted from Henry's slit, and Trip swallowed it all down, enjoying the spicy, sweet cream. He reveled not only in the satisfaction of his lover, but in a job well done.

I gave Henry pleasure.

It was a novel thought to please his partner. His wife had never complained about sex, but she also never made noise. Hell, he'd made more sound than her and he wasn't what could be termed 'vocal'. But Henry didn't hold back, and Trip found he craved the sounds of pleasure from his lover.

Trip released Henry's cock and rolled onto his back. He lay there, catching his breath, and somehow, Henry found the energy to crawl up beside him. They both gasped for a short time, immersed in their own thoughts as their hearts slowed. Trip had never felt such peace and delight as he did in that moment.

"That was the best sixty-nine I've ever had." Henry sounded out of breath but satisfied.

"Me, too." Trip chuckled as Henry rolled onto his side, resting his head on Trip's shoulder. "And the first time I got to suck dick while doin' it."

"But that's a good thing, right?" Despite his more extensive experience with male lovers, Henry sounded hesitant.

"Hell yeah, it's a great thing." Trip met his hazel gaze. "I'm not gonna change my mind, Henry. I like how you touch me, and I like to touch you. You're sexy as hell." He stopped himself before he said *I love you*, but it sat on the tip of his tongue, waiting for its moment.

"Trip..." Henry stared at him, his hair tousled in sexy disarray.

"Yeah?"

"I...I'm really glad you're in my life."

Trip's chest swelled with joy. "I am, too. Hell, I'm really glad you're in my bed. This way neither of us has to go anywhere."

Henry didn't say anything for a moment, trailing his hand over Trip's chest to run his fingers through the hair there. He toyed with the nipples before he rested his hand over Trip's heart and met his gaze again.

"You really want me to move in here with you?"

"Yeah, I do. I like havin' you around me, whether we're eatin', fuckin', or sleepin'."

"What about your family and Mrs. Guthrie? What are you gonna tell them about it?"

Trip stroked Henry's arm where it crossed his chest. "I'm pretty sure Tom and Amber will be okay with it. After all, this is my place. I get to make the rules here." He paused and thought about his late wife's best friend. "As for Estelle Guthrie, she's just gonna have to get used to the idea that you're the man I want. And again, this is my place, and I want you here."

"And you're sure?"

"Hell yeah, I'm sure." Trip paused and met Henry's gaze. "What about you? Do you wanna stay here with me?"

Henry lapsed into silence again and Trip's contentment slowly seeped away. Unease and cold dread filled in behind it. He tried not to fidget, but the idea that Henry didn't want to stay unnerved him.

"Yeah, I do. I just don't wanna cause problems for you." Henry buried his face against Trip's pectoral. "You have enough to worry about with the ranch and your son and Byron bein' gone. You don't need more grief because I'm stayin' with you."

"Hey, now, you let me worry about this 'grief' you're talkin' about." Trip tipped Henry's face up with a finger under his chin. "Havin' you here in my place and in my life makes all the hard stuff easier. I've been alone a long time, and I'd like to have a partner again. So, if it's all the same to you, I'd like you to stay."

Henry stared at him for a long time before he scooted up and laid a soft kiss on Trip's lips. "Okay, I'll stay."

Thank God.

"Good. We'll start workin' on the other room

tomorrow." He rolled over and switched off the light.

"Thanks for the space, but can I sleep here with you?" Henry's voice floated out of the soft darkness.

"I definitely expect you to." Trip pulled Henry close to his side and closed his eyes, enjoying the scent of warm man and sex in the room. "And you're welcome."

Henry sighed and snuggled close, and Trip let himself fall into a warm state of contentment. Life was pretty damn good at the moment.

CHAPTER SIXTEEN

Henry had never been so satisfied with life as he was for the next three weeks. He slowly moved his things from the bungalow into Trip's second bedroom, but he slept most nights in Trip's bed. They shared breakfasts and suppers together like a married couple, and Henry found he loved the domesticity.

It would've been perfect except for the constant barrage of texts and emails from Jordie. Apparently, their aborted dinner date in Fort Collins hadn't deterred the man, and he kept after Henry to reconsider abandoning his music career. Henry pushed them aside, ignoring or deleting them as he focused on spending time with Trip.

The domestic life suited him perfectly. He liked spending time with Trip, whether they cooked or shared the space reading in the evenings. Sex wasn't hurried or desperate, but a sweet exploration of connection between them. Trip still wouldn't let Henry top, but Henry resolved to be patient. The difference in their generations and social mores made him willing to wait Trip out.

The season shifted from cold nights and sunny days to more and more frigid weather as November arrived. Most of the therapy sessions took place in the indoor arena so

STAR LIGHT, STAR BRIGHT

they could still work the animals without freezing in the wet, blustery weather. Old Mags had improved dramatically and even nickered to him each time he came by her stall. Kipling's thrush had cleared up, and the rest of the animals remained healthy.

But that wasn't making Henry frown as he sat in his office.

He'd received another email from Lariat Records of a deposit for his monthly earnings, but he'd checked his bank accounts and there were no new deposits. In fact, there hadn't been any deposits into his accounts for two months now. He rubbed his chin as he looked over the numbers reported in the email and the list of deposits in his accounts. The money didn't exist.

What the fuck is goin' on?

He remembered he'd gotten another email the night he'd left Jordie at the café and scrolled through to find it. Again, he checked that email against his accounts and didn't find the matching deposit. Where the hell was the money they claimed to have paid him?

Picking up the phone, he dialed the number for Lariat Records.

"Lariat Records, how may I direct your call?"

"Billing and payments, please." Henry frowned at his computer screen.

"One moment, please."

His call was transferred to a new woman and her perky voice filled the phone.

"Billing and payments, this is Marylou."

"Hey there, Marylou. My name's Henry Bright and I'm havin' trouble with my royalty deposits. You think you could help me?"

"Sure thing, honey. Let's verify who you say you are and we'll get it all straightened out. What's your social security number?"

He rattled off all the security information to verify his

identity and she went through the checks before telling him to wait a moment as she uploaded the information.

"I see you recently changed accounts, is that true?"

"Yes, ma'am. I moved to Wyoming and needed to have a bank I could access locally."

"Let me see which account number we have on file for your direct deposit." She clicked a few keys then rattled off the last four digits of the account. Henry checked his own account and frowned.

"No, ma'am, that ain't right. Which bank is that with?"

They traded information and it became clear someone had set up an account in his name with his social security number, but it wasn't his current account and he hadn't been the one to do it.

"Who set up this account?"

"It says 'owner of account', but I'm getting the impression someone was pretending to be you."

"Yeah, that's what I'm thinkin' also. Let me give you the proper information and if anyone ever tries to change anythin', please immediately send me an email." He rattled off his personal email address and his bank account with the proper routing number and had her verify every number back to him.

"I'm so sorry about this mix-up, Mr. Bright."

"I'm glad I caught it before it got too expensive. Do you think y'all could do a stop payment on that false account and resend the money to my current account?" Who the hell was stealing his money?

"I think we should definitely make the effort, Mr. Bright. Let me talk to my manager and see what I can do. Let me put you on hold for a moment."

"Thank you, Ms. Marylou."

Henry sat back in his chair and stared, unseeing, at the computer screen. According to what he'd learned, this had happened recently, but he hadn't gotten any notification about it. He rubbed his chin as he thought over what might have happened, but before he could come up with any answers, Marylou was back.

"You're in luck, Mr. Bright. We were able to put an immediate stop-payment on that last disbursal and we'll send out the payment within forty-eight hours to your new account as soon as it's verified."

Henry blew out a sigh of relief. "Thank you so much, ma'am. I truly appreciate it. Y'all have my current email address so you can send me an email when it goes through?"

"Yes, sir, we do. We'll definitely make sure the money gets to you. Do you want to add anyone to your account in case you're unreachable?"

Henry shook his head even if she couldn't see it. "No, ma'am, not at this time. I think it should just be me until I figure out what happened for the last two months."

"All right, then. Anytime you want to change that, you just give us a call. Is there anything else I can help you with today?"

"No, ma'am. I think that's it. Thanks for the help you did give, though."

"You're welcome, Mr. Bright. You have a good day now."

Henry hung up the phone and logged out of his accounts, letting the information sift through his thoughts. How the hell had his income gotten mixed up? He tried to think back to when he'd moved, but all he remembered was trying to get the hell out of Dodge and hightail it back home. Still, he'd never been careless with money, even when he'd been making it hand-over-fist. *I'll definitely be more careful now.*

But how? And where had the previous month's earnings gone?

Before he could make a decision about it, the doors to the clinic burst open and a pretty woman with dark brown hair and large breasts skidded to a halt. A blue heeler mix dog lay in her arms as she looked wildly around the room, searching for something.

"Doc Bright!"

Henry lurched out of his chair and entered the clinic. "Yes, ma'am. I'm here. What's goin' on?"

"It's Nimbus. She's not eating, she's listless, and she hasn't pooped in over a day." She stared at him with eyes full of tears. "I can't lose her. She's my service dog, and I need her to help me with my PTSD. Please."

"All right, now, let me see what I can do for her. Let's put her on the table here." Henry spoke in calm tones, hoping to diffuse some of the woman's anguish. "What don't you tell me your name so I know who I'm talkin' to."

"Oh glory, I'm sorry. I'm Amber Hillcrest, Tom Colton's fiancée." Tears glittered in her eyes as she stared at her dog. "Please, you have to make her better."

"Let me see what's goin' on. Hey there, Nimbus. What's happenin' in your world?" Henry put the stethoscope to his ears and pressed the end to Nimbus's gut. He listened for sounds of digestion and working, but it remained ominously silent. "All right, darlin', I'm gonna check your mouth, tongue, teeth, ears and eyes. Just a bit of lookin' before I do anythin', okay?"

He spoke to the dog, and her golden-brown eyes looked up at him in abject misery in acknowledgement.

"Please, Nimbus, please be okay." Henry heard the desperation in Amber's plea and he turned his attention to the dog in front of him.

He checked the dog over, listening to her breathing and her heart, examining her gums and tongue, and checked her ears and eyes. While he made a show of feeling her body, he opened his other senses to listen to the energies of her body.

Henry sank beneath the confines of Nimbus's skin and followed the lines of energy where they became tangled. Most of the snarled lines centered around her gut, creating an obstruction that kept her from moving it through her system. Conventional wisdom suggested surgery or laxatives, but from what he could feel, he could speed up its dismemberment.

"Okay, what I get from her is she's got an obstruction in her gut." He met Amber's worried gaze. "I don't think it's impossible to move, and I suspect she'll get it out on her own in a day or so. But let me take an X-ray and see what I can see. That okay with you?"

"Yes, that's fine. Is she going to be okay?"

"I think so, but I'd like to be sure. Has she been throwin' up at all?"

Amber shook her head. "She did the first day once or twice, but then she seemed to settle down. Now it's gotten worse and she's been drinking a lot, but nothing's coming out."

Henry nodded. "All right. Let me get an image of her, and we'll go from there."

He picked up the blue heeler and took her into the back room where they kept the x-ray machine. The dog whimpered again, and he patted her head. "It's all right, Nimbus. I'm just gonna take a picture or two of you to see what's goin' on inside." He wanted confirmation of what he'd sensed.

The dog sighed, and he made sure to get the camera lined up to where he wanted before he snapped two pictures. They were delivered directly to the computer, and he opened the digital files to examine the dog's gut. Sure enough, a small mass had lodged itself in the large intestine and remained stubbornly solid.

"All right, honey, let's see if I can get the blockage to move a little here. I promise it won't hurt." He waited for the dog to look at him before he ran his hands over Nimbus's guts. He found the obstruction right where the x-ray said it was and focused on untangling the lines of energy to make the blockage smaller. He massaged a little, but kept his touches light when Nimbus whimpered.

"I know, honey. I'm hopin' this will help." The lines of tangled energy were stubborn, and he had to insist on them moving. At last something popped in his mind's eye and some of the energy smoothed out. The dog heaved a little sigh, and Henry resisted the urge to follow her lead.

"There now, that's better, isn't it?" He stroked Nimbus's coat. "Let's take you back to mama." He picked the dog up and brought her out to the exam room.

"How is she?" Amber stood with her arms wrapped around her middle and her jaw tense.

"She's gonna be fine. Let me show you what's goin' on, but I think we can give her a laxative and it should help her clear out her system." He laid Nimbus on the table again and gestured to the computer screen. "Here's the problem. She's got somethin' stickin' in her gut. Fortunately, it's small and gettin' smaller as we speak, so she'll be able to pass it here soon. But rather than makin' her do it all on her own, I want you to give her the laxative to help."

"Oh thank God. And thank you, Doc Bright."

"You're more than welcome. I'd keep an eye on whatever comes out. More than likely it'll be awful, but it might give you a clue as to what she ate that stopped her up."

"Will do. I don't want to go through this again."

"No, and I bet she doesn't want to, either." He grinned at her. "I'll give you enough for the next couple of days, but I don't think it'll take long." He moved to the cupboards in the back of the room to get out the meds and wrote on the little tag what dosage to take. "One in the mornin' and one at night as needed. Once she's defecatin' normally again you can stop."

"Okay. Thank you." Amber took the pill bottle and returned to her dog, patting her head with a loving caress. "I'm so glad you're here to help." She met his gaze with a warm smile. "And I'm really happy you're here with Trip, too."

Henry blinked and lost his smile. "I'm sorry?"

"Trip Colton. Haven't you moved into his apartment in the lodge?" She raised her eyebrows as she helped Nimbus back to the floor. The dog laid down at her feet, but no longer whimpered.

"Uh, yes, ma'am. I do spend quite a bit of time with Trip." Henry's gut turned cold. What would Amber think? He'd heard from Trip that Tom was okay with it, but in his panic, couldn't remember what he'd said about Amber.

"I think it's so great Trip has found someone to love."

Love?

He hoped that was the case, but they'd never said the words to each other. "Thank you, ma'am. You, uh, you're not bothered by it at all?"

"Not in the least bit. Love is love as far as I'm concerned. As long as you treat each other well, I'm all for it." She smiled at him. "And now that you've helped Nimbus, I'm even more grateful you're here."

He was back on familiar ground again and he offered his best comforting smile. "I'm glad I can help her, too. Just keep an eye on her and I suspect she'll come out of it fine."

"Thanks, I will." Amber nodded as she and Nimbus headed out of the clinic.

Henry blew out a long, relieved breath and cleaned up the table where Nimbus had been lying. Amber wasn't upset about Trip's relationship with him. The last thing Henry wanted was to infuriate all the residents of the ranch. At least he'd helped the service dog.

He finished putting together the clinic before he returned to the office and the problem of where his money had gone. Maybe he could puzzle it out before he went home for supper.

****

Trip knew Estelle had been avoiding him, but he hadn't figured out a way to talk to her about it over the three weeks since Henry had moved in. She'd made the meals for Sunday Supper, but she hadn't stayed. Tom and Amber had remarked on her absence and reminded him he needed to address whatever was bothering her. He agreed, but didn't know how.

As Thanksgiving approached, Trip's unease increased. He wouldn't give up being with Henry for anything. He'd even had a gift made for the younger man, something to show his affection. But Estelle's determined avoidance made life at the lodge harder than it needed to be. Fortunately, he happened to be home one snowy afternoon when she brought in the linens from the laundry for the apartment.

"Oh, Trip, I didn't expect you to be here today. Sorry. I should've knocked." Estelle blushed and her lips tightened into a hard line as she strode past the kitchen table. "I'll just put these in the closet and get back to work."

He didn't have time to say anything, so he rose and poured a second cup of coffee and waited for her to return. She didn't take long and headed straight for the door, but Trip got in her way.

"Can I ask you to please sit down a moment? I have coffee and cream to share." Trip stared her down, though she wouldn't meet his gaze.

"I really have to get goin', Trip. I have a lot of work to get done today." She tried to dodge around him, but he refused to let her pass.

"Come on, sit down with me a moment, Estelle. The chores can wait a bit." He gestured to the table. "Just for a spell. I need to talk to you about Thanksgivin'."

"Oh." Her shoulders released and her lips softened. "All right."

"Thanks." Trip sat down across from her, setting the coffee cup at her place. "Now I'm hopin' you'll be there because it just won't be Thanksgivin' without you, but I understand if you feel you can't make it. Tom and Amber said they'd make the turkey, and I can put together salad and steamed veggies." Trip paused as he met her gaze. "Henry said he makes a mean sweet potato casserole, and I asked Andrew if he'd like to join us, and he said he'd bring his grandmother's pumpkin pie. I'm hopin' you'll bring your mashed potatoes."

Estelle sighed as she wrapped her hands around her mug. She seemed to be picking her words carefully before she said anything, and Trip forced himself to wait her out. She had to understand that Henry would be a part of his life. He wouldn't let something as important as love go because she was uncomfortable with it.

"I'd be happy to bring the mashed potatoes, but I don't know if I'm willin' to stay for the meal." She still wouldn't look at him. "Ever since I met Doc Bright, I've been uncomfortable around him."

"Why? Because he's gay?" Trip shook his head with a frown. "Ransom Knight is gay and you don't have a problem with him."

"This is different." She tightened her jaw.

"How is it different?"

"Because he's made you gay as well!" She raised her gaze and her eyes blazed with hurt and anger. "You weren't gay before he came here, but now he's shacked up with you. What the hell, Trip? You married my best friend, for God's sake."

Trip raised his eyebrows. "I did marry Livvy, and I loved her, no question. But Henry didn't 'make' me gay. If we don't continue our relationship, I'm not gonna go lookin' for another man to be with. I'm bisexual, not gay, Estelle."

She jerked as if he'd slapped her. "Bisexual? How can

you be bisexual?"

He didn't think he could explain the nuances of his sexuality to her, so he kept it simple. "I'm attracted to men or women, depending on the person. It's not their body alone that makes me interested, it's the person inside. And other than Livvy or Henry, no one has attracted me. In fact, I didn't think I'd meet anyone after Livvy died."

"But Livvy was a woman and you married her. You were normal."

Trip frowned a bit. "What does that mean?"

"You were just like everyone else. You had a wife and a child and you ranched. You weren't..." She trailed off with her own frown.

"I wasn't what?"

"Strange, sexually-speakin'."

He wanted to laugh in disbelief, but he couldn't alienate her more than he already was. Instead, he swallowed his anger at her determined ignorance and tried to find a way to get around it.

"I know you don't see men lovin' men as normal, but to be honest, if Henry was a woman, I'd still be interested in her. I'm attracted to more than just the body." He paused and rubbed his chin. "Would you have this much problem if Henry was a woman?"

She opened her mouth to speak, but closed it almost immediately and he suspected she'd reached a conclusion already. But he let her take her time to answer. Either way, it would be a change and they'd have to face it together. He didn't want to find a new housekeeper or ask a long-time friend to leave, but he wasn't going to apologize or change who he spent time with just because she'd known him longer.

"Yes, it would be different if Henry was a woman." Her expression said the answer didn't make her happy. "It would be different because it'd make sense. You married and had sex with a woman all those years ago. You had a son. I don't understand how after all this time you could be interested in a man. And a man who's younger than your son. That ain't right."

Trip sipped his coffee before he blurted out something he'd regret later. He took his time answering just like she had a few moments before.

"I can see how you'd think that, but I've been livin' a long time, and while I might not be the sharpest tool in the shed, I've paid attention to a few things." He raised his chin and met her gaze with compassion. He knew this was hard for her to hear. "I've learned that lovin' other people is important, just like family is. I've learned that attraction doesn't care about gender or age, and people can love more than one person at a time. I've learned that hate only comes from anger and fear, and it's too exhaustin' for me to live with." He gave her a sad smile as her own expression hardened. "I'm in a relationship with Henry and I'm happy. He makes me happy and he's a good person. He treats me, my son and soon-to-be daughter-in-law, and even you, with respect and kindness. Plus, he works great with the animals here at the ranch. I like him and I enjoy bein' with him. That ain't gonna change."

She nodded sharply. "Fine. If that's what you believe, I'm not gonna try to talk you out of it. I just think you're makin' a big mistake and you're just lappin' up the first person to show you more than familial love. Hell, after Livvy died, you wouldn't notice half the things that were right in front of you."

"Now what the hell is that supposed to mean? What didn't I notice?"

"Me, Trip." She rose out of her chair and braced her hands on the tabletop. "Me, this whole time, takin' care of you, makin' sure you ate, and had clean clothes, and clean sheets, and comfort when your son was off ridin' rodeo. I've been here, through thick and thin, and you haven't noticed a damn thing. Over fifteen years I've been here for you, and you haven't seen me."

Trip gaped at her. "Seen you? You've been my friend, and Livvy's best friend. Hell, you were married to John Guthrie up until ten years ago. What haven't I seen?"

"That I'm in love with you, dammit!"

He blinked, his mind completely blank. *Estelle's in love with me?* That didn't make any sense at all. He'd known her for years and she'd never made a move or showed him more than friendship. He tried to get his wayward thoughts under control.

"When did that happen?"

She snorted and scowled. "I've loved you since Livvy and I met you at the dance all those years ago. But you couldn't see me once you set your sights on her. She had you hook, line, and sinker from that moment on. And I bore it because it was obvious you loved her just as much. But when she died and so did my John, I figured now I'd have a chance to be with you, the first man I loved." She shook her head, her scowl deepening. "But you couldn't see me. You were so damn buried in your grief and your PTSD, you couldn't see me helpin' and lovin' you all this time."

She stood and crossed her arms over her chest. "I damn near died when you were gored by that bull. I would've done anything for you. Anything. But again, it was only friendship you wanted. And now you're shackin' up with some young, hot piece of ass, and he isn't even a woman. I could've helped you see a young woman usin' you, but what the hell am I supposed to do when you love a man?"

Trip's voice stuck in his throat. Estelle had loved him all this time? He'd never noticed because he'd never returned the sentiment. He'd loved Livvy with every part of his being and no one had come close, especially after she died. Until Henry. He liked Estelle Guthrie, but after she'd married, he figured they'd found the loves of their lives. He never expected to be hers.

He tried to find something to say, but everything

sounded awful in his head.

"I've never been very good with words, so anything I say to you now is gonna fall short of helpful." He shook his head. "I can't give you the answer to your question. I don't know what you can do. I've only loved one woman in my life and that was Livvy. After she was gone, I didn't think I'd love anyone again. It wasn't that I didn't see you. You were a good friend, someone I cared about, but I didn't love you like that." He grimaced because it sounded harsh even to him. "There ain't no way to soften this, and I'm not the kind of man who likes to hurt anyone. But I gotta be honest and say I never felt that way about you."

All of the anger drained away and stark agony looked back at him from her eyes. "Yeah, I understand that now." She nodded. "I should've known that you'd never love another woman like you loved Livvy, but I hoped I'd be someone who you could spend your later years with. I never thought you'd chose someone younger, or male." She coughed a laugh that sounded more like a sob. "More the fool I. Do you love him?"

Part of him wanted to admit it, to let the world know how he felt about Henry, but another part wanted to share that with Henry first.

"I haven't known him long enough to tell you that. But I can say I like spendin' my time with him."

She nodded again, her expression going stoic. "I guess so if he's livin' here now. I'll tell you what. I'll think about Thanksgivin', but I can't guarantee I'll be there. I have a lot to think about and it's hard to be around you when I've been hopin' to catch your eye for so long."

"I'm sorry."

She held up her hand to stop him from saying more. "It's my own damn fault. I never said anythin' and now it's come to bite me in the ass." She met his gaze, sorrow and exhaustion deepening the lines around her mouth. "Thanks for bein' honest with me."

"Yeah, sure. You're welcome."

She rapped her knuckles against the tabletop and left his apartment. Trip didn't know what to do so he sat at the table, letting the information she'd offered him slide through his mind. *In love with me all this time.* It didn't seem possible, but she'd said it to his face. He didn't doubt her word.

He couldn't change how he felt, or how she did, for that matter, but there didn't seem to be a happy solution. He didn't like to hurt her. It went against everything he'd learned as a man living by the Western Code. The words echoed in his mind.

If I can't help you, I won't hurt you.

I wouldn't ask you for something I wouldn't give you.

I will not cheat, wrong, or defraud anybody in the world knowingly or willingly.

He couldn't help Estelle, and that had hurt her.

"Shit."

He rubbed his hands over his face and shook his head. Intellectually, he knew he couldn't control how she felt or what he'd meant to her. But he still hated hurting her, even inadvertently. He stared out the windows at the snow falling beyond them and realized it had grown dark. *Kinda like my thoughts.*

Trip dragged himself out of his chair and shuffled into the kitchen to decide on supper, his heart as heavy as the darkness outside.

CHAPTER SEVENTEEN

Henry let himself into Trip's apartment and hung his hat and coat on the hat tree. His mind remained on the problems with his royalties, but he didn't know what to do about them. He sighed and looked for Trip, hoping his lover had had a better day than he.

The older man stood at the stove browning some meat in a skillet, but his motions suggested his mind was elsewhere.

"Hey Trip, how's it goin'?"

"Oh, Henry. I didn't hear you come in." He jumped and gave him a guilty look. "How was your day?"

"Frustratin', tirin', and long. Yours?" Henry cracked a smile, but Trip didn't return it.

"About the same." Trip sighed and shoved the meat around a little.

"Here, let me do that. Why don't you sit down with somethin' to drink and tell me what's goin' on?" *Please don't let him be regrettin' our relationship.* He didn't know where the thought came from, but it hovered there like a wraith of bad luck.

"Yeah, okay." Trip retreated to the table and sat down,

his expression troubled.

"You wanna tell me what's goin' on?" Henry sniffed the meat and added some garlic to it.

"Estelle Guthrie stopped by today."

Aw hell. "Oh?" He tried to keep his voice light. "How did it go?"

"She's in love with me."

Henry dropped the spatula. "What?"

"Yeah. Forty-five years and she never said a word until now. Until you."

Oh shit. "Oh." What could he say to that? And would Trip choose an old, easy, heterosexual friend over a new, young, gay one?

"Aren't you going to ask me what I said?" Trip raised an eyebrow.

"Uh, yeah, what did you say to her?"

Trip met his gaze. "I told her I don't love her like that." He swallowed hard. "I, uh, well, to be honest…" He hesitated, his brow creased. "I love you."

"What?" Was that his voice, squeaking?

"I love you, Henry." Trip rose and returned to the kitchen to stand in front of him. "I've been meanin' to tell you, but I couldn't quite get the words out before. I know it hasn't been much time, but I'm too old to let things sit for too long."

He loves me. The words echoed inside of Henry and a roar of jubilation built up in his chest. He wanted to fist-pump the ceiling and do a victory dance around the room, but he settled for a goofy smile.

"You love me?" He blinked at the yearning he heard in his voice. "Are you sure? 'Cause I know it's a new thing for you and—"

"Henry." Trip gripped his arms and met his gaze square on. "I love you, as you are, whatever age you happen to be. It doesn't matter to me beyond you being you. I love you."

Henry swallowed hard as his eyes filled with tears. *I will not blubber, dammit.* But hearing Trip say the words as he looked at him with such sincerity damn near broke him.

"Oh glory, Trip. I don't know what to say."

"You don't have to say anything." Trip gave him a warm smile. "In fact, stay right there. I have somethin' for you." He squeezed Henry's shoulders again before he disappeared into the bedroom. Henry blinked a few times, trying to get his tears under control as he pulled the meat off the stove. *No sense in burning supper. Even if I don't know what it is.*

After a few moments, Trip returned to the dining room with a small leather draw-stringed bag in his hands. He vibrated with excitement, taking several years off his face.

"This here is for you." He handed it to Henry.

"What is it?" Henry glanced up from the bag.

"What kind of fool question is that? You have to open it." Trip mock-scowled and crossed his arms over his chest, but he couldn't hold the scowl for long.

Henry opened the bag and pulled out a braided copper chain bracelet. Each link was brushed to mellow the shine and three linked stars made up the top portion, centered between the clasps. He pulled it out and held it up to the light.

"Wow. That's beautiful. Where did you find it?"

Trip smiled and shrugged. "I know a local copper artist in Lander. I asked him to put this together for you, but I couldn't wait for Christmas."

Henry's heart filled to bursting and the damn tears came back to his eyes. "Wow, I don't know what to say beyond thank you. It's one of the prettiest pieces of jewelry I've ever seen."

"So, you like it?" Trip wore the most adorable look of insecurity on his face.

"Yeah, I love it. Thanks." He leaned forward and brushed his lips across Trip's. "Can you help me put it on?

I could never do bracelets one-handed."

He held it out and a little pink showed in Trip's cheeks as he clipped the bracelet around Henry's wrist. It looked great against his skin and again he found himself fighting tears. *Keep it together, man.* He had to clear his throat before he shot a look at the stove.

"What were you going to do with the meat you were cookin'? I think it's done by now."

Trip blinked. "I dunno, actually. I was pretty much lost in my thoughts."

Henry laughed. "Guess so. Do you have any pasta sauce? We could make spaghetti."

They ended up making a decent meal of spaghetti and meat sauce with a salad and biscuits Trip whipped up. Henry tried not to be distracted by the pretty bracelet hanging on his wrist, but its weight against his arm was comforting. *It's better than an engagement ring.* He started and shot a guilty look at Trip. *Whoa back there, son. He said he loves you, not that he'll marry you.*

And Wyoming still had that issue with the same gender marriages.

Just as they sat down to eat, someone knocked at Trip's door.

"You expectin' someone?" Henry poured them each a beer in a pint glass.

"Nope. I'll see who it is." Trip headed for the door. Henry kept serving them until he returned with Tom in tow. "Hey Henry, Tom dropped by to see you."

"See me?" Henry met Tom's gaze. "Why? Is anything wrong?"

"No, nothin's wrong." Tom sat down in the extra chair. "I just wanted to swing by and say thanks for takin' care of Nimbus."

"You're welcome. How is she doin'? Better at all?"

"Yeah, a lot better. And that mean's Amber's better, too." Tom wore relief like a cloak. "She really depends on that dog to keep her steady. and if Nimbus isn't doin' well, Amber's not doin' well."

"I'm happy to help. Nimbus probably would've recovered on her own, but I'm glad I could cut the recovery time in half." Henry smiled.

"Do you wanna stay for supper, Tom?" Trip settled into the chair beside Henry. "We have plenty to share."

"You sure?" Tom looked at Henry. "I don't want to intrude, but the pregnancy wears Amber out and she's sacked out already so I'm kinda on my own tonight."

"Yeah, sure, not a problem. Let me get another plate." Henry rose and headed to the kitchen.

"She's okay, though, right? Nothin's really wrong with Amber?" Trip's concern came through clearly.

"Yeah, she's fine. Just tends to sleep and eat a lot more often." Tom shrugged. "I read that book about what to expect and this is pretty normal. Basically, she's keepin' herself alive while she builds a whole new body inside. Takes a lot of extra energy."

Trip nodded. "Damn near magic. Definitely miraculous." He winked at Tom. "You'll see what I mean with that little Colton shows up."

Henry returned with the plate of food and set it down in front of Tom before he resumed his seat. "That should be an exciting time. You gonna throw her a shower or anything?"

"A shower?" Tom looked at him blankly.

"Yeah, you know, a baby shower. Where you get all outfitted for the new little one." Henry grinned at their dumbfounded expressions. "Didn't think about that, did you?"

"No, never even crossed my mind. How do you know about that?"

"Back when I was in Nashville, one of the other artists at the label got pregnant while makin' her new album." Henry sipped his beer. "The guy told her he was a free spirit or some shit. Basically, he wanted to freeload off her music career and didn't want the responsibility of bein' a dad, but she wasn't gonna give up the baby. So, a few of us got together and threw a party for her. It was actually pretty fun."

"Oh, yeah, I think Amber's sister-in-law wanted to do somethin', but can't get out here to Wyomin', and Amber can't travel, doc's orders." Tom frowned. "You think we should plan somethin'?"

"Sure, I could help with that, although if Amber has any girlfriends, it might be better. But you don't have to worry about that until closer to the due date." Henry waved his fork dismissively.

"I think we need to plan the weddin' and Thanksgivin' first." Trip pointed to the table. "It's comin' up in two weeks, and we still haven't nailed down where and what time."

"I think we should do it at our house, Dad." Tom swallowed his bite of spaghetti. "That way if Amber gets too tired she can just head on upstairs. Plus, the house is bigger than your apartment here and we have more room for entertainin'."

Henry nodded, but before he could respond, his phone chirped with an incoming email. That was immediately followed by a text notification. He grimaced.

"Excuse me. I gotta check that. Had a situation develop and I kinda have to keep an eye on it."

Trip frowned, but he nodded as Henry left the table to head for his room. He didn't want to ruin dinner with unpleasant news. As soon as he sat down on his bed, he checked the email first. It was a confirmation from Lariat Records that his direct deposit account had been changed and the money had been deposited there. A combination of relief and anger churned through him. At least he had his money now, but where the fuck had it been going?

The text was from Jordie, begging him to reconsider

his decision to stay far away from the music scene. After staring at his phone he counted ten texts from Jordie, alternately begging him to come back and asking him who the hell was he shacking up with in BF Wyoming. Henry scowled and left his phone on the bed as he returned to the dining table.

"Damn, son, you look like someone shot your dog and stole your truck. What's wrong?" Tom raised his eyebrows as Henry sat down.

Henry shook his head. "Just my old manager from when I was in Nashville contactin' me. He's been tryin' to get me to go back and won't take no for an answer. On top of the other things happenin' this week, it's just been one more thing to deal with."

"What other things happened this week, Henry?" Trip frowned as he took a bite of food.

Henry sighed and took a fortifying sip of beer. "Someone's been stealin' my royalty monies, I think."

"What?" Tom barked, his eyebrows raised.

"Yeah. I got an email from the record label and they said they'd deposited my royalties, but my account didn't get the deposit." He focused on his food. "When I called them up to see what the hell was going on, they said they'd been payin' me like usual, but the account they'd been sendin' the money to wasn't mine."

"Holy shit. Where the hell was it goin'?" Tom gaped, anger suffusing his expression.

"I dunno. But I managed to get them to stop the payment on the latest royalties and correct their information on my account." Henry rubbed his forehead as the anger rose again. "The problem is, I don't know how long this has been goin' on. I'm guessin' it's been a while, but I don't know who or when they started doin' it."

"Did you change accounts?" Trip asked.

"Yeah, as soon as I left Nashville."

"Did the record label tell you who set up the account to

receive the money?" Tom's brows lowered as he ate, but he looked more thoughtful than angry.

"No, but then I didn't think to ask. I was too busy worryin' about gettin' the money I was owed this month."

Tom grunted sympathetically. "Yeah, I'd be the same." He sat back in his chair and chewed for a few moments. "You know, I have a buddy who went through somethin' like this a while back. Turned out to be his ex doin' the stealin', but she was pretty crafty. He had to hire a private investigative service to sniff her out. They were thorough and damn good. He said they not only found out about his ex's embezzlement, but also the gigolos she'd been keepin' in silky drawers for months while with him."

"Damn." Trip shook his head.

"Yeah, my buddy was floored with all they found out."

Henry frowned. "They do all sorts of investigations?"

"Yup. But your money issues made me think of them." Tom rubbed his chin with his own frown. "Let me think. I seem to recall their name is... Lost and Found Investigative Service. They operate out of Denver, but that's only a hundred miles from here. My buddy's ex was in Vegas by the time they caught up with her, so I don't suppose Cheyenne is too far to go for them."

"You think they could help?"

Tom shrugged. "Couldn't hurt to ask." He pulled out his phone. "Let me text you their website and you can look 'em up when you have the urge."

"Yeah, thanks." Henry appreciated Tom's help. If nothing else, he could rest knowing someone was tracking things down.

They finished dinner and finalized plans for Thanksgiving. Henry heard his phone chirp a few times with texts from Jordie, but the most important one came from Tom. When he had a moment free, he'd look up Lost and Found Investigative Service, and see if they could help.

CHAPTER EIGHTEEN

Henry scowled out at the snow falling beyond the therapy paddocks. "Why are you callin', Jordie?"

"Because you haven't answered any of my texts. What the hell?"

"You send me fifty a day. I got a life, a job, and a boyfriend. I don't have time to mollycoddle you. What the hell do you want?"

"Let's talk about that boyfriend." Henry could hear the derision in Jordie's voice. "You're really goin' out with the owner of the Triple Star Therapy Ranch?"

Henry gritted his teeth. "I'm not discussin' it with you."

"You know he's pretty much married, right? Some woman with a service dog?" Jordie made a sound of disgust. "I can't believe he'd want to be with anyone who had that PTSD shit. But it's low of him to cheat on her with you."

Anger curled in Henry's gut. Jordie had always had a disdainful streak for anything different. The man was both racist and misogynistic, but now he showed his ableist side. It ignited Henry's temper, but he tried to keep it out of his voice.

"You've been watchin' too many TV shows. He ain't cheatin' on her with me." He sealed his lips over the words he wanted to say, not willing to give that kind of information to his erstwhile manager.

"Come on, she's damaged."

Henry thought about Amber and scowled. The woman was steadier than most people who didn't have PTSD. "You think he's gonna leave her because she's damaged?"

"Wouldn't you?"

He thought about Trip's PTSD and the reason for this ranch, and shook his head. "No, that's not my style. And I'm not goin' out with him, anyway."

"That's not what my source said and—" Jordie stopped and inhaled sharply. "Holy shit, you're not going out with the old man, are you?"

"You said it, not me."

"Oh my god, Henry. He's old enough to be your father!" He heard an audible shiver on the other end of the line. "That's creepy as fuck. And he's a widower. You know that means he was married to a woman, right?"

Glory, some days this man is beyond stupid. "Yup, I'm aware of what 'widower' means."

"You know how you feel about bisexuals. They can't be trusted because they'll fuck anything that walks by."

A pang of unease shot through Henry and he glanced down at the copper bracelet on his wrist. Trip didn't strike him as a man who'd sleep with just anyone, and he'd been single and essentially celibate since his wife had died. Hell, he hadn't even taken Mrs. Guthrie up on her admission of love and they were around the same age. He shoved the unease away, but it fueled some of his unspoken fears.

"He's not like that, and I don't think he's a typical bisexual."

"Come on. He was married to a woman and had a kid."

"So do a lot of gay men from the older generations. That doesn't mean he's bisexual."

But Henry knew Trip had loved his wife. They didn't talk about her much, but every time Trip mentioned her, he spoke with great fondness and devotion. Henry didn't like to be envious of a dead woman, but sometimes he wished Trip would talk about him with such emotion.

"I'm just saying, if he loved a woman once, he could do so again. You know how het men are about boobs and pussies."

"That doesn't make any sense, Jordie. It still doesn't mean he's bi." Henry shook his head. "Look, I gotta get back to work. Somethin' came up and I gotta take care of it."

"All right, fine. But don't say I didn't warn you when he finds some woman his age to hook up with."

"Bye, Jordie."

Henry terminated the call and seethed. *Dammit, Trip's not like that.* Yeah, it had always bothered Henry that Trip was bisexual, but he'd never done anything to make him think he was interested in anyone else, man or woman. Henry glanced down at the copper bracelet again and thought of the night Trip had confessed his love. *Jordie's wrong. Trip is solid.*

But remembering that night also reminded him he needed to call Lost and Found Investigative Service, and he clicked the browser on his computer to find their number.

"Lost and Found Investigative Service, this is Shannon. How can I help you?"

"Uh, hi. My name's Henry Bright and I think I need to hire an investigator."

A soft laugh sounded over the phone. "You think you do, Mr. Bright?"

He matched her chuckle. "Yes, ma'am. I'm pretty sure I do, I've just never done it before. But a friend recommended your firm, so I'm callin'."

"I think we can help you. Let me transfer you to Duncan Wilde, our owner."

"Thank you, ma'am." Henry waited, tapping the desk with his fingers as a melody suddenly jumped into his thoughts. *Like I have time to write down a song now.* He just hoped the melody would come back when he had time.

"Wilde."

The voice on the other end of the phone was gruff and no-nonsense, but some of Henry's unease with exposing his problems to someone else faded.

"Hello, Mr. Wilde. My name's Henry Bright and a friend recommended your firm as the best investigative service in the region. I need someone to investigate somethin' for me."

"I'm glad to hear that, Mr. Bright. What seems to be the problem?"

Henry explained the issues with his royalties and the misplaced money. Mr. Wilde asked several questions to find out the extent of the problem, but at the end of the call agreed to take the case. He said he'd have an investigator get in touch with Henry to clarify any of the details he needed to start the investigation. Henry thanked him and hung up, feeling better about the situation already.

Now if I could just get Jordie off my back, I'd be golden. He didn't have a lot of hope for that.

****

Henry hoped to talk to Trip about Lost and Found, but when he returned to the apartment, Trip wasn't there. A quick text let him know Trip had gone into Cheyenne to see his counselor and visit with Byron. Unfortunately, the weather had gotten rougher that night and he was staying in town just to be safe. Disappointment curled through Henry, but the snow blew horizontal past the windows and he didn't want Trip driving in such weather.

The next day, a man named Brian Calvert from Lost and Found Investigative Service called to get more pertinent details on Henry's case. He was soft spoken, but sharp and asked questions about who had access to his accounts before he'd left Nashville. Henry told him everything he could think of and Brian promised to keep in touch every few days to let him know how it was going.

"Damn, son, aren't you going to take Thanksgivin' off?"

The silence on the other end of the phone made Henry regret his words. "No, sir. This is important for us to finish despite the holiday. If we're lucky, we can solve it by then, but digging through financial records takes time. I'll keep you updated."

"Oh, right. Thank you, Mr. Calvert."

"You're welcome, Mr. Bright."

Trip didn't get home until late that evening and he barely had more than a kiss for Henry before he crashed. Henry tucked him in and turned out the lights, hoping to share his news in the morning.

But a horse breaking out of the barn and tearing up its hind leg got Henry out of bed early and by the time he got the animal patched up and sedated, Trip had returned to Cheyenne. He left a note and a fresh pot of coffee, but Henry couldn't shake the disappointment.

To make the day harder and longer, Jordie sent up a flurry of calls and texts to mirror the snowflakes falling from the sky outside. Henry ignored most of them, but Trip's absence and the barrage of ageism and disdain for bisexuals chipped away at Henry's patience. Trip texted as well, letting him know he was helping Byron move and it might take a few days. He always ended his texts with a heart emoji, but Henry needed more.

As Thanksgiving approached, the days became filled with preparing the ranch for the holiday and lack of staff as well as equine medical emergencies. Trip mostly helped Byron in Cheyenne, and only returned to the ranch to oversee some of the day-to-day chores on the ranch as the staff headed home for the holiday.

As promised, Brian kept Henry up to date on his efforts to find where the money had gone and who'd had access to it. He'd found a few things, but wanted to follow up on some leads before he gave any preliminary findings. Henry's frustration at Trip and the investigation mounted, but he managed to keep his cool and not take it out on Brian.

Trip finally came home on the evening before Thanksgiving, but Henry didn't get a chance to see him before bed because one of the horses got colic. Henry spent the night in the barn walking the horse out to make sure her guts didn't get in a tangled mess. By the time Thanksgiving dawned, Henry was exhausted, dirty, and smelled of horse. He returned to the lodge just as Andrew came in for the morning. The younger man wisely kept his chipper good morning to himself.

Henry took the time to shower before he fell into the bed they'd installed in the second bedroom in Trip's apartment. By the time he woke up again, it was early afternoon and the apartment was quiet. Henry rose and stumbled to the kitchen, hoping Trip would be there. Instead, he found a hand-written note under a plate with a cinnamon roll, and a cold cup of coffee.

Missed you last night. Sorry to hear about Octavia. Hope she's better. Come on over to Tom and Amber's place near the river when you're ready. Love, Trip.

"Sonuvaprick!" Roaring out his frustration felt good, but it didn't change Trip's absence or their only connection being notes and texts. "Dammit all, why the hell didn't you wake me or fuckin' wait for me?"

Henry almost swept the plate and roll onto the floor, but he didn't want to clean up a mess. *You gotta calm down, son. Trip's been busy.* Hell, they'd all been busy, but Henry still felt as if he mattered more as an employee than as a valued member of Trip's family. He threw the coffee in the microwave and warmed it up as he returned to his room to get dressed.

The tote full of his things still sat beside his guitars and he shook his head. It didn't matter where he went, he still only had a few items that meant anything to him. He remembered the melody teasing him the day he'd called Lost and Found Investigative Service, but it was buried in his anger and frustration. He shook his head at his guitars and dressed in his black jeans, a black and gold western shirt, and his good pair of black Ariats. He returned to the kitchen for his coffee and sipped it as he stared out at the gray skies.

Maybe everythin' will be fine. Holidays made everyone crazy with food and celebrations and company. Henry wished it could be just him and Trip, but family was important, and they were expected to attend Thanksgiving with Tom and Amber. All he had to do was get through tonight and they could have a couple of days off from the business of the ranch. He'd still have to check on the animals, but they could be alone and reconnect. *Sweet glory, I wanna reconnect with Trip.*

He set down his mug and headed for the door. He shrugged into his coat and hat then locked the door of the apartment behind him. He considered walking over to Tom's house, but the wind rattled the windows of the lodge hard enough to make him take his truck.

"Hey, Doc Bright. You headin' over to Tom's place for Thanksgivin'?" Andrew appeared with a pie plate wrapped in tinfoil in his hands.

"Yeah, I was just goin' that way. Why?" Henry smiled at the young man.

"Mind if I tag along? Didn't seem to be much point drivin' more cars over there and since we'll all becomin' back here anyway…" He shrugged and Henry nodded.

"Sure. Let me get the door for you." Henry held the door to the lodge open against the wind while Andrew held

215

SIOBHAN MUIR

the pie with both hands. "The wind's blowin' hard tonight. Good thing there's no snow yet."

"Yeah, supposed to be some later, though."

They got into the truck and both sighed in relief. Henry laughed. "Yeah, good to be out of the wind. I didn't miss this in Nashville."

"I bet. The only other place that compares to Wyoming wind I've heard of is Vegas."

"Yeah?" Henry shot an amused look at Andrew. "I didn't notice when I played there."

Andrew bobbed his head as Henry pulled up in front of Tom's house. "Yeah. I read the wind rivals Chicago in fierceness but no one says anythin' to keep tourists from freakin' out. And most of the tourists don't notice 'cause they're inside the casinos all the time anyway."

"That was true for me." Henry turned off the truck. "Let me get the door for you so you don't have to balance the pie."

"Thanks. What about you? Didn't you bring anything?"

Henry paused, blinking as he sifted through his memories. *Aw hell.* He'd forgotten he'd promised to bring a sweet potato casserole. He'd been so caught up with missing Trip and the mess with his royalties, the casserole had slipped his mind. *Fuck.*

"No, I completely spaced it. Too much goin' on this week, and I didn't get the food put together. What a total dick move." He grimaced as he got out and hurried around the truck to open Andrew's door. "Think they'll forgive me?"

"Yeah, I'm sure it'll be fine. Thanksgivin' isn't really about food. It's about family." Andrew slid out and Henry shut the door behind him.

"What about your family? How come you're not sharin' it with them?"

Andrew grimaced and shrugged one shoulder as they

216

stepped up onto the porch. "Most of my brothers have families of their own with kids and stuff. And my folks love the grandchildren. I guess I wanted to hang out with a family that doesn't make anyone feel like the odd-man-out, you know?"

Henry couldn't agree more, but he wasn't sure he'd found that with Trip's family. Especially recently when Trip hadn't been around much. But maybe it would be better at the Thanksgiving celebration with Tom, Amber, and Andrew. He thought he'd heard Trip had invited Byron and Mrs. Guthrie, but he couldn't be sure. And after her admission of love for Trip, Henry didn't expect her to show up.

"Your family sees you as the odd-man-out?"

"Yeah." Andrew shrugged again, his expression tightening. "You know, on account of me not bein' married and all."

Henry wondered if it was more than Andrew's lack of spouse that made him feel his family seemed exclusive, but he didn't push.

They knocked on the door and Amber opened it, a wide smile creasing her lips. "Hey Henry, Andrew. Come on in. It's good to see you."

They stepped into the open-concept home and Henry immediately felt better. The place was warm, homey, lived-in, and comfortable while remaining spacious. He followed Amber and Andrew to the kitchen where Trip and Tom stood arguing over the Broncos' chances for the Superbowl that year.

"Hey Tom, come take this pie from Andrew while I check on the turkey." Amber waved at them to come out of the kitchen from the oven.

"Aw, now you let me do that, darlin'. You're already luggin' around that baby. No need for more effort." Tom smiled indulgently at his fiancée.

"Well then, get to it. We'd like to eat sometime soon."

She shot an amused look at Henry. "I've been smelling that thing all day and it's been teasing me with its deliciousness."

Henry laughed as he shrugged out of his coat and hung it on the hat tree much like Trip's. He removed his hat as well and wondered if Trip would be interested in a kiss. *Probably not amongst company.*

"Hey Henry, I thought you were gonna bring a sweet potato casserole." Trip raised his eyebrows at Henry's empty hands.

"Yeah, I think I finally had a senior moment like my mother used to call it. With everythin' goin' on the last couple of days, I forgot to make it." He shot an apologetic look at Amber. "Can you forgive me? I've been wrapped up in the critters' health at the barn and the mess with my royalties from my music career."

Amber nodded with a smile. "Of course. We have plenty of food." She handed him a corn muffin on a little paper plate. "See? Hot out of the oven." She shot a look at Tom working on the turkey. "Well, sort of. But tell me about that mess you mentioned. Tom said someone was stealing your money?"

"Yes, ma'am." Henry nodded and took a bite of the corn muffin. "Glory be, these are wonderful."

"Thanks." Amber beamed. "One of the few things my sister-in-law taught me before I left Washington. She was a master at them. Mine aren't quite as good as hers, but they're close."

"They're good enough for me." Henry grinned.

"Thank you. I'll make sure to hide hers when she comes out for the wedding with my brother." Amber winked.

Henry laughed, but unease settled in his gut. Trip hadn't come over to greet him or touched him. *What the fuck is that about?*

"Have you told them about the baby yet?" Henry

finished his muffin and set his paper plate down as Amber took the pie from Andrew.

"Oh yeah." Tom laughed as Amber grimaced. "Her sister-in-law wanted to come down here immediately and help Amber, but she and her brother talked the woman out of it."

"I love my sister-in-law, but she kind of takes over." Amber shrugged. "The wedding is soon enough for her to start her organization of my life."

"We won't let it happen, honey." Trip came over and wrapped an arm around her waist, squeezing gently. "Folks in Wyomin' don't like to be managed. We have a way of bein' distractin' from time to time."

Amber laughed and Henry agreed, but his heart shriveled a little bit more when Trip released her and returned to the kitchen without so much as a hug or a wave or a smile.

What the fuck? Are we a couple or not? The copper bracelet on his wrist weighed heavy on his mind. He'd originally thought the gift had been a physical manifestation of their relationship, but over the last two weeks, he'd started to wonder. *Maybe Trip's havin' second doubts.* Maybe he'd found someone else. God knew he'd been spending all of his time in Cheyenne away from the ranch. Could Trip have found someone in town who he liked better than Henry? Someone easier to show affection toward while in public?

The questions and anxiety swirled around in his mind along with Jordie's insinuations, and his gut cramped on the corn muffin. He tried to smile as Amber met his gaze, but he suspected it came out more of a grimace when her brows bunched.

"Everything okay, Henry?"

Her question had Trip meeting his gaze and a tightening of his lips as he looked away.

"Yeah, well, as good as it can be." Henry tried to play

it off with a shrug. "I contacted that firm Tom told me about, Lost and Found Investigative Service, and they've got a guy workin' on my case."

"Yeah, how's that goin'?" Tom nodded as he pulled the turkey onto the counter and opened the tinfoil around it. "Damn, this thing looks pretty good."

"It's goin' pretty well. The guy investigatin' for me said he had a couple of leads he was followin' and would let me know after the holiday."

"He's working through the holiday?" Amber shook her head. "That sucks."

"I think it's more of a choice rather than a work necessity."

"Oh, I'm sorry to hear that. We should've invited him to come here for it." She smiled and Henry thought Tom a lucky guy to have a partner as kind and warm-hearted as Amber.

"He sounded like he was after somethin' that needed his attention, so I didn't think to ask." Henry shrugged. "Next time, Amber."

The doorbell rang and Amber looked up.

"Don't worry, Amber, I'll get that for you." Trip strode for the door and Henry had the oddest feeling that he wanted to get away from him. *Am I just jumpin' at shadows, or is the man purposefully avoiding me?*

Voices sounded from the other room in greeting. Henry helped Amber for a little longer, but when she turned away, he took the opportunity to head toward to door to see who Trip had greeted. An older man, about Trip's age, hobbled in the door with a package of rolls in one hand and a cane in the other. His leg was wrapped in a nylon brace with a knee joint, but he seemed to move pretty well. He laughed with Trip, but that wasn't what froze Henry's blood to solid ice.

A pretty young woman, maybe a few years older than Henry, stood in Trip's arms while he kissed her with joy and greeting. He watched as Trip warmed up to her and turned toward the older man, his arm around her shoulders.

"Glad y'all could come, Byron." Trip squeezed the woman again. "And I didn't expect you to come too, Seychelles. I thought you had other plans."

She smiled up at him with warmth and Henry swallowed bile. "They fell through, and I'm rather glad they did."

Henry turned away and headed back to the kitchen, his mind going over everything he'd seen. *Done, I'm fuckin' done.* Jordie was right. Trip had found a woman more to his liking. Hell, dating a woman, even one as young as Seychelles, was a helluva lot easier in Wyoming than dating a man. Trip could show affection in public and no one would get their tails in a twist.

"Hey, you know, I think I'm going to head out." He gave Amber and Tom a tight smile. "Thanks for the invite tonight, but I'm just not fit for company."

"What? Why? It's Thanksgivin'." Tom's brows came down as Amber's went up.

"Are you sure? There's plenty of food and we'd love to have you." Amber rested a hand on his arm.

"Yeah, I know. But I'm just out of sorts tonight and bein' social isn't gonna work for me. I'm real sorry." He grimaced and turned to find Trip standing behind him with his arm still around the woman. Henry fought to keep from throwing up. "Y'all have a good night and a happy Thanksgivin'."

"Are you leavin', Henry?" Trip frowned as if Henry had done something to embarrass him. "Why? It's Thanksgivin' and we're all here."

"Yes." Henry nodded with a pointed look at Trip's arm around Seychelles' shoulders. "We all are. I think I just need some time alone to work through some stuff. Y'all have a good night."

He brushed past them, heading for the door before he

221

did something he'd regret. He stuffed his hat on his head and shoved his arms through the sleeves of his jacket rough enough to bend a nail back. He bit back a yelp of pain, welcoming it as less than the knife in his heart. *That's a bisexual for you.* Jordie's voice echoed in his head. *Always taking the easy way out with any pretty young thing that walks by.*

"Where are you goin'? It's Thanksgivin' and we're all gathered. Are you seriously leavin' now?" Trip stood behind him, a scowl on his face. "Come on. Supper's ready and we can sit down to eat."

"Yeah, you should get back to that. I'm sure they're waitin' on you." Henry nodded and jerked the door open, heading for his truck.

Trip followed him out onto the porch and caught his arm. "What the hell is wrong with you? Tom and Amber have hosted us. Don't embarrass me like this."

Henry froze, his anger building into a wave that threatened to burst through him as he turned slowly around. "Embarrass you? Embarrass *you*?" He snarled at the older man. "How the fuck am I supposed to feel when you come in after makin' out with that young woman? That was embarrassin' as hell. I'm your lover, your partner, your goddamned roommate, and you're draped over a pretty young thing like a man possessed. What the fuck, Trip?"

"I wasn't makin' out with her or draped over her. She's Byron's daughter, and I was very glad to see her. She's been busy and couldn't help with movin' her father, so it was great to see her."

"Oh, I'm sure it was great to see her." Henry nodded, his lips pulling down into a scowl. "That's what you were doin' in Cheyenne, yeah? Or should I say "whom" you were doin'? You've avoided me for two solid weeks ever since Mrs. Guthrie stopped by and told you she loved you."

"I haven't avoided you, I've been busy—"

"Yeah, I can see that. So was I. But you didn't bother

to catch up with me."

"That's not true, Henry. I texted you all the time."

Henry barked an unhappy laugh. "I might be from a younger generation who's glued to their phones, but even I know we need more than a text now and then in the real world." His lip curled as he shot a look over Trip's shoulder toward the woman in the house behind him. "I should've known it was easier for you to find love with a woman than with me. I guess you and I weren't meant to be, and I'm just wastin' my time. Y'all have a good Thanksgivin' and I won't get in your way with Byron's daughter."

"Henry, wait—" Trip grabbed for his arm, but Henry yanked it out of his reach.

"Fuck you, Trip."

He raised his fist to strike, but couldn't make himself do it. Fury and hurt burned like a brand in his gut and he strode off the porch to his truck without a backward glance.

He didn't even look as he peeled out of the driveway and headed back to the lodge. Tears threatened to overwhelm his sight, but he dashed them from his eyes, using his sleeve when they filled right back up again. He pulled up in front of the lodge and stormed inside. Most of the lights were off except at the front desk where Mrs. Guthrie sat, working on the computer.

"Dr. Bright? What are you doin' here? I thought you'd be at Tom's place for Thanksgivin'."

"You don't have to worry about me anymore. I'm leavin' tonight." He didn't give her a chance to respond as he unlocked the door to Trip's apartment and headed for his room.

Heh, that's just it, isn't it? I only have a room in Trip's apartment.

None of this was his beyond the few belongings he'd brought from Nashville. He'd be out before they'd even carved the turkey. Tears kept blinding him as he threw his clothes into a duffle bag and the rest of his things in the totes. He wanted to curl into a ball and sob, but that wouldn't give him the peace he needed. He stacked the totes and added the duffle bag on top before hauling all of it back to his truck.

"You aren't seriously leavin' tonight, are you?" Mrs. Guthrie looked at him with her brows creased in concern. "Come on, now. Let's have a cup of tea and talk about this. The weather's supposed to turn ugly and most places are closed tonight."

"Thanks for your kind offer, but I don't need to be more of a bother to anyone. I'll be fine." He dropped his gear in the back of his truck and threw the duffle bag in the cab before he returned to the lodge where Mrs. Guthrie stood on the porch. "Here's the keys to the barn, the clinic, the lodge, and Trip's place. I won't be needin' them anymore."

"Are you quittin'?" Mrs. Guthrie's jaw dropped.

"No, ma'am. I'm just takin' some time to myself. Besides, Byron's back so you'll be fine."

"But, where are you headed? Stay the night, Doc. No need to go out now." She tried to give him back the keys.

"That's nice of you to say, but I'll be fine. Y'all take care and have a good night." He waved her away and climbed into his truck, hoping his tears of anger and frustration wouldn't fall.

Why the hell is she bein' nice to me now?

He cranked the engine and backed away from the Lodge. He had to get away, but he didn't know where to go. As he powered up the driveway toward the gate, he thought about heading over to the Fantasy Ranch with Ransom and the Knights. But he couldn't barge in on their family Thanksgiving just because Trip had dumped him for a woman. It hurt to think Trip couldn't handle being with a man at the first sign of difficulty.

Fuck. I trusted you, dammit.

The tears threatened just as his phone pinged. He glanced down, half-hoping it would be Trip, but Jordie's name and number showed on the screen. Fuck it. If Trip didn't want him, he could always hang out with Jordie until he figured out what to do. Something in his gut turned over at the idea of spending more time with Jordie, but he shoved it aside as he pulled over on the onramp to I-25 and sent a text back.

Which hotel are you in? What's the address? What room number?

Henry didn't wait for a response as he accelerated onto the freeway. He had almost sixty miles to go before he reached Fort Collins and Jordie's location. Hell, he'd need those miles just to get himself under control.

Wiping his eyes one last time, he stared out at the night. The freeway was dark without drivers traveling, and the only company he had was the snow starting to fall from the sky.

CHAPTER NINETEEN

Trip stood on the porch for what seemed like a half an hour, trying to figure out what the hell had just happened. One moment, they'd all been enjoying Thanksgiving, and the next Henry was accusing him of cheating with a woman and storming off into the night. Trip tried to think of why Henry would believe he'd cheated, but he couldn't find anything that would lead him to such a conclusion.

Really, Trip? You playin' stupid or just tryin' to avoid somethin'?

He looked up and found Livvy sitting on the porch swing, her arms crossed over her chest as she gave him the "I-expect-better-from-you" look she wore when he acted dim.

Trip squirmed under her gaze. "Yeah. I mean, I didn't cheat on him, and I've been really busy with Byron and the move, and all."

Oh, good, you didn't cheat on him. That's a step in the right direction. Livvy shook her head. *You also didn't make an effort to show him what he means to you even when you're busy, and you had hugs and kisses for everyone but him tonight. What with you avoidin' him after Estelle visited you, is it any wonder he thought you were cheatin' with Seychelles?*

"I wasn't avoidin' him—"

Don't you hand me that load of horseshit, Trip Colton. I ain't got a garden no more.

"I gave him the bracelet. He should know what that means." Trip frowned and resisted the urge to cross his arms over his chest in defense.

Do you hear yourself? He should know what that means? Why would he? Gifts don't mean shit in real life with real actions. The bracelet was lovely, but you didn't follow it up with real affection, and you kissed Seychelles right in front of him.

"But he knows—"

He doesn't know shit. He's young, fragile, stressed, and in love with you. He's needed you these last two weeks, but you ducked away from him to help Byron. And when put to the test, you tucked tail and ran.

Trip flinched at the harshness of her remarks. "I just wasn't ready to do a public display of affection with the family around. I was scared."

I get that. But that family in there—she pointed at the door behind him as she rose to her feet—*already knew you were in love with Henry and didn't have a problem with it. Hell, both Tom and Byron gave you their blessing. Why the hell did you let fear take over?*

Trip's throat closed and he shook his head. He'd been a coward and couldn't face the hurt he'd caused Estelle. When the emergencies took over and Byron needed help, he took the opportunity to be away from the ranch and the obviousness of his relationship with his sexy, young lover.

You're a fool, Trip.

He nodded, his shoulders drooping. "Yeah, I know."

"Dad?" Tom opened the front door and looked out. "Is everythin' okay?"

Trip shook his head without turning around. "No, I don't think so."

"Well, come in out of the cold and we'll talk about it." Tom gestured to the house and its welcoming glow. There was love in that house with Amber and Tom, and Byron and Seychelles. Even Andrew. "Come on."

Trip nodded again and followed Tom back into the house, but he found he didn't really want to be there. *Not without Henry.* He met everyone's concerned faces as he stepped into the kitchen and his regret blazed brighter. *Henry should be here, too.*

"Is Henry going to join us again?" Amber met Trip's gaze, as she loaded some turkey onto a paper plate.

"I don't think so." Trip shook his head.

"What happened? Where did Henry go?" Leave it to Byron to get to the heart of it.

"I don't know. I'm hopin' he went back to the lodge to cool off, but I really should go check." He met everyone's gaze one by one. "I think I'm headed back there, too, to try to talk to him. We have some stuff to work out it seems."

"Aw come on, Dad. Can't you stay for supper?" Tom's face creased into a frown.

"I'd really like to, but I don't want Henry to think I'm too scared to talk to him. It's no fun bein' alone on a holiday." Trip understood that better than most. His holidays without Livvy while Tom was rodeoing had been hell.

"I made up two plates of food for you both." Amber handed him the paper plates wrapped in plastic wrap. "Go and find him. He needs to know we all care about him."

"Yeah." Trip nodded as he took the plates. "Yeah, he does."

"And bring him back here so we can all celebrate." Amber smiled.

"I'll try. Thanks for understandin'."

"Go on. Don't let him stew for too long." Byron waved him out the door. "You need a ride back to the lodge?"

"Yeah, that'd be good. Thanks, Byron."

They shrugged into coats and hats before heading to Byron's minivan. Trip had once teased him about driving it, but it handled well in the snow and it carried all his gear with him when he was called out on emergencies. They didn't speak as Byron drove Trip back to the lodge, but he felt his friend's support.

Unfortunately, Henry's truck no longer sat in front of the porch and Trip's hope for reconciliation dropped to his gut.

"Thanks for the ride. Sorry to mess up your Thanksgivin' plans."

"It won't mess them up if y'all come back to celebrate with us." Byron clapped him on the shoulder. "Go make amends and we'll see you later."

He nodded and swallowed hard at the kindness of his friend. "Thanks." Trip got out of the car and strode up the steps to the door. *Please let his missin' truck not mean anything.*

Inside, Estelle sat at the front desk and she pursed her lips as he stepped in the door. "He ain't here, Trip."

Trip stopped short. "What?"

"He's not here. He lit out of here like this tail was on fire about twenty minutes ago."

"Where was he goin'?" Trip paused at the desk, laying the plates on the surface.

"I don't know." She shook her head, her expression sad. "He didn't say, but he left these." She placed the keys to the barn and clinic beside the plates.

Trip stared at the keys for a moment. *Why the hell doesn't he have his keys?* He lifted his gaze to Estelle's before taking one of the plates toward his apartment. He unlocked the door and pushed inside. Only the light over the stove had been left on, but everything else sat in darkness. Trip set the plate on the table and headed for the second bedroom.

He flipped on the light and looked at the furniture in

the room. The bed sat made and the closet stood open. Henry's guitars and totes were gone. The space remained empty and cold.

Trip's heart dropped along with his shoulders. He turned off the light and returned to the dining area. All that waited for him was a plate of cooling Thanksgiving food. Amber had even included a piece of Andrew's pie.

Trip sat in one of the chairs and pulled out his phone, searching for a message or a text from Henry. But like his apartment, it remained stubbornly silent. His throat closed up and tears threatened. *Aw fuck.* He knew he'd screwed up, but he didn't know how to fix it.

Livvy appeared on the windowsill against the night, the snow sliding past the glass like cottonwood fluff. *Text him, Trip.*

"What good will that do?"

She sighed and shook her head. *Now's not the time to be a pigheaded, stubborn, egotistical jackass. He doesn't know a damn thing about how you feel or what you're thinkin'. You have to tell him.*

"Tell him what? What can I say?"

Sorry, for starters. I miss you, would help. I love you, would be even better.

Trip stared at his phone and opened the text app. He wished he had Livvy's gift for notes. She'd always written sweetly brilliant ones when she was alive, but he'd never been so accomplished. Sniffing hard, he used his sleeve to wipe his eyes before he opened a text to Henry.

Hey Henry. I'm very sorry for how things went down at Thanksgiving supper tonight. I should have hugged you when you arrived.

He bit his bottom lip as he puzzled out what all to say.

I noticed you packed up your things and took them with you. I really hope you're just at the bungalow and I'll see you tomorrow so we can talk. I miss you and wish you were here. I love you. Trip.

He hit Send and set the phone down before he rose to

get himself a fork and knife. No point in waiting hungry. He had a good supper right in front of him. He filled a glass with water and sat down to eat, periodically glancing at his phone. *Come on, Henry. Talk to me.*

But the phone remained silent and Trip eventually went to bed alone, missing him.

****

Henry glanced down at his phone as a text message came in. It was from Trip, but he didn't have the time or the energy to read what it said. Instead he parked his truck at the Rocky Ridge hotel and got out, taking his phone and his duffle bag. The snow kept falling, but at least he didn't have to drive more that night. Despite the holiday, the parking lot was surprisingly full and he had to walk a fair distance to the door. Jordie met him there with a big smile.

"Hey, glad you made it. How was the drive?"

Henry stared at him with confusion. Jordie seemed to think this was a vacation for Henry, a quick jaunt down south to see family or friends. *I don't have any family left.* He wouldn't speculate about the friends.

"Glad to be off the roads. The temperature's droppin' fast." His emotional temperature sat somewhere around frigid.

"Good. Glad you're here. Come on up to the room. Have you eaten? Do you wanna grab somethin'?"

"It's Thanksgivin', Jordie. Nothin's open." He shrugged. "I ate before I left anyway." It didn't matter the only thing he'd eaten was a cornbread muffin. He wasn't hungry. He shook his head. "I think I'm gonna just turn in. It's been a long day."

"Oh, come on, it's a holiday. Surely we can get a beer or something."

Jordie turned on his wheedling voice and Henry paused, narrowing his eyes. He'd had just about enough of

231

whining, dishonesty, and lying that he could stand for one day, and he wasn't about to put up with more.

"You're right. It is a holiday." He turned on his heel and headed for the front reception desk. "I'd like a room, please."

The young woman behind the counter gave him a surprised smile and started moving the mouse to the computer. "Yes, I think that can be arranged. Will your friend be joining you?"

"No, ma'am. He already has his own room. I just need something with a bed and a desk, if that's possible."

"Of course, sir. All our rooms have a desk and a chair." She clicked on the keyboard as Jordie came up.

"Hey now, you can stay in my room with me. It's no problem." Jordie frowned at the woman. "This isn't necessary."

"Yeah, it is. I'm gettin' my own room so I can sleep when I want to and wake when I want to, and get some goddamned time alone." Henry turned off his snarl as he faced the woman. "I'd like my own room, please."

"We do have one available. Which credit card would you like to use?"

Henry arranged for his room and signed the contract before taking his key and heading for the ornate winding staircase to the second floor. Jordie followed, telling him he was being silly, but Henry kept his attention on getting to a place where he could be alone.

When they reached the second floor, Jordie grabbed him and hauled him to a stop. "I don't know what the hell has gotten into you, but you didn't have to make a scene downstairs. And you didn't need your own room."

"I've just had a long drive in a damn snowstorm and I just want to get some sleep. So, I'll see you tomorrow after I wake up. Good night." He opened his door and tried to shut it, but Jordie stuck his foot between the door and the jamb.

"Henry, please."

Henry held up his hand. "Get your foot out of my door and I'll talk to you tomorrow. One night isn't gonna kill you. But I'm tired, I'm pissed off, and I need some sleep, so let it go. Good night." He kicked Jordie's foot backward with his booted toe and closed the door in his face.

"Henry!" Jordie's muffled voice came through the door, but Henry didn't open it. He'd meant it when he said he needed time alone.

Instead, he dropped his duffle bag on the floor beside a double bed and turned on one of the bedside lamps. The room held two beds, a small desk and chair, a flat screen TV that looked out of place on the old 1800s style striped wallpaper. The beds had hand-stitched quilts over featherbeds atop mattresses and Henry damn near sank to the floor when he sat on one.

I'll find a new hotel tomorrow.

Tonight, he just wanted to shower and go to bed, and stop thinking of Trip hugging and kissing that woman after ignoring him for two weeks.

"Fuck!"

Tears started before he was ready to deal, and he stripped off his boots and shirt to distract himself. His heart ached like it had been stabbed, and his breath came in short pants. He stomped into the bathroom and turned on the water in the glass-paned shower. He leaned his hands and head against the cool glass and closed his eyes.

"Oh, God, make it stop hurtin' so damn much." He beat the glass with one hand and the clank of metal against it made him look up.

The copper bracelet Trip had given him sat against the glass and he stared at it, all the anger building up. He jerked his hand down and grasped the chain with the opposite hand, intending to rip it off and throw it away. But the memory of the day Trip had given it to him and the sweet things he'd said stayed his fury.

233

Henry sighed and removed the rest of his clothes before stepping under the spray. He tried to let go of all the thoughts swirling in his head, allowing the water to pound them away with the sweat on his body. And if a few tears leaked out, no one would ever know in the spray of the shower.

He washed his hair and beard, scrubbed his body, and shut off the shower, feeling no better than when he went in. Exhaustion set in and he dragged his damp body to the nearest bed. He hated lying down while his hair remained wet, but fatigue wouldn't be denied and he lay down anyway.

Memories flooded through his mind and released all the pent up hurt and sorrow. He gave a great sob and buried his face in his pillow to keep anyone from hearing him. How the hell had everything gone so wrong? He didn't understand why Trip had backed away or flaunted the woman in front of him. He'd thought they were getting along fine. Great, even. But now it was done and he'd have to figure out what to do the day after Thanksgiving.

Black Friday, for sure.

His phone chirped from his jacket pocket with a threat of dying, and Henry rose to set it on its charging cable. When he plugged it in, he found the text he'd received from Trip and against his better judgment, clicked on the little icon.

Hey Henry. I'm very sorry for how things went down at Thanksgiving supper tonight. I should have hugged you when you arrived. I noticed you packed up your things and took them with you. I really hope you're just at the bungalow and I'll see you tomorrow so we can talk. I miss you and wish you were here. I love you. Trip.

"God dammit, Trip!"

Henry dropped the phone and threw himself back into bed, the tears overwhelming him despite his crying jag in the shower. He laid his head on his pillow and let the grief take him. He hadn't sobbed this hard since his mother had died, but the pain and sorrow cut deeper this time, and he cried himself to sleep.

CHAPTER TWENTY

Trip stood at the window, watching the snow fall as he sipped his coffee. It was a new brand he'd picked up after Henry had moved in, but it didn't bring him the usual pleasure. Hell, not much brought him pleasure these days. Even jacking off didn't give him relief or release the heaviness of his heart.

He'd spent the week after Thanksgiving helping Tom get Byron back up to speed on the ranch and the current animal ailments. Byron had been hesitant to see Old Mags again, but the mare was downright friendly and greeted him like an old friend. Byron was suitably impressed and when he'd praised Henry's abilities, Trip's throat had closed up as the grief hit him hard.

It's still hittin' me hard.

Tom had wanted to fire Henry when they realized the man had left the ranch. Trip's heart had taken another hit and he couldn't find the motivation to do much of anything but exist. And even that hurt. But he did argue for Tom to mark Henry down as taking a leave of absence rather than going AWOL, especially after Estelle relayed what little Henry had said before he left.

Besides, it ain't Henry's fault, it's mine. Trip had tried to live his life by the Western Code, but when push came to shove, he couldn't do it. He couldn't help Henry, but he had hurt him. He'd cheated and wronged his younger lover knowingly and willingly, and in the end, drove him away. Trip couldn't explain that to Tom, but he'd asked his son to give Henry some leeway. Tom wasn't happy, but he dropped the issue.

Amber had tried to cheer Trip up with news about the baby and the wedding, but it was hard to think about attending either event without Henry by his side. Trip berated himself up one side and down the other for being a homophobic asshole. *Doesn't that just beat all.* Here he was a man in love with another man, but he couldn't show it in public. *I'm the worst kind of hypocrite.*

At least he'd sent a text to Henry every night reiterating his apology and stating that he loved him. It wasn't much communication because Henry didn't respond, but Trip felt a little better reminding Henry of his love. *Not that it's doin' much good.*

"Trip? I brought you supper. You hungry?"

He blinked and turned to look at Estelle. She held a tray with her spinach lasagna, a piece of garlic bread, some cut green beans, and a tall glass of water. She gave him a wary look, biting her lip. "Trip?"

"Uh, yeah, that's fine. Thanks."

"All right, now that's it." She set the tray down on the table before stepping up to him and taking the coffee out of his hands. "You come over here right now and sit your ass down to eat. You're wastin' away to nothin' and haven't had a solid meal since Thanksgivin'."

He supposed it was true, but he hadn't been very hungry after Henry had left. Nodding, he sat down at the table and she shoved a knife and fork into his hands before sitting down across from him.

"What the hell is wrong with you?"

"What?" Trip focused on the woman in front of him,

cringing at her fierce look.

"I said, what the hell is wrong with you? You've lost weight, you ain't eatin', you're mopin' around like someone shot your best horse, and you ain't got nothin' to show for it."

Anger sparked in Trip's chest. Where the hell did she get off? First, she was pissed that he didn't love her back, now she was pissed because he was sad at the damage he'd done?

"What the hell are you goin' on about?"

"I'm talking about Henry, you self-centered old mule." She pointed at him with a frown. "You're sittin' here, mopin' about life instead of doin' somethin' about it. Hell, I haven't seen you this miserable since Livvy died."

Trip reared back as if she'd slapped him. "Why are you bringin' her up? I don't need to be reminded about all I've lost."

"Huh, you coulda fooled me the way you're carryin' on, wearin' your own crown of thorns." She shook her head with a disgusted grimace. "I might be a crotchety old woman and stuck in my own head a lot of the time, but I know you're in love with Henry Bright. And I'm pretty sure he's in love with you, what with the desolation I saw in his eyes the night he left. You screwed up. Apologize and bring his ass back home."

Trip barked an unhappy laugh. "What do you think I've been doin' every day? I've been sending him texts and phone calls, apologizin' for my stupidity, and tellin' how I feel. He hasn't responded, not once, to any of them. What the hell am I supposed to do?"

"Track him down, ferret him out, find out where he is and corner him." Estelle shook her head. "I've never known you to give up. If he really is the second love of your life, then you need to go after him. Tell him everythin' and never give up tellin' him. You can't let him get away because you were too scared to make your feelings clear.

Believe me, I know."

Her own pain came back to slap him right between the eyes. "I'm sorry about that, Estelle."

She grimaced again and waved her hand dismissively. "It's done and in the past. Can't change it now and I'm not gonna dwell on it. But I can't sit here and watch you give up on somethin' you love just because you hit a bump in the road. If Henry is the person you want and love most in this world, then you gotta do somethin' about it, and never give up on him." She snorted. "He's young and doesn't have the perspective we do. Which is why he needs you. He needs you to not give up on him."

Trip swallowed hard. "What if he doesn't want me anymore?"

She shrugged, her lips pulling down at the corners. "That's a possibility, but you can't bank on that until you talk to him. More than likely that young pup thinks you don't want him." She shook her head. "Look, I can't tell you how to run your love life. It's fairly obvious I'm the least successful of the two of us. But that said, I do know showin' up, makin' your needs, wants, and intentions known, day after day, is probably the most important. No one can read each other's minds, and guessin' in a relationship ain't fun. If Henry's who you want, you never give up on tellin' him."

Estelle gave him a sad smile. "I'm gonna let you eat. I got a lot to do to get this place decked out for Christmas and it's already the eleventh of the month. You have a good night, Trip."

She left him with his meal and his thoughts, and he tried to eat as much as possible just to keep her from reprimanding him. But he still wasn't very hungry and put the lasagna in the fridge to eat later. Darkness had fallen hours earlier and his energy to stay awake went with the light. *Damn, I'm gettin' old if I'm ready for bed at seven-thirty.* It didn't stop him from undressing and crawling into bed.

He lay back, wishing he could curl up next to someone, but the emptiness of the mattress mocked his desire. The apartment seemed too quiet and empty despite his comfort living there alone for years. He rolled onto his side and tried to ignore the recriminations rattling around in his thoughts.

****

"Trip, wake up. I need to talk to you."

He knew that voice, but it had been years since he'd heard the serious tone in it. He frowned, but opened his eyes and rolled over in bed, scanning the room. Snow still fell outside, but the lights in the room glowed with extra warmth like the holiday cards he'd seen in stores around this time of year. Rolling his head enough to see the room, he found Livvy sitting in his armchair where he'd draped the last quilt she'd made for them at the start of their marriage.

"You awake or do I need to jump on the bed?"

"Livvy? What're you doin' here?" He blinked blearily at her.

"Now what kind of a fool question is that? Why wouldn't I be here?"

"'Cause you're dead. Have been for years." He'd never been so blunt in his life, but being woken up out of a sound sleep had stripped his manners.

"Just because my body died doesn't mean I'm not around. Don't I talk to you most days?" She dipped her chin and looked at him from under her brows.

"Yeah, but I just thought it was my subconscious or somethin'." He closed his eyes and shook his head before he opened them again. "What are you doin' here now, tonight, bein' so solid and all?"

She snorted and her lips quirked into a half-smile. "I

need to talk to you about Henry Bright."

"Aw hell, not you, too. Estelle grilled me about him already."

Livvy chuckled. "Oh, I know she did, and everything she said was right on. But here's the thing. She doesn't know what I do about Henry."

Trip shook his head as he sat up and leaned against the headboard. "What the hell is that supposed to mean?"

"It means that if you'd been payin' attention, you would've heard the truth when it was told to you instead of bumblin' around like a jackass and lettin' fear rile you up."

He took a breath to respond, but closed his mouth tight on anything he would've said. Livvy had often gotten him riled up about something and he'd only come out looking more stupid than he already was.

"Okay, I'm listenin' and tryin' not to be more of a jackass. What truth are you talkin' about?"

Livvy gifted him with one of her glorious smiles, the one that had attracted him from the moment he'd met her. "You're gettin' smarter in your old age. You remember when you talked to Byron about your relationship with Henry the first time?"

"Yeah, I remember. What about it?"

"Byron was right about me." She met his gaze, no teasing smile, no laugh, no wink. Serene calm looked back at him and he shivered.

"What do you mean, Byron was right about you? Right about what?"

"Come on, Trip. Think back." She raised an eyebrow and dropped her chin.

Trip frowned and let his gaze fall to the blanket over his hips. What had Byron said? He remembered talking about his friend Bo, and why he'd quit rodeoing. *Is that what she's referrin' to?* That didn't seem right. He kept thinking over the conversation as Livvy rose from the chair and sat down beside him on the bed, her gaze fixed on him.

Trip scrubbed his face as he went over the conversation with Byron. The old vet had asked him how long Livvy had been gone and how old Henry was. He frowned. There'd been something about the correlation between her death and Henry's age. *What was it again?*

"Are you talkin' about the part when Byron said Henry's a reincarnation of you?"

Livvy smiled. "Yup."

"Oh, come now, darlin'. How does that work? You're sittin' right here, talkin' to me. And you've been with me for years. How can Henry be you startin' again?"

She sighed, but her smile remained. "When we're alive, we have limited views. We can't see everythin'. We live in duality. Light and dark, love and hate, left and right, up and down. The thing is, the universe doesn't really fit into such extremes. I can't explain to you how I've been with you this whole time, because you know I have, and yet Henry is my way of bein' with you again."

She reached out and he felt her warm hand on his for the first time in almost thirty years. "I was so happy when Henry got here. I knew you'd be okay. But you both have so much to learn about love. You and I, we didn't have enough time to learn the lessons and I didn't want to leave you hangin'. Henry's my gift to you." She squeezed his hand before her smile faded. "But you can't screw this up. You need to do a better job learnin' about love and effort and determination than you did with me."

Trip opened his mouth to protest, but she held up a hand to forestall him.

"It's not your fault. I died too early in our marriage for either of us to learn nearly enough. And I wish I could've been there for you when you got gored by that bull. But Henry could be here for you now, and he has abilities I never did. Plus, he can talk to you, man to man, that speaks to your lovely cowboy heart." She smiled, love and sorrow mixing in her expression. "I've waited until Henry could make his appearance to know you'd be okay. And you will, Trip. I promise. But you have to make him understand that you'll be there for him and love only him."

"How do I do that? I screwed up real bad at Thanksgivin' because I was too scared to show how much I loved him in front of others." Trip grimaced. "I was a fuckin' coward and I hurt him. Now he won't answer my texts or calls."

"You don't give up on him. You keep callin' and textin', and never let him doubt you meant it when you said you loved him." She tilted her head and smiled the secret smile she wore whenever she knew something he didn't. "And when he calls you for help, don't hesitate to give it to him."

Trip snorted. "I don't think he's gonna call for help."

She shrugged. "Just don't hesitate, Trip."

He sighed. "Yes, ma'am." He raised his gaze to hers. "You know I'm gonna be a grampa?"

She broke out her brilliant smile again. "Yes, I do. I'm very happy for you and Tom. Amber is a wonderful addition to our family. Henry will be, too."

"Even if I'm so much older than him?" He bit his bottom lip.

Livvy snorted again, rolling her eyes. "Age is a number used to determine social security payments and meal discounts. It's got nothin' to do with love."

"Henry said somethin' like that, too."

She winked. "See? I told you. I've been tryin' to tell you from the start."

He frowned, rubbing his lower jaw. "Yeah, but reincarnation? That's crazy talk."

"Don't make it less true." Livvy winked as she stood. "Now you get some more rest. Christmas is comin' and you need to be ready."

Trip yawned as he settled back into bed. "Ready for what?"

"Ready to fight for what you love. Never give up on Henry, okay?"

"Okay, Livvy. I love you." Trip yawned again and closed his eyes.

"I love you, too. I always will."

CHAPTER TWENTY-ONE

Henry strummed his guitar and stared out the window of his hotel room. He'd been restless with nothing to do beyond think and wait, but what he was waiting for, he didn't know. It had been just over two weeks since he'd left, and Trip had texted and called him every day, apologizing and asking him to talk. But Henry didn't have the energy to call or text back.

The Christmas holiday was still two weeks away, but it looked as if he'd spend it alone. *Or with Jordie.* Somehow that seemed even worse. Brian had called a few days before and said he was close to finishing his investigation. He'd call and email the report when done.

Maybe that's what I'm waiting for.

To be honest, he really wanted to get back to the Triple Star and work with the animals again. But the way he left it, he wasn't sure they'd let him back on the property. He suspected Tom would be furious with him and he couldn't blame him at all. Until the Triple Star, Henry had never walked out on a job before in his life. But he hadn't been able to face Trip and needed to get away.

Two weeks is a helluva long time to 'get away'.

But he'd been waiting for something. He'd moved to

an extended stay hotel so he wouldn't have to go out as much while he worked on the melody plaguing him. He had the song and he had the chords and bridge, but the words remained out of reach. It frustrated him that the song wouldn't come through clearly even while he had nothing else to do.

Irritated, he rose to make some coffee and his phone rang. He almost didn't check it, assuming it to be one of Trip's daily attempts to connect, but his anger had waned and only fear remained. Fear that Trip would keep calling. Fear that he wouldn't. Glancing at the phone, he caught sight of Ransom's name and he immediately picked it up.

"Hey Ransom, how are you?"

"I'm good, gettin' ready for Christmas. But what I want to know is what the fuck is goin' on with you?" Anger sizzled across the digital lines and Henry swallowed hard.

"What are you talkin' about?"

"I told you Trip Colton couldn't be a fling, Henry. The man is a friend and a damn good neighbor. You can't fuck with him and then run out on him. What the hell were you thinkin'?"

"I know that, Ransom. What the hell? This happened two weeks ago. Why are you just callin' me about it now?"

"Because I needed some help with somethin' from Tom and he was really down in the mouth. When I asked, he said his dad is havin' relationship troubles." Henry heard the frown in Ransom's voice. "I can only assume that meant you. What the hell happened?"

"Don't get mad at me. *He* cheated on me. With a woman." Anger still sparked every time Henry thought about it.

"What? With whom?"

"Byron's daughter. Trip spent the two weeks before Thanksgivin' in Cheyenne with Byron and his daughter. He avoided me when he was at the ranch, and wouldn't come near me at Thanksgivin'." Henry shook his head to keep the tears from building and falling again. *Damn, I'm a fuckin' sap.* "You wanna talk about flings? Talk to Trip."

"Do you know for sure he was cheatin' on you, Henry?" Ransom's voice had softened.

"Not for sure, no, but based on the way he was actin', it seemed a pretty sure thing."

"Has he tried to talk to you since then?"

Henry sighed, thinking about all the calls and texts he'd received. "Yeah, he's tried, but I was too angry to respond. I've been givin' myself some time to cool down."

"Have you cooled down enough to answer him? Because you at least owe him that." Ransom snorted, his disgust coming through loud and clear. "Look, I may not be the best partner or lover, but I know one thing for sure. You have to communicate with the person you care about most or you can't fix shit. He's been tryin' to connect with you and you're actin' like a goddamn teenager. Don't his efforts mean anythin'?"

"Yeah, they're actually workin'." Henry sighed again. "I just didn't want to come back to him without havin' worked shit out on my end."

"What are you waitin' on?"

"I got stuff weighin' on me. Like somethin's comin' and I need to be alone for it. You know?"

Ransom sighed. "I think you're bein' an idiot. Why the hell would you want to be alone when the shit hits the fan? But I won't argue. You gotta do what's right for you. Just don't wait too long. Trip's patient, but he won't wait forever. At least text him back so he knows he's not shoutin' into the wind."

"Yeah, okay."

"I'm serious, Henry. Trip deserves at least that."

"Yeah, I got it."

"Good. So, will you be comin' back here for Christmas? You're always welcome at the Fantasy Ranch." Ransom's voice lightened again. "Don't stay in Colorado alone for the holiday, okay? It ain't fun or healthy."

What if I deserve to be alone? But he couldn't voice that to Ransom. He didn't need his friend ranting at him about being an idiot again.

"I'll see. It'll depend on the weather." And whether he could face his friends again.

"Just think on it, okay? I'd like to see you and I know Tawny hopes you will come so we can all sing carols together."

Henry laughed. "Yeah, yeah. I know it's because I used to sing for a livin'."

"Well, yeah." Ransom chuckled. "But seriously, don't be a stranger. You'll always have a place here in Wyoming."

"Yeah, thanks." Henry paused as his phone chirped with an incoming call. "Hey, Ransom, I gotta go. I'll talk to you later, okay?"

"Yeah, later."

Henry clicked over to the other call. "This is Henry."

"Hey, Henry, it's Jordie."

Henry's mood plummeted. "Hey, Jordie. What's up?"

"I have great news." Jordie damn near chortled over the phone. "Let's go out to celebrate."

Henry raised his eyebrows. "Celebrate what? You haven't told me what it is yet."

"I know. I want it to be a surprise, like a pre-Christmas gift. Come on. Dinner will be my treat."

He opened his mouth to refuse, but it would be nice to have someone cook him something better than grilled cheese sandwiches or brats. He could cook more than that, but it hadn't been worth it without Trip around to enjoy it.

Glory be, I miss him. His anger had morphed into sorrow. *Then call him, you dumbass.*

"Yeah, okay. Where do you wanna go?"

"Let's go to the Essential Gourmet. I love their filet mignon."

Henry grimaced. He'd lost his taste for eating much beef after he found out Trip couldn't digest it. *Dammit, why the hell am I thinkin' about Trip?* But he'd changed a lot of his habits because they were healthier or Trip did something similiar.

"Sounds good." Henry glanced at the digital clock above the stove in the kitchenette. "See you there at six?"

"How about I come pick you up? We can carpool."

Henry shivered. "Thanks, but I'm gonna do a little grocery shoppin' on my way back so I'll be ready for the holiday."

"All right. I'll see you there at six." Jordie fairly cackled. "This is gonna be stellar. You'll see."

"Bye, Jordie."

Henry clicked off the phone and dropped it on the counter. He didn't want to go out with Jordie, but the restless feeling had returned. He headed for the shower to wash the restlessness away. But the gut feeling of something coming wouldn't leave him alone.

He tried to ignore it as he got dressed for supper, but he found himself packing his things as if he planned to leave the hotel. It didn't make sense. *Where the hell am I gonna go?* Maybe he could drive up to the Fantasy Ranch and stay there a while. But he'd be awfully close to the Triple Star. Still, he put all his clothes into the duffle bag and the rest of his things back into his totes. Just in case.

He stacked his things near the door and surveyed the room. Nothing remained except the items furnished by the hotel and he had a moment of déjà vu. *That pretty much sums up my life, don't it?* He didn't have much except his memories, and lately those hadn't been enough for him anymore. He missed the Triple Star ranch and the people there, even Estelle Guthrie. *And I want to go back.*

Shaking his head, he threw on his coat and gloves, and headed out to his truck.

****

"So, what's the big news?" Henry settled into the chair across from Jordie at the restaurant and eyed his former manager. The other man wore a manic excitement as if he'd been under a lot of strain lately.

Jordie grinned, but it didn't quite hide the exhaustion around his eyes. "Let's order before I divulge all my secrets. This is a night of celebration even if it ain't quite Christmas."

Henry nodded. It was only the twelfth and he didn't feel much like celebrating. *Maybe if I was with Trip.* And that wasn't likely to happen unless he answered at least one of Trip's texts. Henry looked over the menu and selected a chicken alfredo before he set his menu down.

"How are the new songs coming along?" Jordie's eyes sparkled.

"Good, I think. I haven't been working very hard. You know, just lettin' the muse go where it will." He shrugged, not willing to tell Jordie about the one song plaguing him.

"Good, good." Jordie practically vibrated, but the waiter came to take their order.

Henry kept his peace until the waiter left, his curiosity overriding his usual lack of interest. "What has you so damn riled up? You're damn near bouncin' over there."

"Oh, son, I got some terrific news today and I've been wanting to share it with you all day. You ready?"

Henry frowned. "Stop draggin' it out. What's goin' on?"

"I got in touch with Lariat Records today and asked them if they'd take you back as an artist." Jordie grinned as he opened his cloth napkin for his lap. "They've been so pleased with the sales from your last album, they were happy to negotiate a deal with me. They're willing to give you a larger cut of your royalties, especially with places like Pandora and Spotify. Isn't that great?"

The water turned to sludge in Henry's mouth as he stared. *What the hell is he talkin' about?* He had no interest in going back to the music industry and he'd made that clear months ago. Yeah, the muse had come back and he'd starting writing music again, but he wouldn't return to the world of sex, drugs, and rock n' roll. He'd done that dream and enjoyed it for a time, but he'd moved on to something else now.

"Jordie." Henry put his glass down and met the other man's bright gaze. "I'm pretty sure I made it clear I wasn't goin' back to the music industry. You got a hearin' problem?"

Jordie snorted and waved a dismissive hand. "No, I don't. That was months ago before you left the ranch. Before you started writing music again."

"I might be writin' music again, but I haven't changed my mind. That's not what I want to do for the rest of my life." Henry shook his head. "I wasn't kiddin' when I said I was done, even if it was months ago."

"What the hell else are you gonna do?" Jordie's mouth tightened. "You left the ranch in nowhere Wyoming because that piece-of-shit bi-fucker cheated on you as I said he would, and you don't got a job anymore. This is a great opportunity."

"I'm a veterinarian, Jordie. That's what I want to do. There are other ranches beyond the Triple Star." He met Jordie's gaze with his jaw set. "I'm not goin' back to the music biz."

"Oh, for fuck's sake." Jordie scowled. "You can't quit now, not when everyone is expecting you to come back. Sure, they were okay with you taking a sabbatical to get your head on straight, but this was your dream to hit the big time. We're at the edge of greatness here."

Henry matched his scowl. "What greatness? That isn't what I wanted a few months ago, and it ain't what I want now. I wasn't kiddin'. Shit-oh-dear, I got out of the music scene on purpose and I meant to stay out."

"But if you don't take this opportunity, you may never get another one."

Part of Henry hesitated. Hadn't he always wanted to play music and get paid for it? Hadn't he wanted the notoriety and recognition of his hard work and creativity? If he walked away now, Lariat would never take him back.

But do I really want them to take me back? He knew the answer before the end of the question echoed in his mind. No, he didn't want to go back. While the people at Lariat Records were kind enough and not the worst by far, he had no interest in the life anymore. He didn't want the glitz and glitter. He yearned for quiet evenings watching the sunset or walking along the river while the horses grazed nearby. He needed the smells of hay, leather, horses, and sunshine of the Triple Star barn. And most of all, he wanted Trip Colton.

I love him.

There it was. No matter what had happened at Thanksgiving or what would happen after, Henry wanted Trip. He wanted to see if they could make it work, through thick and thin, sunshine or rain, wind and snow. He wanted his quiet life at the Triple Star and his sexy, hot nights with Trip in the lodge.

He opened his mouth to reply when his phone rang. It wasn't Trip because he'd set a specific ring tone for his calls. *Glory be, I hope he calls again tonight.* Hearing the man's voice would give him the courage to apologize once and for all. He pulled it out and saw Brian Calvert's name on the readout.

"Excuse me one minute. I gotta take this." Henry rose as Jordie gaped. "Keep your shirt on. I'll just be a minute."

He retreated toward the front of the restaurant near the doors and stood out of the way of the diners coming in. No one paid him much attention as he leaned against the wall with a large potted palm.

"This is Henry."

"Hey Henry, Brian Calvert. I've finished my investigation. You got a moment or three?"

"Yes, sir. I'm all ears. What have you found out?"

"It looks like you've had some embezzling issues for awhile now, I'd say going back to about the time you started with Lariat Records, though it could be longer than that."

Shit, that's over six years ago. "Okay. Was it someone at the company?"

"Nope. The person doing it was pretty smooth until recently. The amounts taken were small and usually on top of other expenses so you wouldn't notice. Things like paying too much for food or drink at parties. Or extra for rooms at hotels. Little things that wouldn't necessarily set of any alarms."

Henry frowned. "So, they were mostly expenses?"

"Yeah, until just before you left Lariat Records. In a two-week period before you took off, the amounts became bigger, by an order of magnitude, and for things you weren't necessarily a part of. The guy got sloppy." A rustling of papers sounded on the other end. "Things like clothing purchases at high end men's shops in Nashville, a vehicle purchase...looks like a new Lexus. And a country club membership costing the same as a Caribbean cruise for two."

"Holy shit. Who the fuck was usin' my money like that?"

"The same guy who set up the false accounts when you left Lariat. Jordie Heathrow."

Henry's world narrowed down to a small spot on the floor between his boots. "What did you say?"

"Jordie Heathrow, the guy listed as your manager at Lariat Records."

"Sonuvaprick! Are you sure?"

"Yeah. Like I said, at first he was really careful where

he skimmed off the top, but the longer he did it, the more sloppy he got. The big payout was your first royalty statement after you left Lariat in late September. He set up a dummy account and all thirty-six thousand three hundred and twenty-eight dollars went into it."

"Holy fuck." Anger rose in Henry's chest. "So, when I called Lariat to ask about my royalties, that next check would've gone to him, too?"

"Yep. It was all good to go until you switched the account with Lariat's financial people. Whatever the guy's doing, he's living off your September royalties."

Oh, I know what the sonuvaprick is doin'. Henry shot a gaze back through the restaurant where Jordie sat talking to the waiter. *That asshole is takin' me out to dinner with my own fuckin' money.*

"Unfuckin'-believable. And you have all the proof of this?"

"Yep. I have careful documentation and backups on my backups. I'll make sure it's all available to you both in your email and a hardcopy as well if you want to sue."

"Oh, I'll be thinkin' about that. But the first step is to get his ass arrested for embezzlement." Henry took a deep breath. "Thank you, Brian. I appreciate your hard work and effort through the holidays."

"Not a problem, Mr. Bright. I'll have all the electronic information sent to your email and drop the hardcopy in the mail. You got an address I can use?"

"Hold off on sendin' the hardcopy until I set up more of a permanent address. I'm between residences at the moment. But I'll email you as soon as I have somethin' more concrete."

"Sounds good, Mr. Bright. I'll let Duncan Wilde know that I've found what you're looking for and have him contact you about the final bill from Lost and Found."

"Thanks. I'm real grateful. You have a good holiday now."

"Thank you, Mr. Bright."

"Oh, Brian?" Henry hoped the man hadn't quite hung up yet.

"Yeah, Mr. Bright?"

"A friend wanted me to pass on to you if you ever needed somewhere to go for the holidays, you'd be welcome up at the Triple Star Ranch. She didn't want you to be alone." He hoped he wouldn't have to be alone, either. *Maybe the invitation is still open for me, too.*

A surprised silence ticked away a few seconds on the other end of the phone. "Uh, wow. Thank you, Mr. Bright. That's very kind."

"Yeah, Ms. Amber is pretty kind. You're always welcome. She wanted me to extend the invitation and I promised her I would."

"Thank her for me. I'll keep that in mind." He sounded reluctant, but maybe he'd change his mind. "I have your number if I need company."

"Sounds good, Brian. Thanks again."

"Have a good night, Henry."

"Thanks. You, too."

Henry ended the call and shook his head. He hoped the man took Amber up on her invitation. But the reason for Brian's call returned and he took a deep breath to keep from throwing his phone across the entryway of the restaurant.

Motherfuckin' sonuvaprick cheatin' thief! He clenched his jaw and closed his eyes. Jordie sat right across from him and told him he'd pick up the check while living on Henry's money. Fury burned away any doubts about returning to Lariat Records. He had nothing against the company, but he'd be damned before he let Jordie anywhere near his financial holdings.

Taking a deep breath to beat back the rage, Henry returned to the table. Jordie spoke into his phone with confidence, a wide smile on his lips as he negotiated some deal. *I'll bet he is.* Probably figured to use Henry's money while doing it. He looked down at the plate of pasta and meat in alfredo sauce and his appetite evaporated. The anger made his stomach curdle.

He glanced up as Jordie laughed, waving his hand to illustrate some point while he talked on the phone. *Probably lettin' everyone know he's got his cash cow back, and he'll be milkin' me for the rest of my life.* Henry tightened his jaw to keep from hollering at his tablemate and looked for the waiter. He couldn't stand to be in Jordie's presence any longer.

"Excuse me, can I get a box for this? Somethin' came up and I need to leave."

"Of course, sir. Let me take that for you." The waiter reached for the plate and Henry snagged his sleeve.

"And my companion will be payin' for both of us. I think he might be stayin'." Henry nodded to Jordie who hadn't noticed the interruption.

"Of course, sir."

The waiter retreated with Henry's plate and he sipped his water to calm himself down. Damn, but he wanted to yank Jordie out of his chair and pummel the shit out of him. Instead, he waited for Jordie to finish his call, trying to figure out the best way to break away.

"Yep, yep. It's all good. All right. Talk to you later, Eddie. Yep, bye." Jordie swiped the phone with satisfaction and set it on the table. "All set. Eddie will see us in Nashville after New Year's." He glanced down at Henry's empty place. "Where's your dinner? Something wrong with it?"

"No, but somethin' came up. I gotta get goin' and deal with it." *Yeah, without makin' a scene here at the restaurant.* "I'm headin' back to my hotel to take care of everythin'."

"Oh no. Here, let me get the check and I'll come with you."

Henry wanted to snarl at him not to bother, but that would likely be followed up with a fist to his jaw. Instead, he nodded and accepted the to-go box from the waiter. *No point in wastin' good food seein' as I've paid for it and all.* The idea that Jordie had been stealing from him since the moment he'd signed with Lariat Records infuriated him. He kept his gaze down as he slid his arms into his jacket and zipped it up.

"I'll see you at my hotel, Jordie." He swung away from the table, catching the concerned expression on Jordie's face, but he couldn't care less.

Outside in the parking lot, Henry fumed, but forced himself to think about what he'd do next. He needed a good local lawyer. He made phone calls on the way to the hotel, calling on his lawyer back in Nashville. The man gave him a name of a local firm in Cheyenne and said he'd offer a recommendation. Henry's determination firmed as the snow started falling hard and heavy. He cranked up the heat in the truck and headed for his hotel.

When he arrived, he spent the time before Jordie joined him hauling his shit down to his truck. He'd leave first thing in the morning. He didn't know where he'd go, but he'd start by calling Ransom. He stopped at the front desk and settled his bill, letting them know he'd be checking out in the morning, then he returned to his room to check his email.

Brian Calvert had sent the full report with all the attachments and he was tempted to open it, but Jordie knocked on his room door. Henry closed the email program and the computer before he answered the door. He let Jordie in before he shoved the computer in his duffle bag and settled himself on one of the armchairs in the room.

"Everything okay, Henry?" Jordie wore a realistic look of concern.

Who knows, it might be real.

"No, it's not. The phone call was serious." Henry

shook his head, trying to keep his voice even. "When were you gonna tell me?"

"Tell you? Tell you what?" Jordie frowned as he sat down on the other chair, wiping his hands on his pants. "What's going on?"

"That's what I'd like to know." Henry met his gaze, fighting to keep from roaring at the other man. "I'd like to know when you were gonna tell me you were embezzlin' from me."

"What? What the hell are you talking about?" Jordie rubbed his hands on his pants again, his face blanching white.

"You heard me. I have proof, Jordie. I hired an investigator to find out where the hell my money was goin'." Henry rose, but stayed back for fear he'd do something violent. "Everythin' tracked back to you. You stole from me. You took my hard-earned money and bought shit with it. What the fuck, Jordie?"

"Hang on, now." Jordie held up his hands in placating gesture. "I think you're overreacting. I'd never steal from you. We've been in this together from the beginning."

"Yeah, we have. I trusted you to deal with me fairly." Henry refrained from pointing at his duffle bag, but he held up his phone. "I have the proof you've been stealin' from me since I signed with Lariat. And I know you stole my September royalties and have been livin' off them this whole time." He shook his head. "Why, Jordie? Why would you take my money?"

"What the fuck do you care?" Jordie scowled. "You were gonna be a goddamned vet in Bumfuck Wyoming. You didn't need that money. I had to see something for my efforts."

"Something for *your* efforts? I earned every penny of that money."

"Bullshit! All you did was strum your guitar and look pretty." Jordie's face twisted in to an ugly grimace. "*I got* you the sponsors and the backers. *I* negotiated the deals. *I* made sure you were paid what you were worth with Lariat. *I* earned that money."

"I didn't see you out there playin' all night and takin' pictures of your naked ass. That was my work you were livin' off of." Henry tightened his hands into fists.

"Oh, Henry." Jordie sighed and shook his head. "I did it for us, you know? For you and me, so we'd always have a nest egg when you either got too old or too tired to play music anymore. I figured you and I'd always be together, living like kings." He scowled. "And we would've too, if you hadn't gone running off to Wyoming on a fucking whim. Hell, you just up and left me in Nashville. You didn't even say goodbye."

"I didn't say goodbye because you loved that lifestyle and I was done. You didn't listen every time I told you I didn't want it. I couldn't make you hear me so I left." Henry narrowed his eyes. "But you've been stealin' longer than just the last few months. You've been stealin' since the beginning."

"I told you I work on commission—"

"Yeah, but you took more than you fair share and I paid you well. You were never hurtin'."

"I had certain needs—"

"Fuck you! So did I!" Henry grabbed Jordie's shirtfront and jerked him nose-to-nose. "My needs might've been simpler, but I never would've stolen from anyone to get them." He abruptly released Jordie and stood back. "You know, since I returned to Wyoming, I learned somethin' called the Western Code. Trip Colton actually taught it to me. It goes like this:

"If I can't help you, I won't hurt you. I wouldn't ask you for something I wouldn't give you. I will not cheat, wrong, or defraud anybody in the world knowingly or willingly." Henry narrowed his eyes. "You did the opposite of everything I stand for. You couldn't help me, so you hurt me. You asked for things you wouldn't give anyone. And you cheated, wronged, and defrauded me, your client and friend, knowingly and willingly. I'm fuckin' done with you. You didn't embezzle money from me for a nest egg. You did it because you're greedy and you're a cheat."

Henry shook his head and turned to grab his jacket. "Good back to Nashville, and get yourself a good lawyer 'cause I'm sendin' my proof to the cops."

"You sonuvaprick!" Jordie launched himself at Henry's back, but he whirled and met Jordie's face with his fist. "Ow!"

Henry shook out his hand, scowling. "Fuck, that really hurts. The stunt men in the movies make it look so easy." He threw his jacket on and zipped it up before grabbing his keys and his duffle bag and heading for the door. "Feel free to stay the night here. The room's paid through tomorrow."

"Sonuvaprick, that fuckin' hurt, Henry."

"Good." Henry yanked open the door.

"You'll be back, you hear me? You'll be back when you realize this was a mistake. And you'll see I was right." Jordie stood with blood on his lips.

"Keep tellin' yourself that. Maybe you'll believe your own lies."

Henry stepped out of the door and headed for the stairs. There was no way in hell he'd allow himself to get cornered in a little steel box with Jordie if the man came after him. He trotted down the stairs, his footsteps echoing in the concrete stairwell, but he felt better than he had in weeks. Between Jordie's wheedling and the investigation into his missing money, Henry had been wound tighter than a spring. Now his shoulders loosened and he finally had a sense of freedom.

He headed out the side door to his truck and stopped, surprised. Several inches of snow had already accumulated on the hood and the temperature had dropped to bone-chilling since he'd gone inside. His breath plumed out in front of him as he clicked the doors open, shivering as snow dropped down the collar of his coat. The snow fell thickly, reducing the visibility to drive.

Fuck that. I'm goin' home.

He threw his duffle into the cab and started the truck, allowing the engine to warm as he climbed out to scrape off the windshield. He hurried because he wanted to get back to Wyoming. He was done with Nashville, done with Colorado, and done with Jordie Heathrow. Anger fueled his efforts as he jumped back in the truck and headed for the interstate.

Henry hoped Ransom would have a place for him, but he couldn't call while driving. The snow fell too heavily for him to do anything but concentrate on the road. He held tight to the wheel and squinted into the plumes of snow beyond his headlights. The storm worsened the closer he got to the border between Colorado and Wyoming, and he had to slow to around thirty-five MPH, squinting through the whiteout.

He'd just passed the large outcropping of rocks on the western side of the freeway at the state line when he realized the plumes of white were coming from his truck. He glanced down at the temperature gauge on his engine and swore a blue streak, easing his truck over onto the shoulder.

"What the fuck?"

He put the truck in park and shut it off, watching steam rise from under the hood. He pulled on the hood release and shoved out into the blowing snow. The temperature at the border sat even colder than at the hotel, and he shivered in his jacket as he reached for the hood.

"Sonuvaprick!"

The release latch burned his fingers and he yanked them back before stomping to the passenger door to grab his gloves. *What the fuck is wrong with my truck?* Armed with his gloves, he opened the hood and steam billowed out into the frigid air like a mushroom cloud. The radiator hissed with each flake of snow hitting its scalding surface and Henry's heart sank. *No water or fluids.* The radiator sat empty and his truck wasn't going any farther that night.

"Shit!" He slammed the hood closed and squinted into the whitened gloom.

No one else was stupid enough to try to drive I-25 in these conditions and he was all alone until the plows came by. *If they don't close the interstate first.*

Fortunately, he'd charged his phone before he left Fort Collins and his truck had power if not driving capability. The only problem would be heat. While the engine had overheated, he couldn't run it to pump that heat into the cabin. He climbed back inside and grabbed his phone, tapping out Ransom's number.

The phone rang until it went to voicemail and Henry's heart sank.

"Hey Ransom, I hope you get this message soon. I'm stuck on the side of I-25 in the blizzard with an overheated engine. If you get this, would you be willin' to come get me? The phone has power and bars so I should be able to get your call. Thanks."

He hung up and stared out at the gathering snow on his windshield. He turned the key one click and let the wipers sweep it off, wondering how long it would take to go cold. He had blankets and could probably last the night. Hell, he even had his uneaten supper.

Shaking his head, he tried to call Ransom back, but again it went to voicemail. He didn't bother to leave a second message. Instead, he looked down at his phone and flipped through the contacts to Tom and Trip Colton. Should he call them? *Would they even answer?* Tom would probably shout at him to go fuck himself, and he deserved it. But he didn't really want to talk to Tom anyway.

Call Trip. The voice of his inner wisdom rarely spoke to him except when writing music or signing contracts, but it came through clearly now. *Bite your pride in the ass and call him. Don't be a fool.*

He clicked on Trip's name and stared at the number illuminated on the screen. He missed Trip so much his eyes filled with tears. *Dammit, I wish I could say I'm sorry for bein' such a dumbass.* He swore he heard his wisdom voice snort before it added, *Then call him and ask for his help. No one in Wyoming leaves anyone stranded on the side of the road in a blizzard.*

Swallowing hard, Henry punched Trip's number. He held the phone to his ear with a shaking hand and listened to it ring, barely breathing.

"This is Trip."

Just the sound of his voice made Henry's breath catch and his eyes fill with tears. *I gotta get a handle on all this emotion.*

"Trip?"

"Yeah?"

"I–I need your help."

A long pause sounded on the other end of the phone and Henry's breath stopped. "What kind of help are we talkin' here, Henry?"

"I'm stuck on the side of I-25 and the snow is comin' hard and fast. The truck overheated and it ain't goin' anywhere tonight." He cleared his throat and swallowed hard. "Would you be willin' to come get me? Please?"

Trip didn't make him wait. "Where are you? I won't be able to see you very well from the southbound side."

"I'm right below the bison silhouette at the border, about ten miles south of Cheyenne." He ran the wipers again. "No one else is out here, not even the plows yet. I'm gonna save my lights until you get close, but I'll turn 'em on again in about a half hour."

"You got enough blankets and food if it takes me a while?"

"Yeah. I can stay warm until you get here."

"All right. You hang tight, Henry. I'm on my way. I'll bring my tow-cable and we'll get your truck back to the ranch, no problem."

Henry's throat closed with relief and gratitude. "Thank you, Trip."

"Yeah. You hang in there. We'll be there soon."

The call ended and Henry let the tears he'd been holding back fall. They splashed on the screen of his phone. No one had ever done so much for him and he realized he didn't want to live without Trip. Yeah, he still had hang-ups about bisexuality, and Trip might worry about public displays of affection, but those were small things in comparison to living without the man.

I love him.

It wasn't a question. He sat back in his driver's seat, the wipers intermittently cleaning the windshield of snow, and settled into the feeling of loving Trip Colton. He had to repair the relationship he'd fucked up. He'd do everything he could to show Trip he meant his love no matter what.

Without warning, the lyrics to the song he'd been working on came into clear focus and he scrambled to pull up the Memo option on his phone to type them out. The words came so fast he almost couldn't keep up as the melody burst through his imagination in full song. He hummed the tune, chanting the words in his head before grabbing his acoustic guitar and strumming the chords. The music poured out of him as the tears flooded down his cheeks and the love filled his heart.

CHAPTER TWENTY-TWO

Trip shoved his phone in his pocket, Livvy's voice echoing in his memory. *When Henry calls you for help, don't hesitate to give it to him.* Trip looked at his son. "I need to go get Henry."

"What? Why?" Tom gaped at him.

"He's stranded on the northbound side of I-25 just under the bison cut-out. His truck's overheated."

"Fuck. In this blizzard?" Tom shook his head and strode for the hat tree. "Let me tell Amber where we're goin' and get my gloves."

"Thanks, Tom."

Trip thanked his lucky stars for both Tom and Livvy. He'd been blessed, thrice now, with the addition of Henry. But Tom, for all his disappointment in Henry's actions at Thanksgiving, didn't hesitate to help someone stuck out in a Wyoming blizzard.

You taught him well. Livvy appeared beside the couch as he shrugged into his jacket.

"Thanks, Livvy. We both did."

She nodded, her smile a little sad. *Are you gonna tell him who Henry is?*

Trip grimaced and shook his head. "I dunno. I'm not

sure he'd believe me, and Henry himself would probably laugh. I think it's enough that I know who he is at his core."

And who's that?

"The love of my life, no matter what form he's taken."

Her sad smile widened. *That's exactly who he is. I love you, Trip. Know that, but it's time for you to find your own way without this last remnant to haunt you.*

"You're leavin'?" Fear grabbed him by the gut and he paused with his keys in his hand.

It's time. You need to focus on Henry. You aren't losin' anything if I'm not here. You'll always have me in your heart. And in the love you give to him.

"Aw, Livvy." Tears welled up and he blinked his eyes to keep her in focus.

Now don't cry. You're strong enough to do this, and Henry has more wisdom than he knows. You're gonna be okay if you keep workin' at lovin' and takin' care of him. He's the best person to come into your life in a long time. Her smile turned sweet. *I love you. I always will.*

"But Livvy…"

Go help Henry.

She faded from sight just as Tom called to him from the hallway outside. "Come on, Dad! The snow is gettin' heavier."

Trip swallowed his sorrow and hurried out of his apartment. "You remember where we put the tow cable?"

"Yeah. Already in the cab of my truck. Let's go get Henry."

****

The drive to the border made Trip reevaluate his sanity. Visibility had been reduced to no more than a few feet beyond the hood of Tom's truck and he thanked his lucky stars they hadn't closed the freeway yet.

"Okay, we're close to the border. Call Henry." Tom hunched over the steering wheel as they rolled along through the thick snow. They had to use the Garmin to figure out where the actual roadway sat and couldn't drive faster than about thirty-five miles per hour.

Trip dialed Henry's number, hoping he'd still be able to connect.

"Trip?" Henry's voice came through.

"Yeah. Turn on your lights. We're almost to you headed southbound." Trip hoped they'd be able to see the lights in the fierce whiteout.

Clicks sounded from the other end of the call. "Lights on."

Trip strained his eyes through the snowy night. "There!"

A brighter spot across the freeway blazed out damn near beside them and Tom slid to a stop.

"We see you. We're comin'. We're gonna cross the divider strip and try to pull up in front. Hang tight."

Tom turned his truck and nosed down into the median between the two strips of asphalt. *Please let the ground be frozen.* The last thing they needed was to sink into mud. But the truck churned its way through the deeper snow and eventually dragged itself out onto the other side. Trip gripped his phone tight as they inched toward Henry's truck. The damn thing had lost its color in the monochromatic world of the blizzard, but the wipers kept the snow off the windshield and the headlights blazed in the darkness.

They slid past and pulled over in front of it just as Henry opened the driver's door. Trip ended the call and jumped out his own door, happier than he'd been in weeks.

"Are you all right?" He trudged through the snow until he reached the younger man, his throat tight. "You're not hurt or anythin'?"

"No, I'm fine. Really." Henry threw himself into

Trip's arms. "Thank you for comin' for me."

Nothing had felt right until that moment and Trip hugged Henry as tight as he dared. "You're welcome. I'm just glad you called." He pushed Henry back to look at him. "Come on. Let's get your truck hitched up so we can get home safe. It's a long way in this kind of weather."

"Right." Henry looked up as Tom stepped out of his truck. "Tom? Boy, am I glad to see you. Thanks for the help."

"Yeah, let's get this hooked up and get out of here. The storm's getting worse." Tom nodded and hauled the tow cable to the front of Henry's truck. "Dad, hold this while I crawl under the front."

Trip grabbed the tow cable and held it steady while Tom scrambled under Henry's truck. Trip could barely take his eyes off his lover, looking for some sign of Livvy in him, but he couldn't see anything. *That's because he's his own person, you fool.* He snorted at Livvy's voice in his head and nodded.

"What?" Henry secured the tow cable to the bed of Tom's truck.

"Nothin'. Just very glad to see you."

"Glory be, me too."

"There. It's good to go. Henry, I need you to steer your truck while I pull you. Dad, why don't you ride with him? I can make the drive back."

Trip wanted to do as he suggested, but the drive down was harrowing and the weather progressed toward more dangerous.

"Are you sure, Tom? The weather's gettin' worse. And Amber will kill me if you get hurt."

"Yeah, I'm sure. I got the Garmin."

Trip shook his head. "You can't watch it and the road at the same time." He shot an apologetic look at Henry. "We'll all get home safe if I ride with Tom."

Henry nodded. "I'd rather be safe than have company.

Take Trip with you, Tom. I'll be right behind you. Literally."

Tom's shoulders relaxed. "Okay. Let's get goin'." He headed for the driver's door and got in.

Trip turned back to Henry. "I would've ridden with you. Never doubt that. I just don't want Tom to get too tired or drive off the road."

Henry gripped his arm. "I know, and I appreciate it. I'd rather get home safe."

"Okay." Trip didn't want to walk away. "I have a lot to tell you, but I'll wait for when we get home. And you're sleepin' in our bed tonight, hear me?"

Henry grinned. "Yes, sir, I do. Let's go home."

"Yeah, okay."

There didn't seem to be anything else to say, but Trip couldn't let go. Instead, he jerked Henry close and took his lips with a hard kiss. Henry's flavor burst across his tongue and the younger man gave as good as he got. They stood in the light of Henry's truck, the snow falling on their shoulders, and Trip had never been happier.

When they broke apart, Henry stared at him, his lips swollen and his eyes glazed with pleasure.

"Drive safe now. I'll see you at the ranch and we'll pick up from there." He took a step away, then paused and turned back. "I love you, Henry. Never forget that."

"I won't."

"Good."

They went their separate ways and got into the different trucks, but Trip's gut had loosened and hope blazed in his heart.

"Y'all good?" Tom turned on the wipers and shoved the truck into gear.

"Yup. Let's go home."

"Fuck yeah."

Tom eased the truck onto the road. The wheels slipped a little on the snow-covered asphalt when the tow cable grew taut, but eventually everything shifted into motion and Henry's truck followed along. Tom blew out a relieved breath and Trip concurred. Now all they had to do was make it the twenty-six miles to home.

Glory be, let us make it home.

****

Trip had never been so glad to see the gate at the Triple Star Ranch as he did when they slid under it that night. The snow hadn't slackened at all the whole way, and it had taken them well over an hour to get from the state line to Route 224, but they'd made it. Tom had done a magnificent job fighting the drifts while Trip kept them on the road. He couldn't have been more proud of the man Tom had become.

About halfway home, Tom shot Trip a look. "Are you really gonna forgive him?"

"Yup." It was already a done deal anyway. No point in denying it.

"Why?"

"Because what happened at Thanksgivin' wasn't just his fault. You're driftin' a bit right."

Tom adjusted the wheel, but said nothing.

"I screwed up too, Tom."

"How? You didn't drive him off." Tom scoffed.

"That ain't entirely true." Trip shook his head as he stared out at the driving snow as they passed the Vandehei exit. "Mrs. Guthrie stopped by about two months ago and told me she'd been in love with me for forty-five years."

"What? Seriously? Mrs. Guthrie has loved you since you met Mom?"

"Apparently. I had no idea, but after she stopped by, I started to worry about how it would look to be with Henry, and that maybe I was missin' somethin' with women." Trip grimaced, his gut cramping with shame. "So, I spent as much time with Byron and Seychelles as I could, helping Byron move back to his place. I avoided Henry as much as possible."

"She-it."

Trip nodded. "Yeah. And when the Abernathys arrived at your place for Thanksgivin', it was easier to show Seychelles and Amber some affection because I'd gotten so good at avoidin' Henry. Nobody cares if I hug and kiss them."

"Damn, Dad. That's cold."

"Yeah, I was an asshole, and Henry knew it. He doesn't deserve to be a guilty secret of mine. He deserves to be a full, visible member of the family. My partner and lover, without the ugliness of rejection."

"None of us had a problem with that, you know. Not even me."

"I know. But I did. I was scared to show everyone how I felt about him." Trip glanced down at the Garmin. "The road turns a bit to the right here."

Tom turned the wheel and Henry's headlights swung behind them. "How are you gonna change when we get home? Henry might be younger than me, but he doesn't deserve to be treated like that."

"I'm gonna work on my issues with Dr. Emily, and I'm gonna be honest with Henry. I don't like bein' wrong or scared, but it's better to be wrong and scared with him than without him."

Tom nodded as his hands tightened on the steering wheel. "That's how I feel about Amber." He glanced at his review mirror before turning back to the road. "I like Henry, and I see how you are with him. Plus he's a damn good vet. Don't fuck it up with him again, okay? He's good people and I don't want either of you hurt."

Trip chuckled. "I seem to remember sayin' somethin' like that to you."

"Yup."

That's the last thing they'd said beyond directions before they arrived at the Triple Star, and Trip's heart had swollen with gratitude for his son's acceptance. *He's a great man, Livvy.*

I know, Trip. You done good.

They pulled up in front of the lodge, and Tom maneuvered Henry's truck as close as he could before parking. Trip shoved out the door and headed for the back to unhook the tow cable. Henry met him at the front of his truck and they worked together to dislodge the cable. Tom joined them as they got it loose, shoving his phone into his pocket.

"I just talked to Coal Lostmoon. He'll look over your truck in the next couple of days to find out what's wrong."

Henry frowned. "Coal Lostmoon?"

"Yeah, he's the mechanic Ransom Knight shares with us to fix our equipment and cut costs. Good man." Tom coiled the cable. "He got a scholarship to MIT for mechanical engineering. Aced school and came home to Wyoming to help family. We're lucky to have him workin' with us."

"Damn, I'd say you're really lucky." Henry nodded. "Thanks again for comin' to get me. I really appreciate it."

"Hell, I wouldn't leave anyone stranded in one of these blizzards." He squinted as snow hit him in the face. "Speakin' of which, I'm headed home. Y'all might want to get inside. Temperature's dropping and it'll freeze your balls off."

Trip laughed. "Gotta love Wyoming. Thanks for drivin', Tom."

"Not a problem. I'll talk to you tomorrow."

They waved Tom on and he drove off before Trip turned back to Henry. "Grab everything. We're takin' it in the house."

"Everything?" Henry raised his eyebrows.

"Damn right. Your room is too damn empty." Trip

grasped one of the totes covered in snow and hauled it up onto the porch before coming back for the second one.

"All right, all right, don't hurt yourself." Henry grabbed the second one before Trip could and took it to the porch. "The guitars and my duffle bag are in the cab."

"I'll get them." Trip returned to the truck and opened the door. The damn thing smelled just like Henry and he couldn't help but inhaling the scent. Peace and contentment stole over Trip and some of his worry slipped away.

"Hey, are you gonna get the stuff or what? It's snowin' out here." Henry appeared at his side, poking him with an elbow.

"Yeah. Since you're here, you take your duffle and a guitar. I'll get the other one." Trip grabbed one of the two cases and backed out of the truck to give Henry room. "I'm gonna take this to the apartment and come back for the totes."

"See you there."

Trip headed inside and unlocked his door, so glad he was home. Storms like the one raging outside always made him nervous, especially when he had friends or family out in them. Plus, his side ached from the old goring injury. He left the door open and hauled the guitar case back to Henry's room. It would always be Henry's room. Trip had no need of a man-cave unless it came with the man bringing his stuff back in.

They brought in the totes and Henry paused at his old room, gazing at the bed. His shoulders slumped and he looked as tired as Trip felt.

"Hey, why don't you go take a shower? It was a helluva drive and the shower will help you relax." Trip rested a hand on Henry's shoulder.

Henry looked like he wanted to say something, but in the end only nodded.

"I left a robe in there for you. It's a nice fluffy one. I think Amber got it for me a while ago and I haven't gotten around to usin' it yet."

"Thanks." Henry nodded again. "Hey, Trip, I'm real sorry I left."

"Hey, shower first, then we'll talk. We both got a lot of stuff to get off our chests."

"Yeah, okay."

Henry disappeared into the bathroom and Trip made some coffee. He hung his coat and hat on the hat tree and pulled off his boots. *I'm gonna talk to him tonight, Livvy, and tell him that I wanna be with him forever.*

She didn't respond, but a sense of happiness warmed his chest. He started a fire in the fireplace and had two cups of coffee sitting on the table when Henry returned to the main room.

"I made some coffee. Have a seat. Feel better?"

Henry nodded quickly and glanced down, studying his toes. "Thanks for the robe. And for comin' to rescue me. Even after I was such a damn jackass at Thanksgivin'."

"Yeah, well, you know the Western Code, don't you?"

Henry laughed. "Yeah, I know it." He rubbed the towel over his hair and sat down beside Trip on the couch. "I actually learned the opposite of it just tonight."

"Oh yeah?"

"Yeah. I found out who was stealin' from me all this time."

Trip sat up and met his gaze. "Who?"

"My manager, Jordie Heathrow." Henry scowled and his hands tightened around the towel. "The sonuvaprick has been embezzlin' from me since I got signed with Lariat Records."

Trip gaped. "Unbelievable. How did you find out?"

"Those Lost and Found folks Tom told me about. They've been researchin' since early November."

"Shit. I'm sorry, Henry." Trip leaned forward with his elbows on his knees. "I hope the man goes down in flames for it."

"Oh, he will. I'll make sure of it. I have all the proof and I'll be sendin' it to the cops." Henry grimaced. "I was stayin' with him in Fort Collins."

"Is that where you went on Thanksgivin'?" Trip's gut clenched with unease. *What if he liked Jordie better?* A feminine snort in the back of his mind made him dismiss the notion. *None of that. You know better.*

"Yeah. I was the big, dumb jackass who thought he was my friend." Henry scowled. "But he'd been tryin' to convince me you wouldn't love me or be faithful to me because you were bi, and I believed his poison." He paused and met Trip's gaze. "I'm sorry. I was a stupid bigot."

"Hey, don't take all the responsibility, now." Trip grimaced with a shrug. "I was scared of showin' how I felt about you in front of folks. Old habits die hard, but that's no excuse. I meant it when I said I loved you, but I was too scared to practice what I preached." He swallowed hard. "I'm sorry for bein' the jackass at Thanksgivin'. I shouldn't have avoided you for the two weeks before the holiday, and I should've hugged you when you arrived."

Henry nodded. "I missed that hug. I was tryin' to get back to the way we were before Mrs. Guthrie stopped by. The night you gave me the bracelet." He held up his hand. "I kept it. I couldn't take it off even if I said all that terrible shit to you when I left. I'm sorry. Really sorry. Can we start again? I—I love you. I was miserable in Colorado."

"Aw hell." Trip rose at the same time as Henry and opened his arms. "I don't want to be without you ever again if I can help it." He closed his arms around the younger man, relief and love cascading through him at the feel of Henry's body against him. "You gotta stay with me, okay? Or I'm gonna go insane"

Henry coughed a laugh that sounded suspiciously like a sob. "Just try to get rid of me. I need you in my life. I might be young, but I try not to be stupid very often, and I've already had my quota for the year. I love you and I need you. You're the love of my life."

His own words echoed back at him made him squeeze Henry tight. "You're the love of my life, too. I've never missed anyone as much as I've missed you in the last couple of weeks. Why didn't you answer any of my texts or calls?"

"I was too stupid and stubborn." Henry shook his head against Trip's chest. "Ransom called me and told me not to be a jackass, but I guess I had more jackassery to do. I appreciated the texts and calls, though. Thank you for tryin'."

"Aw hell, I just couldn't let it lie. You're too important to me."

"Thank God." Henry backed up and met Trip's gaze. "I started writin' and playin' music again. Every time I heard your voice on my phone, it set me to thinkin', and I've got damn near a whole album's worth of new music written down. It's all because of you."

Trip allowed a goofy smile to curl his lips. "Do I get to hear this here music?"

"Maybe I'll play it for you. But not tonight. Tonight, I just need to be with you."

"That's damn good to hear, because I need to be with you, too." Trip cupped Henry's face with both hands as he met his gaze. "Tonight, I want you to make love with me. I want you to remind me of your love, physically."

"You wanna fuck me?"

"No." Trip swallowed hard and met Henry's gaze steadily. "I want you to fuck me."

CHAPTER TWENTY-THREE

Henry stared at Trip, but the older man's gaze never wavered. *Holy shit, he wants me to top him.* Trip had never been comfortable with the idea of Henry's cock in his ass and Henry understood. For someone who'd been straight for most of his life, anal sex freaked him out. Helping Trip learn about gay lovemaking hadn't been a burden for Henry, but he'd missed the tight heat of a lover's sheath.

"Are you sure?" Henry searched his face. "I know we've been apart for a while, but I don't mind the way we did this before."

Trip shook his head. "You've been patient with me, but I want to do this. It's a way for me to show you I love and trust you. I need you to know I don't want to be with anyone but you." He ducked his head and kissed Henry on his neck below his ear. "Please, Henry."

"Oh glory." The soft kisses paired with Trip's beard sent blood shooting straight to his cock. "Yeah, let's go to bed. I've missed your body next to mine for weeks."

Trip pulled back to look at Henry. "I'm really sorry I was such a coward."

"And I'm really sorry I was such a bigoted asshole. But I think we've both apologized enough, and I'd like to move on to bein' together full time. Whaduya say?"

Trip's lips curled into a sexy smile. "I say, hell yeah."

"Good. I'm gonna clean up the coffee. Why don't you get ready for bed? I'll be in in a minute."

Trip nodded and headed for his bedroom with another one of those toe-curling smiles. Damn, the man was sexy. Henry carried the coffee mugs to the kitchen and set them in the sink, his excitement and arousal rising with his cock. Glory be, he'd wanted to fuck Trip for months, but hadn't wanted to push him away. *Yeah, instead you ran away, you halfwit.* But now he had his moment and excitement filled him in more ways beyond sexual.

I get to make love to Trip.

The overwhelming joy made him want to fist-pump the air, but he settled for a grin and headed for the bedroom. *Our bedroom.* At least for the nights when he didn't have to take care of the sick animals.

Henry paused at the doorway as he watched Trip strip down to nothing. The scars on his side and leg gave him character and Henry wanted to lick them again. The silver hair on his chest and belly made his mouth water. Glory, he wanted to suck on Trip's nipples while he massaged the big cock and heavy balls between his legs.

And tonight I get to fuck that ass.

"Glory be, you're beautiful."

Trip raised his eyebrows as he settled, naked, on the bed. "You think so?"

"Hell yeah, I do. You're my silver fox." Henry opened the ties of the robe and slid it off his shoulders. "I'm gonna enjoy rubbing all the muscles under that sexy hair."

"I still haven't manscaped. I hope you don't mind."

Trip sounded so hesitant, Henry crawled onto the bed and planted his face between his pectorals, Trip's thick cock rubbing his belly. Henry inhaled deeply, taking in his lover's scent. He loved the feel of the soft hairs on his cheeks as Trip's fragrance settled in his nose with a feeling of home.

"No sir, I don't need you to shave for me. I like you just the way you are."

Henry kissed his way up to Trip's lips and took them in a sweet, erotic kiss. Trip didn't hold back and groaned as their tongues dueled, sliding over one another. Henry rocked his hips, rubbing his cock against Trip's thick shaft and they both moaned.

"Fuck, it's been too long." He gasped as Henry rocked again.

"I agree." Henry backed off a little and stroked Trip's cock. "But I want to take my time."

Trip grunted. "I dunno if I can last, especially with you strokin' like that."

"I'll just have to take it slow and teasin'." Henry winked as he pushed Trip's legs apart. "Glory be, I love your cock and balls. They're fuckin' sexy." He nuzzled the soft, crinkled skin of his scrotum, inhaling his musky scent. "And you smell so damn good."

Trip laughed. "You like that smell?"

"Oh, hell yeah. You smell like sex, man, and erotic pleasure. I'm gonna revel in it all night tonight."

Trip lost his smile. "Just tonight?"

Henry paused and met his gaze from between his legs. "No, not if you want me here. I love you, Trip. I wanna be with you every night I can." He licked his way up to the tip of Trip's thick cock. "And I'll suck on your cock anytime you want me to."

"Fuuuccckkk." Trip threw his head back with a sigh. "You surely have a way with words."

Henry didn't bother to answer as he sucked on Trip's shaft. He slid his tongue over the flared head and dipped it into the slit, enjoying the tangy flavor of his pre-cum. Pleasure tightened his own cock and he dropped one hand down to massage his shaft while he sucked on Trip.

Holy shit, I've missed this. He wanted more of the

exquisite pleasure, but he hadn't had sex in too long. If he kept going this way, neither of them would get what they wanted. He pulled back with a few more licks of Trip's shaft and he sat up, staring at the masculine body of his sexy lover.

"I have to admit I don't think I can hold out very long. I've missed you too much." Henry reached for the lube on the bedside table. "But I want to make it good for you. Are you ready for me to prepare you?"

Trip stilled, his pupils still blown, and his cock jerked with arousal. "Yeah. I'm ready for you to fuck me."

"Oh, I'm not gonna fuck you." Henry settled belly-down between Trip's legs as he squirted lube on his fingers.

"You're not?"

"Nope, I'm gonna make love to you until you come so hard, it takes your breath away." He slid his fingers into Trip's crack and massaged his hole as he kissed his balls. "Relax for me, braveheart."

Trip's cock flexed as Henry brushed his lips over the tender skin of the scrotum. He rubbed the anal ring with gentle fingers and Trip moaned. Henry's cock responded in kind by hardening with arousal. *Glory, I want him so much.* But he had to go slow. Trip had never had anal sex himself and too much pain would ruin it for him.

"Oh, glory, Henry. It feels amazin'."

Henry enjoyed the pleasure in Trip's voice as he added more lube to his fingers before inserting one into his grasping sheath. Trip grunted with surprise, but didn't try to move away.

"Relax. Push against my finger. That's it." Henry kept sliding his finger in and out of Trip's hole while he licked his balls, making sure the pleasure outweighed the unusual discomfort. He remembered his first time with anal sex and he was determined to make it better than even he'd experienced.

He rocked his hand against Trip's ass, enjoying the reactions of the hard cock in front of him. He was tempted to suck it into his mouth, but he didn't know if Trip could hold back. Instead, he licked and kissed the heavy testicles resting above his hand, before adding a second finger into Trip's tight hole.

"Oh, she-it." Trip groaned and rocked his hips, sucking in more of Henry's fingers. "Holy shit, that feels fuckin' amazin'."

Henry grabbed Trip's cock with his free hand and stroked slowly in the same rhythm as he pumped his fingers. Trip moaned and rolled his hips in time, forcing Henry's fingers in harder and faster. As much as Henry enjoyed the view of Trip getting off on being finger-fucked, he refused to let Trip's first time be without a cock.

"Ah ah ah." Henry withdrew his hand and reached for a condom in the drawer beside the bed.

"Aw hell, why'd you stop?" He'd never heard Trip so plaintive.

"Because I want to be in you for your first time with anal penetration." Henry held out the condom. "Would you do the honors?"

Trip met his gaze and licked his lips, but sat up and took the condom with a hungry expression on his face. His eyes were black with how large his pupils had grown and a ruddy hue suffused his cheeks. Before he stretched the latex over Henry's shaft, he leaned forward and sucked the head into his mouth, damn near taking Henry to his knees.

"Sweet glory. You're so fuckin' sexy when you suck my cock."

Trip hummed against Henry's rigid flesh, but he pulled off and rolled the condom on, his pleasure obvious. He raised his gaze to Henry's and smiled.

"You're fuckin' sexy all the time, my handsome Kick-ass Cowboy."

Henry grabbed his head and planted a harsh, wet kiss

on Trip's mouth. The older man held his hips in an iron grip, as if he couldn't stand to only touch by lips. When they broke apart, their breath sawed between them.

"Love me, Henry."

"Yes, sir." He pushed Trip back and smeared lube on his latex-covered cock before crawling up Trip's body to brace himself, one handed, nose-to-nose. "Are you ready?"

"Yeah, I need you."

"Damn, Trip. You're gonna make me come with words like that. Push against me, now."

Henry lined up his cockhead with Trip's hole and pressed inward. Trip tightened at first, his eyes growing wide as his body made room for Henry's shaft. Henry forced himself to go slow, despite the overwhelming heat and pleasure of entering Trip's body. *Sweet glory, he's so fuckin' tight.*

Once the head popped behind the tight ring of muscle, they both froze. Henry held his breath with the intensity of the hot pressure on his dick, but he tried to watch Trip's reactions to make sure he wasn't causing pain.

"You okay, Trip?" He was impressed he could fit three words together coherently.

"Oh, god, yeah."

"Do you want me to move?" *Please, let him say yes.*

"Okay."

Close enough. Henry slid a little more of his shaft into Trip and the man clenched around him with a groan. Henry backed out, then reversed, each time pushing more of his shaft into his lover until he sat seated to the hilt with Trip's balls resting against his groin. *Fuck, he's so hot and tight.* Henry never wanted to leave, but with every passing moment and each squeeze of Trip's body, his control slipped further from his grasp.

"Damn, I'm so fuckin' full." Trip held perfectly still, his hands tightened into fists in the bed covers.

"What color are you, Trip? We still good."

"Color?" Trip's brows lowered as he tried to understand. "Oh, green. I'm green."

Henry inwardly sighed. "Good, 'cause I gotta move."

"Move?"

"Yeah, like this." Henry pulled his cock slowly from Trip's body before sliding it back in.

"Oh, fuck. Yeah, do that again. It feels so good."

Music to his ears. Henry rocked his hips, sliding in and out of Trip's ass, the pleasure making him damn near breathless. Trip's body squeezed him each time he slid home and he saw stars. He wouldn't last very long so he reached down and grasped Trip's thick shaft in his hand as he pulled out again.

"You're so fuckin' sexy. You make me hard just thinkin' about you each day. You're the love of my life." He shoved in a little faster and harder, and Trip gasped as his eyes slitted to half-mast while he watched Henry move. "I need you in my bed, braveheart. I need you in my life. I need you so much. Aw shit, I'm not gonna be able to hold back."

He squeezed Trip's cock. "Come for me, braveheart. Come hard, 'cause I'm gonna fuckin' blow. Aw yeeeaaahhhh."

Henry's orgasm blew through him like a shock wave, shooting up from the base of his spine all the way to the top of his head and beyond. Hot jets of cum exploded out of his cock, filling Trip's hole and he couldn't keep from slamming his shaft into his lover.

Trip followed him with deep pulses of cum splattering onto this chest as he cried out. His sheath clamped down on Henry's cock and Henry saw more stars than he'd ever spied in the Wyoming sky. He was home, this was his lover and the man he never wanted to leave.

"I love you, Henry."

The rough, emotional words brought him back to the present, and he met Trip's gaze as they both stilled. Henry released Trip's cock and braced himself on his hands so he wouldn't lose the moment.

"I love you and I don't ever want you to leave. I can't promise I'll always get it right, but I can promise I'll always try." Trip's eyes filled with tears and they spilled over onto his cheeks. "You're the love of my life and I don't want to let you go. Ever."

"Oh, glory, Trip. You don't have to let me go." Henry gently pulled out of Trip's body and rolled over on his side, gathering the older man against his chest. "I'm not goin' anywhere. This is where I want and need to be. Right here, with you. I love you, braveheart."

He kissed Trip's cheeks and smoothed the tears away as Trip sobbed out his emotion. He didn't mind Trip crying, and he certainly didn't mind holding him. He'd be there forever if he had any say in it. He stroked Trip's head and settled into the scents of sex, sweat, and sexy man, happy for the first time in over a month.

After some time, Trip calmed and Henry kissed his forehead.

"I'm gonna get rid of the condom and clean up. You okay now?"

"Yeah, I'm good."

"Hell yeah, you are." Henry winked as he rolled out of bed and Trip laughed.

Pleasure from that sound zinged through Henry as he cleaned himself up. He looked into the mirror of the bathroom and grinned at the sated, happy expression on his face. This was where he needed and wanted to be. At home in Wyoming with the animals on the Triple Star Ranch and in the arms of his partner. *Husband. I want him to be my husband.*

The thought only half-shocked him. It seemed strange to think of Trip as his husband, yet it had familiarity as if he'd done something like this before. *Don't be silly.* But he couldn't quite push the feeling away without merit.

Shaking his head, he brought a warm washcloth out to Trip and lovingly cleaned his crack and belly, each time kissing the wet skin left behind.

"I love you, Trip." He gazed into the steel-blue eyes of his handsome lover. "Would you ever consider marryin' again?"

Trip's eyes widened. "Marryin'? Who?"

"Me." Henry cleared his throat, feeling a blush work its way up his cheeks. "I mean, if you can see yourself with me long term. I know I'm young and don't have the experience of an older man, and I might be a bit stupid when it comes to—"

Trip sat up and silenced him with a kiss. "Hell yeah, I'd consider marryin' you." He grasped Henry's wrist and held up the copper bracelet. "I think I kinda meant this as an engagement promise back then. I just didn't have the courage to ask."

Henry blinked at the bracelet before he raised his gaze to Trip's. "You were thinkin' about it way back then?"

"Yeah." Trip gave him a goofy grin. "I pretty much knew from the moment you moved in that I wanted you to stay for good. I ain't been sure of much in my life, but I was sure of you."

Henry slammed his mouth to Trip's and kissed him deep. "Hot damn, I love you, and I'll get you an engagement promise as soon as I can. Please marry me, Trip. Whenever we can. I don't wanna upstage Tom and Amber, but I wanna be yours forever."

"Oh, you're gonna be mine forever. Because I'm already yours. I love you."

"So, is that a yes?"

"Nope. It's a hell yes." Trip grinned as he pulled Henry down into his arms in the bed. "Now let me keep you warm tonight and tomorrow we'll decorate this place for Christmas."

Henry laughed as he snuggled up close to his fiancé. "I

was wonderin' why it wasn't festive in here."

"I didn't feel real festive without you." Trip sighed and closed his eyes as Henry settled his head against his shoulder. "But now that you're home, I think it's gonna be the best Christmas ever."

"Yeah. It'll definitely be mine. I love you, Trip."

"I love you, too, Henry."

THE END

AUTHOR'S NOTE
ABOUT TRIPLE STAR RANCH, BOOK 2

This story between Trip Colton and Henry Bright was inspired by LIFE AFTER YOU by Daughtry. In my mind, this was the song Henry wrote while he was stuck on the side of I-25 just before Christmas. While I can't quote the lyrics in the story for copyrighted reasons, I can send you to the following link to read the lyrics and listen to the song on YouTube. The lyrics encompass everything Henry felt for Trip.

The moment I heard this song I was driving Mr. SM to work in Cheyenne and my Muse squealed like woman at her first rock concert. I made Mr. SM turn the song up and I had the whole final scene of Henry stuck in the snowstorm below the bison cut out at the state line mapped out in front of me.

Be sure to check out J.M. Madden's Lost & Found Series where you can meet all the combat-modified veterans who work with Duncan Wilde as investigators. In fact, you can meet investigator Brian Calvert in LOVING LILLY and find out more about him specifically.

I hope you enjoyed Trip and Henry's tale, and be sure to read how Tom Colton met Amber Hillcrest in ROPE A FALLING STAR, book 1 in the Triple Star Ranch series. Keep your eyes open for more of the #CheyenneCowboys with tales about Seychelles Abernathy, Andrew Martindale, and Coal Lostmoon.

Thanks so much for reading.

Siobhan

ROPE A FALLING STAR
TRIPLE STAR RANCH, BOOK 1
SNEEK PEEK

Only the best stars fall...

Three time bronc-riding champion Tom Colton's dream of a fourth title ends when he draws Wooden Nickel, a mean little bronc with more twists than a maze. With his heart no longer in rodeo, he figures it's time to go home to the Triple Star Ranch, the PTSD therapy ranch he and his dad founded to help others with trauma in their pasts. Tom just wants a little time to nurse his hurts and consider his next move.

Amber Hillcrest started out as a Triple Star client and stayed on as a massage therapist. Her dog Nimbus keeps her PTSD in check, but her heart remains bruised. She knows she's too old and too broken for love, especially with the son of her boss, but he's hot enough to fill her fantasies for years to come.

Amber tries to keep it professional between them, but Tom proves too irresistible with his big heart and charm. But someone is sabotaging the Triple Star and the neighboring Fantasy Ranch, and an ex-girlfriend keeps coming around, trying to reconnect with Tom. Tom's hands are full of problems instead of the luscious massage therapist. But when Amber gets kidnapped, Tom will move heaven and earth to get her back and tell her how he truly feels.

OTHER BOOKS BY SIOBHAN MUIR

Her Devoted Vampire (from Three Lakes Books)
Queen Bitch of the Callowwood Pack (from Siren Publishing)
Not a Dragon's Standard Virgin (from Siren Publishing)
Second Chance Succubus (from Three Lakes Books)
Darwin's Evolution (from Amazon)

Cloudburst Colorado Series
A Hell Hound's Fire (from Three Lakes Books)
The Beltane Witch (from Three Lakes Books)
Christmas I.C.E. Magic (from Three Lakes Books)
Cloudburst Ice Magic (from Three Lakes Books)

Rifts Series
Take the Reins (from Three Lakes Books)
A Centaur's Solstice Wish (from Three Lakes Books)
In Death's Shadow (from Three Lakes Books)

Bad Boys of Beta Squad Series
Bronco's Rough Ride (from Three Lakes Books)
The Navy's Ghost (from Three Lakes Books)
Rimshot's Hard Target (from Amazon)
Bam-Bam's Inked Hart (from Three Lakes Books)

The Ivory Road
A Walk in the Sand (from Three Lakes Books)
Outback Dreams (from Three Lakes Books)

Triple Star Ranch Series
Rope a Falling Star (from Three Lakes Books)
Star Light, Star Bright (from Three Lakes Books)

Warbler Peninsula Series

Order of the Dragon (from Three Lakes Books)
The Valkyrie's Sword (from Three Lakes Books)

Coming Soon
Deli's Take Out (Bad Boys of Beta Squad #4)
Wildfire's Heart (Elemental Hearts #1)
Loch'd Hearts (Elemental Hearts #2)

ABOUT THE AUTHOR

Siobhan Muir lives in Cheyenne, Wyoming, with her husband, two daughters, and a vegetarian cat she swears is a shape-shifter, though he's never shifted when she can see him. When not writing, she can be found looking down a microscope at fossil fox teeth, pursuing her other love, paleontology. An avid reader of science fiction/fantasy, her husband gave her a paranormal romance for Christmas one year, and she was hooked for good.

In previous lives, Siobhan has been an actor at the Colorado Renaissance Festival, a field geologist in the Aleutian Islands, and restored inter-planetary imagery at the USGS. She's hiked to the top of Mount St. Helens and to the bottom of Meteor Crater.

Siobhan writes kick-ass adventure with hot sex for men and women to enjoy. She believes in happily ever after, redemption, and communication, all of which you will find in her paranormal romance stories.

Connect with Siobhan online at:

http://siobhanmuir.com
http://www.facebook.com/siobhan.muir.35
http://twitter.com/SiobhanMuir
http://siobhanmuir.com/siobhans-blog
http://pinterest.com/siobhanmuir.35